She couldn't stand not having him a minute longer

Claudia wanted Leandro, and she knew he wanted her. She felt like the sexiest woman in the world standing in front of her mirror fresh from her shower. Dropping the towel behind her, she waltzed into the living room, desire giving her all the confidence she needed.

"I was thinking we could skip dinner and go straight to dessert. What do you think?" she asked him, pausing in the doorway.

His head came up and she saw his jaw tense as he registered her nakedness.

"You are full of good ideas tonight," he said.

Holding his eye, she walked slowly toward him, loving the way his eyes followed the bounce of her breasts.

"You have no idea," she said as she pushed him farther back onto the couch and straddled him. She could feel the firmness of his thighs beneath hers, the rasp of his denim against her skin. His hands found her torso on either side, sliding up until they were resting just beneath her breasts.

This man was going to be hers at last.

Blaze™

Dear Reader,

Welcome to Claudia's story. This book pretty much wrote itself—Claudia leaped off the page, grabbed me by the throat and wouldn't let go until I'd left her happy and whole. It's so cool to write a strong, gutsy character. I had a lot of fun with the contrast between her larger-than-life personality and her actual physical presence—as Grace once commented, Claudia can be one scary little lady sometimes!

I hope you enjoyed getting to know Sadie, Grace and Claudia in the SECRET LIVES OF DAYTIME DIVAS miniseries over the past few months, and meeting their hunky other halves, Dylan, Mac and Leandro. I also hope you enjoyed the behind-the-scenes world of soap production. It's a grueling business, but it has been a great training ground for me over the years and I love it.

I love to hear from readers! You can contact me through my Web site—www.sarahmayberryauthor.com— via e-mail at sarahjmayberry@hotmail.com, or c/o Harlequin Books, 225 Duncan Mill Road, Don Mills, Ontario M3B 3K9, Canada.

Until next time, stay well,

Sarah Mayberry

HOT FOR HIM
Sarah Mayberry

HARLEQUIN®

TORONTO • NEW YORK • LONDON
AMSTERDAM • PARIS • SYDNEY • HAMBURG
STOCKHOLM • ATHENS • TOKYO • MILAN • MADRID
PRAGUE • WARSAW • BUDAPEST • AUCKLAND

ISBN-13: 978-0-373-79330-3
ISBN-10:   0-373-79330-8

HOT FOR HIM

www.eHarlequin.com

Printed in U.S.A.

ABOUT THE AUTHOR

Sarah Mayberry lives in Melbourne, Australia, with her partner, Chris. In addition to writing romance, she writes scripts for television. Like all her characters, she loves sexy cars, chocolate, a good glass of wine and a great laugh. Unlike her characters, she has to pay for the chocolate on the treadmill. Long live fiction.

Books by Sarah Mayberry

HARLEQUIN BLAZE
211—CAN'T GET ENOUGH
251—CRUISE CONTROL*
278—ANYTHING FOR YOU*
314—TAKE ON ME†
320—ALL OVER YOU†

*It's All About Attitude
†Secret Lives of Daytime Divas

Thanks to Chris for holding my hand throughout this book and the previous two, and to Wanda the Wonderful, the good editor from the north, for listening to hours of rambling madness. Here's to walking the streets of Paris with you both again sometime in the near future.

1

HE SMELLED OF LEATHER and musk and warm skin, and his shoulder was a solid wall of muscle against her left arm. Every time he spoke, his deep voice vibrated through her whole body. And every time he laughed, she had to fight the urge to squirm in her chair.

Claudia Dostis was seriously in danger of screaming out loud. In fact, if Leandro Mandalor's big, beefy arm knocked against hers one more time, she was not going to be answerable for the consequences.

It was the organizers' fault. They'd squashed too many people at too few tables at the open forum sessions for the Daytime Television Convention, then they'd compounded their mistake by seating her next to her arch rival.

How was she supposed to concentrate on answering questions from the floor when she was pressed up against Captain Butthead?

He was easily the most obnoxious man she'd ever met. Hands down, without even trying. All he had to do was walk into a room and she was instantly annoyed. It had a lot to do with her innate competitive spirit—his soap, *Heartlands,* competed on a daily basis with *Ocean Boulevard,* her baby. It had even more to do with the fact that six months ago he'd tried to get the jump on her by poaching the *Boulevard*'s idea to run a feature-length wedding episode in the winter months.

But mostly it was just *him*.

He was too tall—six four, or something equally ridiculous. He was too dark—olive skinned, with glossy black curly hair that he wore cropped close to his head. And he was too, too, too cocky. The man oozed confidence and take-charge charisma. He liked to call the shots, and he expected people to give him what he wanted, when he wanted it, stat.

And the way he looked at her—as though she were a private joke that only he understood. His dark brown eyes always held a hint of laughter when they lit on her, and it made her long for a large, heavy object to aim at his big, fat head.

For about the millionth time that afternoon, she felt the warm press of his body alongside hers as he shifted in his seat. Her fingers curled around the edges of her notes as she fought the need to punch him and tell him to keep his distance.

"…it's an interesting point, but I'm not sure that I agree with it," he said in his deep baritone. "What do you think, Claudia?"

She stiffened. She'd been so busy grinding her teeth over their forced intimacy she'd completely missed the comment from the floor.

Shit.

Her stomach tightening with panic, she ran her mind back over the past few minutes. They'd been talking about audience expectations for daytime drama, and the challenge of both meeting those expectations and providing fresh formats and ideas. Unfortunately, about the time when the discussion had gotten more specific, she'd been mentally sticking pins in his voodoo doll.

In short, she had no idea what she was supposed to agree or disagree with.

Her chin came up and she cocked an eyebrow at the giant hulking next to her. When in doubt, come out fighting was her motto. It had never failed her yet.

"Nice try, Leandro," she said, "but I think we're all interested in hearing what you've got to say."

He held her eye for a beat, a small smile curling his mouth. She couldn't help noticing that he had full, sensuous lips, and that his mouth was bracketed by laugh lines.

"How can I resist when you ask so nicely?" he said. He held her eye for a moment longer—just long enough to make her feel distinctly…uncomfortable—before turning back to face the room full of eager wannabe writers, producers and directors.

"Television is a visual medium, we all know that. The simple answer is that there are always going to be beautiful people on our screens. But it doesn't mean there isn't a place for character actors. In all honesty I can say that when I sit down to cast a part, I'm thinking about the role, the character, not the sexual appeal or looks or body of the actor or actress trying for the part," he said.

Signaling he had finished, he gestured for Claudia to pick up the gauntlet.

"As much as it kills me, I'm going to have to agree with Leandro," she said.

A ripple of laughter washed through the room. Their rivalry was becoming an industry in-joke, she knew.

"The reality is, some of the most popular long-term characters on *Ocean Boulevard* are played by actors and actresses who fall outside the accepted norms for physical beauty in our culture," she said, warming to her topic.

"Particularly in daytime drama, the audience falls in love with people and personalities, not faces and bodies. They spend a lot of time with our characters every week. They love them and hate them—after a while, what they look like becomes almost irrelevant. Having said all that, however…I will plead guilty to casting for beefcake occasionally. I figure our stay-at-home moms deserve a bit of eye candy every now and then."

That scored her a laugh. She sat back in her chair, waiting for the next question. When it was directed to the producer of the *Kelly Larson* talk show, on her right, she risked a glance at her watch. Ten more minutes and her official obligations for the convention were over. Hallelujah.

"*Beefcake.* I wonder how they'd react if I said I cast for tits and ass?"

Leandro had leaned close to her ear to deliver his *sotto voce* comment, and she could feel his breath against her cheek.

"You should try it, see how they like it," she suggested sweetly.

He grinned, his teeth very white against his tanned skin. She wondered if he had them whitened, or if he visited a tanning salon, or both. Surely Mother Nature hadn't bestowed all that height and breadth on him as well as great teeth and a year-round tan?

"Would you promise to tend my wounds after they tear me to shreds?" he asked.

"I've got a large container of salt out the back, ready and waiting," she said.

He laughed, a full-throated sound that drew the eyes of their interested audience.

Suddenly realizing how it must look, the two of them whispering with each other and grinning like schoolkids, she concentrated on her notes. The problem was, she wanted to wipe the smug smile off his face so badly, she leaped at any opportunity to lock horns with him.

But then she'd always been stubborn. From a young age she'd learned to look out for herself, and it had been good preparation for her career. She'd had to fight many prejudices in her battle to be taken seriously in the world of network television. Now, fighting was so much a part of her life it was second nature.

"Well, folks, that's all we've got time for today. Let's join together in thanking our special guests from the industry for their time and expertise in answering our questions today," their chairperson, Bonnie Randall, said.

Claudia acknowledged the round of polite applause with a small smile. The truth was, of the five-hundred-or-so hopefuls crowded into this session, only a handful would achieve their dream to become part of the entertainment industry. It made her sad to see all the expectant faces sometimes.

Pushing back her chair, she stood for the first time in two hours and winced at how tight her back and butt were. She really had to think about adding some stretching to her work-out routine—Pilates or yoga or something. She was turning into an old lady with all the hours she was clocking behind her desk.

"This way," Leandro said from behind her, and she felt a large hand land on her back as he steered her toward the closest exit.

Instinctively she dug her heels in, not liking how small she felt standing next to him. On a good day she was the shortest person in the room at five foot one, but she felt positively childlike next to Leandro's towering height.

"I can find the door on my own," she said coolly.

His mouth quirked. "Just trying to be a gentleman," he said.

"*Trying* being the operative word. Why don't you quit pretending you're anything other than what you are—a pirate," she said.

"A pirate? Why am I not getting Johnny Depp vibes when you say that?" he said wryly.

"You know why."

He cocked his head to one side as he looked down at her. "You're not still upset about the wedding episode?" he asked incredulously, as though she'd brought up a spat they'd had on the playground in elementary school.

"Yeah, I am. And I will continue to be as long as originality and reward for effort remain important to me," she said stiffly.

He shook his head, clearly amused. She hated that she amused him. It made her want to kick him in the shin, or any other part of his body she had ready access to.

"Claudia, when are you going to let it rest?" he asked mockingly. His hand landed in the middle of her back again and she found herself being steered toward the exit once more.

She was so busy being irritated by his condescending attitude that she went without protest.

"It's really not the conspiracy that you're imagining, you know. I heard through a reliable source—who came to me, by the way, and not the other way around—that my biggest rival was running a feature-length special. What would you have done if the same opportunity fell into your lap?"

"Let me think for a moment… Come up with my own bright idea? Decide to be original?" she suggested.

"Sure you would have. And then you would have decided to fight fire with fire. You're a beat 'em at their own game kind of woman. You wouldn't be where you are today if you weren't," Leandro said.

They were out in the foyer of the Universal Hilton by now, and somehow they'd managed to find a quiet, secluded corner to stand in. Claudia was oblivious to everyone and everything else as she glared at the man looming over her.

"Don't put me in the same grubby little basket as you, bucko," she said, jabbing a finger at his chest. He was standing so close she actually hit him, her finger driving home into firm, resilient muscle.

To her consternation, he threw back his head and laughed.

"Don't laugh at me," she warned him through gritted teeth.

"Then stop being so cute," he said. "Did you know that your nostrils flare when you get really angry?"

It was too much. It had been a long day, and an even longer convention, and Leandro Mandalor had been a dark, disturbing presence throughout the whole damned thing. Giving in to base impulse, she hauled back her foot and kicked him, hard, in the shin.

"Yow!" he howled, skipping backward and bending to clutch at his calf.

"*Cute* my ass. And my nostrils are none of your business, flaring or otherwise," she said before spinning on her heel and making for the elevator bank.

The sound of his laughter followed her across the marbled foyer.

She ground her teeth together and called him four-letter

words all the way up to her floor. He thought she was a joke. A Kewpie doll he could poke a stick at and get some laughs out of. Her stride morphing into a stalk, she made her way to her hotel suite and swiped her key card.

Sadie and Grace looked up from where they were lounging in the living room when she entered.

"Uh-oh. Mandalor alert," Sadie said as she saw Claudia's face.

"The man is an arrogant ass. A patronizing pig. A…a…" Claudia spluttered, running out of appropriately vitriolic insults.

"Slippery snake? Jittery jerk? How about leprotic loser?" Grace suggested, poker-faced.

"It's not funny," Claudia wailed, throwing herself into an armchair and toeing her high heels off with a relieved sigh.

Sadie grimaced apologetically. "It *is* kind of funny. Sorry, sweetie," she said. "Every day you've left the convention fuming at him. Even you have to admit that it's a teensy, weensy bit amusing."

Jumping to her feet again, Claudia crossed to the minibar and grabbed herself a bottle of mineral water.

"Have I been that bad?" she asked as she cracked the seal on the bottle.

Grace and Sadie made eye contact with each other, then nodded in unison.

"Yup."

Taking a slug of mineral water, Claudia pushed her shoulder-length straight black hair away from her face.

"He reminds me of my brothers," she admitted. "It's not just that he's Greek, either. Although that doesn't help. There's this whole macho man thing that Greek guys have—like they're God's gift to women. My brother

Cosmo walks into a room and absolutely believes that all the women there want to have sex with him. Leandro is exactly the same."

"Yeah, except that Leandro is probably not that far from the truth, whereas your brother is definitely on the deluded side," Grace said wryly.

Claudia pulled a face and made a gagging noise. Sadie laughed.

"Come on, Claud, are you telling me you don't find Leandro attractive?" Sadie asked.

"He's a giant. And he's got that big nose and those girly lips," Claudia said, shaking her head dismissively.

Grace rolled her eyes. "You mean that sexy, masculine Greek nose and those lips that look like they could win Olympic gold in all the important oral events?"

"Sorry, can't see it," Claudia said firmly. It was true, too, she assured herself. She'd sat next to him for two hours today and felt nothing but irritation at being hemmed in and imposed upon. "He does absolutely nothing for me."

"So, what did he say this time?" Sadie asked. She leaned forward, obviously eager for the latest installment in the Leandro Mandalor saga.

Claudia briskly filled in her two best friends and colleagues, feeling warmed when they gasped with outrage at the appropriate points and hooted their approval when Claudia reported her zingers.

"You're definitely ahead on points," Grace announced when Claudia had summed up the shin-kicking incident.

"Definitely. He'd have to do something really audacious to beat physical assault," Sadie said.

Claudia winced. "Put like that, it sounds kind of…childish," she admitted.

"Never say die, Claud," Grace said. "And never, ever apologize."

"Hmm. That's so interesting, Gracie, because I swear when I picked you up from your place the other day, I heard you say sorry to Mac for using all the hot water in the shower…" Sadie said teasingly.

"Strategy. Mac thinks he's got me where he wants me, but it's *so* the other way around," Grace said.

Claudia didn't bother calling her friend on her faux feminist stance. Grace and Mac had long since ironed out the problems in their relationship and had been living with each other for nearly three months now. As for Mrs. Sadie Anderson…the content look behind her eyes was testament to how happy she was with Dylan.

"God, we'd better win tonight," Claudia said. "If he walks away with that award, I am seriously going to need sedating for a few days."

"We'll win," Grace said confidently.

"You don't know that," Claudia fretted.

"Yeah, I do. Mac made that episode look so perfect. And it rated through the roof. Of course it's going to win," Grace said.

"Really?" Claudia asked, her pulse surging with excitement as she thought about walking up on stage tonight and accepting a People's Vote Award on behalf of the show. It would mean so much to her, both personally and professionally. The show hadn't received a People's Vote for nearly five years, and to win this year would put the seal on the success of their wedding feature. They already had another feature scheduled for next winter—with the story line very tightly under wraps—but the win would give them the cherry on top that Claudia craved.

The awards show wasn't televised in prime time like the Emmys or the Oscars, but a cut-down version of the ceremony with highlights would be shown during the day. She wouldn't be human if she didn't want her mom and dad to see her on that podium accepting a crystal statuette. It would be a very public vindication of her battle to assert herself and her dreams.

The old sadness welled up inside her as she admitted to herself that she would probably never know if her parents had even seen the show, let alone if they had it in them to be proud of her still…

"We're going to kick ass," Sadie said, stretching out languorously.

"What are you going to wear?" Grace asked. "Please tell me it's not black."

Claudia threw one of the suite's heavily tasseled cushions at her friend.

"It's red, if you must know." Sadie and Grace teased her a lot about always wearing black. Partly it was because she was too busy to shop, and black always went with black. But partly it was because she felt as though people took her seriously when she was dressed in dark colors. She was small and she was female—she wasn't about to disadvantage herself further by dressing like a sex kitten or a vamp.

"Gracie?" Sadie asked, switching her attention to the other woman.

"Vintage Dior. Mac bought it for me. That's all I'm saying," she said, waggling her eyebrows mysteriously.

"What about you, Sade?" Claudia asked.

"I'm recycling. The black-and-white sheath I wore a few years ago." She shrugged.

"You know, usually I hate these things, but I have a

good feeling about this one," Grace said, suppressed excitement in her voice.

Claudia met her friends' eyes and held up both her crossed fingers.

She really wanted to win this award. And not just because it meant she could rub Leandro Mandalor's big Greek nose in her triumph.

Although that was definitely part of the appeal.

LEANDRO TURNED the shower on, waiting till the water was good and hot before stepping beneath the stream. His old soccer injury was aching after a day of sitting in one position for too long, and he rolled his shoulder for a few minutes, letting the heat work the stiffness out of his muscles. Reaching for the tiny bottles of toiletries supplied by the hotel, he squeezed shampoo into his palm and massaged it into his hair. Immediately, he was surrounded by a scent that was strangely familiar and beguiling. Definitely floral, but with a warm undertone that hinted at something darker and deeper. Inhaling deeply, he closed his eyes and tried to think. A vague image swam across his mind's eye, and then it came to him: Claudia Dostis. The shampoo smelled exactly like Claudia Dostis.

He smiled into the shower spray as he rinsed the lather from his hair. His shin had already turned a pleasing shade of bruise from her well-planted kick a few hours ago, and he knew he should be more pissed than tickled by her display of temper, but he couldn't help himself. She reminded him of all the best things about his feisty female relatives—full of pluck and opinion and zest for life. She might be one step up from midget status, but she was all energy—a vibrant, dynamic woman who took life by the scruff of the neck and shook it for all it was worth.

Plus he'd always had a thing for short women. Easy to say when he checked in at six feet four inches, since almost every woman was shorter than he was, but Claudia was genuinely on the miniature side. Just like most of his girl-friends since high school. And his soon-to-be ex-wife, Peta.

Thinking about Peta effectively killed any buzz he'd generated thinking about the feisty Ms. Dostis. He'd had the divorce papers couriered over to Peta last week, but she was still stalling on signing. They hadn't been married for long enough for the delay to be about the money—they'd both agreed to walk away with what they'd brought to the relationship. The reality was, Peta didn't need his money. As it turned out, she hadn't needed his anything. Their marriage had been a joke from beginning to end—a joke perpetrated by his raging hormones and his stubborn belief that he could make their relationship work.

Now he just wanted it to be over. It was bad enough that he was the only member of his large family to have a divorce under his belt. His brothers and sisters had all chosen well when they gave away their hearts. His mama hadn't stopped telling him that she'd known from the moment she set eyes on Peta that she was wrong for her boy. Too blond. Too skinny. Too ambitious.

While he still didn't agree with his mother on points one or two, he had to bow to her superior wisdom on three; Peta, it turned out, had cared more about her career as an up-and-coming agent than she did about her fledgling marriage. When she'd opted to use confidential informa-tion that he'd shared with her in the privacy of their bedroom to further her career, he'd gotten the message loud and clear. Peta had a fire in her belly—but it wasn't big enough to warm the both of them. It had only been a matter of time after that before their marriage had died a quiet, painful death.

Turning his back to the shower spray, Leandro planted his hands on the wall opposite and ducked his head, letting the water run down the column of his spine.

Was he bitter? He didn't think so. More…wary. He still wanted a wife, children. He wanted the warmth and belonging of building his own little family unit. But next time around, he would choose more wisely. No more career women in their stiletto heels and neat little suits. No more business lunches that turned into personal dinners and then something much more personal. This time, he'd use his head as well as his heart and regions farther south when he picked his life mate.

His thoughts flew to the delicious Ms. Dostis again, and regions farther south gave a definite twitch of approval. Yeah, she was hot. A pocket rocket, his brothers would call her— small of frame and stature, but with curves in all the right places. She was all woman, and if she attacked sex with one fraction of the energy she attacked the rest of life, he figured bedtime with her would be a death-defying experience.

Reluctantly, he pushed the tempting thoughts from his mind. She was his competitor, for starters. And even if there wasn't *that* major stumbling block to consider, there was the fact that he was about to become a newly divorced man at the age of thirty-six. His days of playing the field were behind him—he wanted to be young enough to kick a soccer ball with his children. There was no time to stop and smell the flowers anymore, even if Claudia was a particularly enticing bloom. He was a man on a mission—meet, mate, procreate.

Exiting the shower, he toweled himself dry and wandered, naked, into the bedroom. His suit was hanging on the back of the closet door and he eyed it with misgiving for a long beat. Monkey suits were the curse of the industry, in his opinion. No matter how well-cut the suit, he always felt as though he was wearing a straitjacket. Shrugging into his shirt, his mind drifted to the night ahead. Speeches, announcements, daytime stars, writers, directors and producers swanning about with too much champagne and too little food. It was going to be duller than dull. There was only one moment of possible interest—the Best Special Feature Award. There were four contenders in the category, but *Heartland*'s only real competition was *Ocean Boulevard*.

He was quietly confident they'd pull it off. He'd lavished money, time and effort on their white wedding episode. They'd shot on location in Aspen, bought a couture dress and sprung for extra publicity. True, *Ocean Boulevard*'s special had just beaten them in the ratings. But Leandro was sure the production values of his effort would tip the balance in their favor.

Slipping on boxer briefs, he pulled his suit trousers on. Claudia would breathe fire when he stood on the podium and accepted the award. Did it make him a cad that he was looking forward to seeing her delicate nostrils flare out in anger yet again?

Just the thought of it brought a smile to his face as he tied his shoelaces.

He couldn't remember the last time a little friendly rivalry had been so much fun.

LIAR, LIAR, *pants on fire.*

The words ran across Claudia's mind as she stopped

dead in her tracks at the sight of Leandro Mandalor in full black tie. Good Lord, he looked stunning—a veritable man mountain in elegant black. His hair shone in the discreet lighting of the hotel's ballroom, and the crisp white of his shirt was the perfect foil for his olive skin.

In contrast to what she'd told her friends earlier, he was a very, very attractive man.

There, she'd admitted it, if only to herself. And she'd be damned if she ever said the words out loud—it was embarrassing enough having the hots for a man so beneath her contempt.

Although…she'd been thinking quite a bit about what he'd said to her earlier at the convention—about what she would have done in his shoes. If she'd learned he was trying to stitch up the winter ratings period, she'd have seen red…then she'd have tried to out-maneuver him. Which was pretty much what he'd done. He'd announced his wedding episode, proclaimed it to the world as the last word in lavish soap excess, then dared her to best him. So maybe he wasn't quite as contemptuous as she'd first thought.

But he was still her arch rival—conniving sneakery or no conniving sneakery. He still lusted after her ratings points, just as she salivated over his. And he was Greek. She never, ever dated Greek men. They reminded her of her brothers and her father and her cousins, and they brought to mind every family gathering she'd ever attended since before she could remember. They were too traditional, too alpha, too domineering. Not that she was in any danger of being dominated—she simply had better things to do with her time than to manage some lunkhead with a bee in his bonnet about looking after her, or something equally medieval. She preferred men with more modern outlooks, men who played by the same rules she did.

"Wow. Check out those sissy lips and that big Greek honker," Grace said, eating up Leandro with her eyes.

"*Oooh* yeah, he just about makes me feel sick to my stomach," Sadie chimed in.

Standing on Grace's other side, Mac cleared his throat and shot Dylan a world-weary look.

"A little consideration for the chopped liver over here, ladies," Mac said. "At least wait until we're not around before you start scoring the other studs out of ten."

"The *other* studs?" Grace asked, one eyebrow arched imperiously.

"We still qualify, even if we are spoken for," Dylan said, smoothing a hand down the sleeve of his midnight-blue tux.

Sadie stepped close to straighten his tie. "I'm willing to concede the point," she said huskily, smiling up at him from under her lashes.

Claudia tore her eyes from Leandro and tried to remember what she'd been thinking before she got hit by the freight train that was her rival's sex appeal.

Right. Their table. She'd been looking for their table. Consulting the notes her assistant had provided, she began scanning the room for table five. It was flatteringly close to the stage, and Claudia told herself it was a good sign— easy access to the podium. The organizers wouldn't do that unless she actually needed to get up there, right?

"We're over here, guys," she said, directing them toward the round banquet table marked for *Ocean Boulevard*.

As she turned away, something tugged at her awareness. She knew Leandro was looking at her before she glanced his way. His near-black eyes were unreadable from a distance, but his acknowledging nod and the quirk of his mouth told her he was laughing at her again. In an instant she went from self-conscious to annoyed. More than anything, she'd like to flip him the finger. Instead, she smoothed a hand down her hip and over her butt, all of it hugged to perfection in deep red velvet, and turned her back on him.

She could feel him watching her all the way to her table, and she thanked her guardian angel that she didn't stumble in her high heels and long skirt. Just what she needed, to go ass-over-tit in front of Mr. Machismo.

"Claud, you sit between me and Grace," Sadie said. "That way we won't have to talk across Mac and Dylan all night."

"See? Chopped liver again," Mac joked as he took his seat. Grace slid her hand beneath the table and an arrested expression crossed Mac's handsome face.

"Still feeling like chopped liver?" Grace asked in a sultry tone.

"N-no, not exactly," Mac said, his eyes finding Grace's substantial cleavage.

"Settle, children. Don't make me go find the fire hose," Claudia warned them.

Lately she'd found herself feeling like a spinster aunt with two sets of lovebirds twittering around her constantly. Most of the time she was too busy to regret her lack of a love life, but when she saw a fine specimen of manhood such as Leandro dressed up in all his finery, she couldn't help remembering that there were definite perks to having a man in her life.

Sex being the major perk on her mind right this minute as she watched Leandro weave his way through the tables. For a big man, he moved with surprising grace. And even though she'd made a few cracks about his Greek nose, it suited him. It was a man's nose—a take-no-prisoners kind of nose.

Realizing that she was staring, Claudia concentrated on unfolding her napkin and spreading it across her lap.

Off-limits, she reminded herself. But perhaps a timely reminder that it had been a while since she'd caught up with either Harry or Simon, her two bed buddies. Although last time she'd seen him, Harry had been all doe-eyed over a woman in his office. One of the hazards of bed buddies—sometimes they fell in love with someone and left a girl stranded.

Sliding her slim-lined cell phone from her small clutch purse, Claudia punched in a quick text message to Simon. If he was free tonight, there was no reason why he couldn't meet her at the hotel after the ceremony. Instead of spending the night on her own, ricocheting around the lavish suite the production company had provided for the duration of the convention, she and Simon could see how many rooms they could christen.

Her finger hovering over the Send key, Claudia glanced up and was caught in the magnetic darkness of Leandro's gaze. His table was the one across from hers, and he was seated facing her. She'd be looking at him all night. At those shoulders. Those firm, full lips. And he'd be looking right back at her, his eyes full of heat and curiosity and challenge.

Her finger descended on the Send key, and she sent a prayer to the goddess that Simon was sitting at home twiddling his thumbs tonight. If she had any luck, he'd be twiddling something a lot more interesting later this evening.

Feeling distinctly jittery, she fidgeted with her silverware and wineglass and pretended she was listening to what her friends were saying on either side of her while she waited for her old lover to respond.

It had been a few months since she'd scratched the particular itch that was bugging her tonight, she realized as she did a mental calendar check. How had that happened? No wonder she was feeling like a cat on a hot tin roof. She was well overdue for a good roll in the hay.

Her phone beeped in her purse and she almost leaped on it. Her breath hissed out between her teeth as she saw Simon's response: Can't make it. Wish me luck—just got engaged! S.

Good Lord. Claudia stared at the screen for a full minute, feeling as though someone had pulled the rug out from under her. First Harry, now Simon. She really *was* a hard-up spinster. Automatically she sent a text back, offering her congratulations and best wishes. Simon was a nice guy. She really did wish him well.

She was so distracted, she didn't notice the waiter leaning close to pour her wine, and her glass was full before she could protest. Grace solved the problem by placing her hand over her own glass, then swapping with Claudia's full one when the waiter had moved on.

"Thanks," Claudia said, reaching for her water glass.

"No problem," Grace said. "Relax, Claud—if we win it's great, if we lose it doesn't mean anything."

"Okay. I'm not quite sure how the logic of that works, but I'll try to go with it," Claudia said.

She *was* nervous about the stupid award. That was probably half the reason why her stomach was tied up in knots. As for being sexually frustrated…well, it wasn't like she was going to lose control and start humping Leandro Mandalor's leg or anything, was it? She could survive one evening of being attracted to a handsome man without taking a one-way trip to Desperado-ville.

"Ladies and gentleman, please take your seats if you haven't already. We're thrilled to have you all here this evening to celebrate the twenty-third annual People's Vote Awards," a smooth voice announced over the speakers.

Claudia sat up straighter. Grace and Sadie grabbed one of her hands each.

"Two hours, a million speeches, and too much wine from now, it will all be over," Grace said.

"We're going to win," Sadie said.

"Definitely we're going to win," Dylan agreed.

Claudia forced a smile. Suddenly she felt twelve years old again, standing in school assembly, waiting to hear her name called for the academic achievement awards. It was stupid to place so much weight on something that was essentially meaningless in her day-to-day life. She earned a good salary, the show was rating well, she had great friends. This award wouldn't add or subtract from her life in any way.

But she was still ridiculously excited and nervous and apprehensive.

Against her will, her gaze found Leandro at his table. He was watching her, but she'd already known that. Lifting his champagne flute, he mouthed the words, "Good Luck," to her. She inclined her head in regal acknowledgment.

May the best woman win.

LEANDRO SPUN his wineglass around and around on the white linen tablecloth and tried to keep his eyes from wandering to Claudia Dostis again. It was useless, however—she looked spectacular in a deep red velvet evening gown, and he was powerless to stop himself from seeking out the deeply shadowed V between her breasts. Idly he wondered if she was worried about one of her girls accidentally popping out to say "hello" during the evening—her dress was seriously cut almost down to her belly button. She must be using a hell of a lot of Hollywood tape, he figured. But it didn't stop him fantasizing about the neckline of her top gaping or sliding open a fraction more. Just enough for him to see some nipple. One would be enough. For some reason, he'd developed something of a preoccupation regarding her nipples since she'd set foot in the room. He wanted to know what they looked like—whether they were small and pouty or large and swollen—what color they were, how they would feel beneath his hands, in his mouth, against his tongue. What sort of noises she'd make when he sucked on them, thumbed them, bit them.

Just your garden-variety obsession, really. One that had kept him in his seat for most of the evening, concealing the kind of hard-on he hadn't *enjoyed* since senior high.

The bummer was, he wasn't ever going to find out the answer to all those sensual conundrums. Claudia's nipples would remain her little secret, for a host of good reasons he'd already gone over in his suite upstairs. Damn it.

A round of applause cut across his thoughts and he automatically brought his hands together. Dragging his eyes from the scarlet vixen across the way, he ran a finger down the awards list for the evening. One more announcement, and then they were up. He felt in his pocket to see if the speech he'd written earlier was still there, then surreptitiously used the back of his spoon to check that he didn't have spinach stuck in his teeth.

When he glanced back at Claudia, she was smoothing on fresh lipstick and patting her sleek, shiny bob into place.

A waste of good makeup, he thought wryly. *Sure hope she's a good loser.*

CLAUDIA SAT on the very edge of her chair, her hands hidden beneath the table as she clutched her speech between icy-cold hands.

She could feel her heartbeat echoing in her belly, and her head felt as though it was balanced precariously on the end of her neck. What if she won, but couldn't make it on stage because she was so nervous? Or, worse, what if she tripped on the stairs, and went sprawling in front of the entire industry? Or—absolute disaster—what if she stood on her hem and her skirt tore off and she was left standing in nothing but the skimpy lace thong she was wearing beneath all the velvet?

The absurdity of the last thought brought a smile to her lips. She could walk. She could talk. Somehow, she'd manage to combine the two and get up on the stage if her name was called.

"…and our last two finalists in this category, *Heartlands* for their feature-length special *White Wedding,* and *Ocean Boulevard* for their feature-length special, *Paradise Found.* A great year for this category, I think you'd all agree, with some top-drawer competition," the MC said.

Sadie's hand squeezed Claudia's knee beneath the table, and Grace shot her a look loaded with anticipation and excitement.

"And the winner of the People's Vote Award for Best Special Feature is…*Ocean Boulevard* for *Paradise Lost.* Give a big hand to producer, Claudia Dostis, everyone!"

Absolute astonishment shot through Claudia like a jet of ice-cold water. Then a warm flush raced through her body and up into her face.

"We won," she said stupidly.

Grace and Sadie were laughing and jumping up out of their seats to hug her and drag her to her feet. All around them, people were clapping and looking her way with congratulatory smiles. At the back of the stage, a huge screen showed selected highlights from their wedding special.

"We did it, Claud, we did it," Sadie said, squealing with excitement.

"Go get 'em, tiger," Grace said, pushing Claudia toward the stage.

Claudia blinked, then took a step forward. Then another. An agent she'd wrangled with just last week stepped forward to kiss her cheek in congratulations. A former boss clapped her on the back and told her he'd always known she had what it took. The MC smiled down at her as she mounted the steps, her head floating about a mile above her body now.

Then she was standing at the podium, and she came back into her body with a jerk. A thousand faces stared up at her, waiting. She forgot about her speech and spoke from the heart instead.

"One of the great things about working on *Ocean Boulevard* is the genuine passion that we all have for what we do," she said. "I think that shows in every episode, but this special was a real labor of love from the word 'go.' I have to thank Dylan Anderson for his amazing idea and story magic, and my incredibly talented script producer, Sadie Post—sorry, it's Anderson now, I keep forgetting—for pulling it all together. I also have to thank the gifted, the brilliant Grace Wellington for bringing Sadie and Dylan's story to life with her wonderful script, and Mac Harrison for his inventiveness and creativity in realizing our shared vision when he directed the episode. Lastly, I have to thank the cast for once again giving their everything and making us all believe. Everyone here knows that television is a collaborative medium, and that behind the scenes are hundreds of people whose efforts make what we do possible. We have the best cast, an outstanding, can-do crew, and a supportive network. We're all tremendously proud of this special, and we're proud of the fact that it won the ratings, and it's fantastic to stand up here tonight with this award. Thank you!"

Holding the award high, Claudia grinned broadly.

She'd imagined this moment for so long. The buzz of triumph. The satisfied knowledge that all their hard work had been recognized. The approval—even envy—of her peers.

And the vindication that originality and creativity would win over strategy and cunning any day of the week.

Moving toward the stairs offstage, her gaze tracked across the tables full of smiling, applauding people until they stopped on one man. His eyes held hers for a long beat before he nodded his head in acknowledgment and slowly clapped his hands in a private round of applause meant just for her.

Victory, it turned out, was sweet indeed.

The next few minutes dissolved into a blur of handshakes and kisses and jumping up and down from the *Ocean Boulevard* contingent as they passed around their trophy, took photos of each other and generally gloated and celebrated. Sadie and Grace stood on either side of Claudia, arms wrapped around her waist, big smiles on their faces. For a moment Claudia was choked with emotion. These women were so important to her, and together they'd made something great, and it had been recognized in front of the industry.

Despite her determination to keep things positive, her thoughts turned to her parents. If things were right between them, she would be out in the foyer right now, calling them to tell them she'd won. Her father would bellow loudly and break into excited Greek and want to hang up and phone the whole extended family to brag. Her mother would ask what she was wearing and insist that Claudia get plenty of photographs for later.

But things were not right with her parents. And they never would be.

Feeling an unaccustomed lump of emotion in her throat, Claudia excused herself from the celebrations and made her way to the ladies' room.

It was cool and quiet in there amongst the marble and gold-plated taps, and she took a few deep breaths to calm herself. Her color was high, she saw in the mirror, and she ran some cool water over her wrists before drying them and exiting to the foyer.

She'd almost made her way back to the ballroom when a warm hand wound itself around her elbow and tugged her into a darkened corner. She found herself facing Leandro—staring up at him, more accurately. Up close, he was devastatingly attractive in his formal wear and her heart instantly kicked up a gear.

"Claudia. I just wanted to tell you that dress is…spectacular," he said, his dark gaze dipping into her cleavage.

"Thank you. You scrub up okay yourself," she said.

He shrugged dismissively, then reached out a hand. She watched, for all intents and purposes paralyzed, as his fingers found the neckline of her dress just above the swell of her right breast. Catching the velvet between thumb and forefinger, he gave a murmur of appreciation as he ran his thumb back and forth over the pile of the velvet.

"Velvet is so tactile, don't you think?" he said. "Makes you want to reach out and touch."

She could feel the backs of his fingers against her skin, and she knew she should knock his hand away. But for some reason, she didn't.

"Aren't you going to congratulate me?" she asked, trying to find some solid ground, some reason to not take him up on the invitation in his eyes.

"Definitely," he said, and then he lowered his head and she knew he was going to kiss her.

She could have taken a step back, said no, pushed him away. She did none of those things. She stood on her tiptoes, swayed forward, met him halfway, her mouth already open. He gave a growl of approval as their lips met, heat on heat, silk on silk, and then she was leaning against the never-ending wall of his chest, and his arms were around her and his tongue was in her mouth.

She felt surrounded by him. Invaded by him. And she'd never been more turned-on in her life. His tongue brushed over hers, his hands splayed across her bottom and lifted her into the firmness of his erection, his teeth nibbled at her lower lip, his five o'clock shadow brushed her cheeks and neck.

Her breasts hardened into two demanding, greedy peaks, and even the thickness of the velvet was not proof against her need as her nipples jutted into his chest. Between her thighs, desire throbbed, thick and heavy as treacle. On fire for him, she thought feverishly of the suite upstairs, of the big bed, of getting this giant of a man naked and inside her where he belonged, where he could take away the ache he'd created inside her…

And then he broke the kiss, and stepped away from her.

It was like walking out of a sauna and straight into a plunge pool. She'd been so absorbed in him, in what they'd created between them.

"Congratulations, Claudia," he said, his voice husky with desire.

Then he walked away.

2

CLAUDIA WAS STILL FUMING the next day when she arrived at work. She hadn't seen Leandro Mandalor's face when he'd walked away from her, but she'd bet her house, her car and her job that he'd been smiling. The smug bastard.

Her responding to his kiss didn't mean a thing. He was obviously a practiced seducer, a charmer from way back. She'd allowed him to work his wiles on her, and it had been amusing. Entertaining, for a brief, unimportant moment in time. Then she'd gone back into the ballroom and reveled in her win and hadn't looked at him once more all night.

So there was no need for him to feel as though he'd achieved something, just because she hadn't slapped his face or gagged with disgust. It had been a kiss, nothing more. No big deal.

Slamming her car door shut, Claudia grimaced at her reflection in the tinted glass of her side window. Her eyes were deeply shadowed from lack of sleep—and not because she'd been partying endlessly all night with the gang from work. As usual, she hadn't touched a drop of alcohol and she'd rolled into bed and closed her eyes at the very respectable time of midnight.

And promptly not slept a wink for the entire night.

And not because of excitement, either. At least, not excitement over their win.

No. Unfortunately, it had been the other kind of excitement that had kept her up. The Leandro-Mandalor-induced kind.

One kiss, and she'd been ready to drag him up to her suite and ride him like a pony at the fair. She closed her eyes as she imagined how monumental her regret would be this morning if she'd actually followed through on that instinct instead of limiting her transgression to a single kiss.

Although, technically, it hadn't been her who had limited it. Leandro had been the one who had walked away.

Which brought her back to her favorite two words for the day: *smug bastard.* Why hadn't she been the one to push him away, to smile up into his face and deliver a sassy line? Why, why, why?

Thank God she wasn't still at the convention. A small saving grace. With a bit of luck, she wouldn't have to look him in the eye again for a full twelve months.

Collecting the award from her back seat, she clicked her car shut and made her way into the building. The news of their win had spread through the office and she was mobbed the moment she walked in the door.

It took her a full half hour to make it to her desk, but by then her mood had improved dramatically. It was great to see how proud her staff was of the award. As she'd said last night, television was a collaborative medium. No one person could take credit for the success of the show, and it was great to be able to pass the joy around. There was an official display cabinet for awards in the conference room, but she decided that this latest gong might find a home on the reception desk for the first few months. That way everyone could remember their win when they walked into work each morning.

Crossing to her office, she saw Sadie was at her desk already, looking bright-eyed and not in the least hungover. Claudia narrowed her gaze on her friend, taking in Sadie's glowing complexion and suddenly remembering the untouched wineglass at her friend's place setting last night.

Suspicion hardened into certainty as she walked into Sadie's office and Sadie fumbled to hastily open a new screen on her Web browser.

Claudia smiled, propping her butt on the edge of Sadie's desk and swinging her foot casually.

"Have a good time last night?" she asked idly.

"Of course. Not every day we get a People's Vote Award," Sadie said.

"So you're not tired at all?" Claudia probed.

Sadie shrugged. "Not really. We didn't tie one on, since both Dylan and I had to work today. I don't understand why they hold the awards night on a Monday."

Claudia nodded, then stood. "It's so we don't enjoy ourselves too much. God forbid that anyone ever feels comfortable in this industry."

Moving toward the door, Claudia waited until she was on the threshold before she spoke over her shoulder. "And by the way, I think Amazon is having a special on baby books this month."

"Yeah? Thanks," Sadie said brightly, then she bit her lip and blushed hotly.

"Huh! Gotcha!" Claudia said, pouncing. "You're pregnant."

Sadie just smiled ruefully. "I told Dylan there was no point trying to keep it from you and Grace. He doesn't understand about female intuition."

Claudia ignored the small flicker of hurt that her friend

would want to keep such great news from her in the first place. Plenty of couples liked to wait until they'd passed the crucial first trimester before spreading their good news far and wide. There was nothing unusual in Sadie and Dylan wanting to hold tight to their secret for a little bit longer. Except…for a while now, it had been just the three of them—her, Sadie and Grace. Perhaps it was an index of how wrong Sadie's first engagement to Greg had been that Claudia had never felt this way about their relationship. But Sadie and Dylan were utterly committed to each other. They'd been married for just six months, and now they had a baby on the way. The friendship between her, Sadie and Grace would never be the same again.

Of course things were going to change, she scolded herself impatiently. She knew that; it was a part of life. Grace and Sadie had fallen in love and settled down. Claudia had simply been too busy working and looking in the other direction to really notice what was happening around her.

"How many weeks?" she asked, pushing her own feelings aside to celebrate her friend's great news.

"We think eight. I've got a doctor's appointment tomorrow," Sadie said.

Claudia rounded her friend's desk to hug her.

"I'm so happy for you. For both of you. A little Sadie or Dylan. I can't wait to meet him or her," Claudia said.

"I still can't quite believe it. A little person is going to grow inside me. How weird and amazing is that? I keep thinking about those scenes in *Alien*. Is that wrong, do you think?" Sadie asked worriedly. "Shouldn't I be knitting booties or something instead of worrying about a monster bursting out of my abdomen?"

Claudia laughed. "Leave it to you to turn pregnancy into a science fiction gore fest. You'll be fine, Sade. Worse comes to worst, you can sleep through the whole birth these days and watch it on video later."

"Now you're talking," Sadie said with enthusiasm. "I know I'm supposed to want the whole yoga-aromatherapy-natural-birth thing, but pain is not my friend. I want whatever they've got in big, industrial doses."

"A woman after my own heart. If I ever had a kid, I'd want them to just induce a coma in the last week of pregnancy and then wake me when the kid's toilet trained," Claudia said.

Sadie blinked with surprise.

"You know, that's the first time I've ever heard you talk about having children," she said.

"Hey, you're the one who's pregnant, not me. I was speaking hypothetically. You know I don't want kids," Claudia said, picking a piece of lint off her trousers.

A groan sounded behind them.

"All I want to know is, does one of you have a handgun?"

They both turned to find Grace standing in the doorway, her already pale complexion alabaster and her eyes hidden behind her cat's eye sunglasses.

"It would be a mercy killing. You could take me out to the car park and do it quietly," she moaned, flopping into Sadie's visitor's chair. Swooning theatrically, she pressed a hand to her forehead.

"I feel like Tallulah Bankhead," she said.

Sadie and Claudia exchanged amused looks.

"Too much champagne, Gracie?" Claudia said in her loudest, no-nonsense voice.

Grace winced and held up a hand. "Don't be cruel. It's not nice to taunt the animals," she said.

Sadie shook her head and reached into her desk drawer. "Here, have some aspirin," she said, tossing the pack over. Then she caught Claudia's eye and lifted an eyebrow. Claudia shrugged a shoulder in response to her friend's unspoken question. The cat was out of the bag already, after all.

"But before you go off to nurse your hangover," Sadie added, "I've got some news. Well, really, it's mine and Dylan's news."

Grace sat up as though someone had goosed her. Her glasses slid down to the end of her nose as she looked over them at Sadie.

"Get out of town," she said. "You're not pregnant!"

"Incorrect. Do not pass go, do not collect two hundred dollars," Claudia said.

Leaping to her feet, Grace raced around the desk and threw herself into Sadie's arms.

"You and Dylan are going to make the best parents," she said, hugging Sadie fiercely. "The absolute best. Imagine the bedtime stories that kid's going to hear."

They spent another twenty minutes combing over the few bare details of Sadie's pregnancy so far—two missed periods, no nausea, no tiredness, definite increase in bust size—and discussing Sadie's *Alien* fears before peeling off to go to their respective offices.

Claudia found a pile of phone message slips on her desk, all of them congratulation messages bar two. Her voice mail was likewise clogged, and she put a call through to her assistant to ask her to sort through the backlog and let her know if there were any genuine callbacks required.

Then she sat back and stared at her office wall. Sadie was going to have a baby. She and Dylan were going to have a little family. If Grace's rapt expression and intent questioning were anything to go by, she and Mac wouldn't be far behind, either. Grace had a couple of years on Sadie, after all.

And Claudia was older than both of them.

It wasn't something she'd ever really registered before. They'd all met at university when they joined the Undergraduate Film Festival Committee, and soon formed a firm friendship. Even though Sadie had skipped a year at school, and Claudia had tried her hand out in the workforce for a few years before opting for higher education, age had always been irrelevant in their bonding.

Frowning, Claudia checked her e-mail. She didn't care about her ovaries aging. They could self-combust for all she'd notice—she'd fought too long and too hard to get where she was to walk away from it all to serve up puréed apple and change diapers twenty-four hours a day. Babies were fine for other women, but not for her.

Ruthlessly she squashed the memory of holding her eldest brother's first son in the hospital. She'd been surprised by the fierce tug of love she'd felt, the instinctive desire to protect and nurture the tiny red person bundled in the blanket. Almost as though to eliminate any maternal longing, a grim memory pulled at Claudia: an image of a woman huddled on a bed, sobbing her heart out.

Impatient with her self-indulgence this morning, Claudia brushed it away. While she was contemplating her navel, *Ocean Boulevard* awaited.

It was mid-morning when her assistant, Gabby, buzzed a call through to her.

"I have Leandro Mandalor on line one," Gabby said. She sounded faintly scandalized that the competition would dare to call.

Claudia pursed her lips.

"Tell him I'm unavailable," she said. "Tell him to call back in an hour."

Smiling to herself, she bent to her work again. Did he really think he could just call her after what had happened and she'd jump at the chance to talk to him like a good little girl?

Probably he did, she knew. That ego. That self-assurance—of course he did.

Well, he had another think coming.

Exactly an hour later, Gabby buzzed her again.

"I've got Mr. Mandalor again," she said.

"Tell him my meeting has run overtime. He should try again in another hour," Claudia said.

An hour later, Gabby came through to Claudia's office.

"It's him again," she said. She looked faintly harassed. "I think he knows I'm lying."

"I'm a busy person, Gabby. He has no way of knowing if I'm in a meeting or not. Tell him I went straight out to my lunch meeting without checking my messages. You don't know when I'll be back."

Looking distinctly uncomfortable, Gabby picked up the line from Claudia's office.

"Mr. Mandalor? I'm terribly sorry, but Ms. Dostis has gone straight out to her luncheon appointment. Perhaps if you tried later this afternoon…?"

Claudia could hear the low bass of Leandro's voice without being able to discern actual words. She frowned as Gabby flinched, then went pale.

"Um, just hold on a moment," Gabby said, reaching for the hold key as though it were a lifeline.

"What?" Claudia asked. "Did he bully you? What an asshole."

"He said that you've had your fun, but that he wasn't

calling about the kiss. He said that something very important has come up and unless you want to see it across the front page of *The National Enquirer,* you should take his call."

To her everlasting shame, Claudia felt herself blush with self-consciousness. How dare he mention that stupid kiss to her assistant?

"Give me that," she said, wresting the phone from Gabby's unresisting fingers.

Her finger punched down onto the hold button.

"What do you want?" she asked bluntly as soon as the line went live.

"My, my. What a terribly quick lunch that must have been," Leandro said.

It was the first time she'd heard his voice over the phone. To her astonishment, the deep vibrato of his baritone made something utterly primitive and feminine within her snap to quivering attention.

"Do you or do you not have a business matter to discuss with me?" she said.

Gabby was standing in her doorway, hovering curiously. Claudia gave her a thumbs-up to indicate all was well and sent her on her way.

"That kiss was hot, but not hot enough for me to jump through all those flaming hoops like a dumb circus pony, Claudia. Yes, I have a business issue to discuss."

Not hot enough? Where did this guy get off? Claudia puffed her cheeks out and put her free hand on her hip, really ticked off now. Then she noticed Gabby still hovering.

This time she waved her hand at her sticky-beak assistant, indicating she should go, and Gabby had no choice but to slink away unsatisfied.

"Fire away, then, Mr. Mandalor. I'm a busy woman."

"Not too busy for this. Are you aware that a member of your cast is, shall we say, getting it on with a member of mine?" he asked.

Claudia blinked and sat back in her chair. She usually had a pretty good grip on who was doing what with whom. It was part of the job—she needed to know who might be at risk, and who was putting the show at risk.

"No. Who are we talking about here?"

"Alicia Morrison on your side, Wes Brooks on mine," he said.

Claudia winced. Alicia was just seventeen, Wes in his thirties. Not a particularly good look, especially when Alicia played a character called Angel.

"But wait, there's more," Claudia said, anticipating Leandro's next line.

"Clever lady. The reason I know about this little…fling…is that Alicia and Wes were dumb enough to videotape themselves in action."

Shit.

"Please tell me that tape has not disappeared," she said.

"House break-in. Just your usual grab and run. But guess which tape was still in the video machine?"

Claudia mouthed a four-letter word.

"So Wes came to you and confessed all?" Claudia asked. "And now we're just waiting for the other shoe to drop?"

"It's worse than that. I got a call this morning from some scuzzball. He wants to meet tonight to find out what this tape is worth to both of us."

Claudia frowned. "Blackmail?" Her stomach tensed. This was a first for her.

"In a word."

Claudia stared at her desk, her mind racing as she calculated what was at stake. Alicia was a popular, up-and-coming young actress. She'd played a virginal innocent since joining the show at age fourteen. Lord only knew when and how she'd met Wes, but Claudia couldn't help feeling some responsibility for the situation she was in. Who was to say what Alicia's life would be like if *Boulevard* hadn't plucked her out of a shopping center talent competition and put her on national television? Not that Alicia was crying herself to sleep at night over her great career or anything—but perhaps she shouldn't have to suffer publicly for her bad decisions just yet.

Then there was the damage this would cause to the show. They had a strong core audience in the Midwest. She could just imagine the kind of mail she'd get if triple X-rated footage began to do the rounds. She'd be forced to lose Alicia, which would mean months of rewriting and stress for her team…

"Where does our budding entrepreneur want to meet?" she asked, grabbing a pen and pulling her notepad toward her.

"He gave me an address for a bar on the Strip. Here's what I was thinking—I go along representing both of us tonight, see what he's got, whether it's anything to worry about. Then we reconvene to discuss our options."

"Sure. What address and what time?" Claudia said impatiently, brushing aside his offer to be the front man for both of them.

"I don't think—"

"I can see that. Don't worry, I'm smart enough for both of us. Can I have the address, please?"

She heard him swear under his breath, then the shuffle of paper on the other end of the phone.

"It's called Monkey Shine," he said, reading out an address on Sunset Strip. "He wants to meet at nine tonight."

"Fine. I'll meet you there at eight-thirty," Claudia said, underlining the address and time on her notepad.

"You really want to do this? Even though I'm giving you an out?" Leandro asked.

Claudia lifted the phone away from her ear and stared at the receiver. What planet was this guy from? Some place where women still met their men at the door with pipe and slippers in hand?

"News flash—having a penis doesn't make you more capable of doing anything except urinating while standing up," she said. "I'll see you at eight-thirty. Don't be late."

THE LITTLE GRUB flexing his extortion muscles had picked a suitably sleazy locale to begin his apprenticeship, Leandro decided. Monkey Shine had grimy painted-over windows out front and a neon sign with several letters burned out. Inside wasn't much better—sticky carpet, the stink of stale beer and cigarettes, and lighting so dim he could barely see his hand in front of his face.

Booths lined the left-hand wall, a bar the right. He made his way to the latter on the basis that the illuminated Jack Daniel's sign above the glass rack offered marginally more light. He was early—Claudia wasn't due for another ten minutes—but he'd wanted to check the place out first. If it was beyond the pale, he'd meet her at the door and lay down the law. He was sure she could hold her own in the boardroom or on the studio floor, but this was different. This was shady underbelly stuff, and she was so small he could pick her up and carry her around in his shirt pocket. He didn't want to be responsible for her getting hurt.

Ordering a Miller, he narrowed his eyes and scanned the room. There was a doorway at the back with a sign hanging over it announcing that pool tables and toilets could be found on the other side. It was a seedy place, but it didn't seem to have more than its fair share of bums, drunks, louts and hookers. He figured he'd have trouble convincing Claudia she should go home without bullet holes or a forensic body outline to support his case.

He'd just taken his first mouthful of beer when something sharp and hard hit him on the back of the neck. Frowning, he shot a look to the ceiling to see if the sky was, indeed, falling, then flicked a look over his shoulder. The second peanut caught him just below the eye, and he jerked his head back instinctively.

She was seated in the shadows of the third booth from the door, and Leandro shook his head as he slid in opposite her.

"Had to check it out on your own, didn't you?" he said.

"Great minds think alike," she said.

She was wearing a sleeveless black turtleneck sweater, and he couldn't stop himself from admiring the way the thin knit clung to her breasts. She might be small, but her breasts looked more than enough to satisfy any man.

"Fancy that, my breasts are in the same place they were last night. A miracle," she said dryly.

As always with her, he found himself smiling.

"You're a sexy lady. I'm only human." He shrugged.

"Subhuman, you mean," she sniffed.

"There's nothing sub about me, babe," he said with a cocky grin.

She eyed him steadily. "I'll take your word for it."

He took a mouthful of beer, noticing that she was nursing a cola and something.

"Did you talk to Alicia?" he asked.

"Tried. She started crying the moment I said the words *Wes* and *videotape* in the same sentence. I think she's been holding out on us," she said dryly.

"How so?"

"It was an Academy Award winning performance—innocent-damsel-in-distress stuff. I felt like Dr. Mengele by the time I'd confirmed the facts. Wish I got that kind of performance from her on set."

"You think they were crocodile tears?" he asked skeptically. "She's seventeen, on her way up. Pretty legitimate to be freaked out that one moment of weakness might ruin it all."

She wrinkled her nose, tilted her head to one side. "In my experience, women who do the whole sex tape thing are not wilting flowers. But I reserve my judgment until I see the footage. Maybe Wes had to lay a trail of breadcrumbs to coax my innocent little Bambi to the bed. But I think not."

Leandro eyed her over his beer.

"You're a real hard-ass, is that it?" he asked.

"I'm a realist. And, unlike Alicia, I don't think there's anything wrong with sex how you like it. The stinger for her is that she's got a profile, but maybe this will teach her to be a little smarter in the future. Shoot, watch, erase. I'll get a T-shirt made for her."

"You sound like you know what you're talking about," he said.

Her near-black eyes glinted in the dim light. She looked mysterious and sexy and forbidden.

"I've seen *Sex, Lies and Videotape,*" she said, shrugging one shoulder negligently.

"Hmm," he said, grinning at her. "And the rest."

Suddenly she slid along the booth seat and stood, crossing to his side.

"Shove over," she said.

He stared at her. "What…?"

She rolled her eyes. "So the con man has somewhere to sit. I don't want to rub elbows with him. He might have cooties," she said.

"Right."

He felt like a real dumb-ass as he slid along the bench seat to make room for her. What had he thought was going to happen? That she was about to give him a little demonstration of sex how she liked it?

The booths were designed for intimacy, and he found himself brushing against her as she sat beside him. Her scent enveloped him, and he inhaled surreptitiously.

"Bulgari," she said matter-of-factly. "Drives men nuts."

He let out a crack of laughter. She never missed a trick.

"You sure it's the perfume?" he asked.

She turned her face toward him, and he admired the sweep of her cheekbones and the heart-shaped fullness of her mouth. Her nose was straight and proud, a delicate, feminized version of his own Greek prow, and her teeth flashed white against the plum of her lipstick.

He was as hard as a rock, thanks to her perfume, her tight little top, the sass of her conversation and the chemistry between them. He reminded himself again that she was forbidden fruit—his greatest competitor—but tonight little head was prevailing over big head. And little head was only thinking of one thing: getting Claudia naked as soon as possible.

She opened her mouth to respond just as a skinny guy

wearing a cap pulled down low over his face slid into the booth opposite them. Leandro felt Claudia stiffen beside him and he instinctively put a reassuring hand on her knee. Her elbow jabbed him sharply in the ribs and he slid his hand free. For a moment there he'd forgotten who he was sitting next to. God forbid that Claudia Dostis need reassurance.

"I know who you are," the guy said, gaze flickering over Leandro. He was more interested in Claudia, however. "You're the producer of *Ocean Boulevard,* huh? Figured you'd be older. And uglier."

His tone was lascivious.

"And I figured you'd be smarter. Life's full of disappointments. Where's this tape you say you have?" she said.

The guy's rat-sharp face hardened as he processed her insult, but he placed a notebook computer case on the table.

"I don't *say* I have anything—I've got it. And if you want it, you're going to have to pay," Rat Man said.

Claudia looked bored. Leandro dropped an elbow onto the table and leaned forward.

"More showy, less talky," he said. "Then we can discuss what it's worth. For all we know you've got footage of a pajama party."

Rat Man laughed. "No pajamas at this party, buddy," he said.

Unzipping the bag, he flipped open the lid on a seen-better-days notebook computer and pressed a button. The screen sprang to life, and Rat Man flicked them both a look of anticipation before hitting the touch pad.

Leandro met Claudia's sideways glance and correctly interpreted the dismay in her guarded expression. Whatever was on the original tape, it had already been converted to digital. Which meant it was just a few mouse clicks away from finding its way, via the Internet, into every teen boy's hard drive across the country.

The screen started out black, then a naked body walked in front of the camera and Leandro recognized Wes, naked and sporting a very respectable hard-on. A second body entered the frame, moving in a blur of motion, launching herself at Wes so that he fell backward onto the bed, the woman on top. Leandro recognized her as Alicia Morrison only because he knew it was supposed to be her—the woman on the screen could not have been further removed from the "pure as the driven snow" character she played on *Boulevard,* or the sweet girl next door she presented as in real life. Naked, full-breasted, and sporting a tattoo of a miniature devil with a pitchfork on her left butt cheek, she was very much in charge. Straddling Wes's body, she wriggled her hips until she had him placed just right, then she glanced over her shoulder toward the camera.

The look on her face was pure naughtiness as she slid down onto Wes's erection. She licked her lips, closed her eyes and mouthed the word "Yum" to the camera. Then she started to work her hips like a seasoned pole dancer, and Rat Man clicked the screen to blackness.

"I want five hundred thousand," he said.

Leandro didn't bother checking with Claudia.

"What do you think we are, Bank of America? You think we've got that kind of money lying around?"

"I don't give a shit," Rat Man said, supremely cocky now. "You get me the money by Friday, or this goes public. She's pretty hot stuff, that little blond girl, isn't she? I reckon I'll be able to spin a few bucks out of folks watching her shaking her tail feather."

"Spare us the yap, Sparky," Claudia snapped. "How are

we going to make this exchange? And how do we know you won't take the money and release the footage anyway?"

"You'll just have to trust me, won't you? I'm the one calling the shots. Which means we'll meet back here, this booth, this time on Friday. No cops, no smart stuff, nothing—or my partner smears this across the world," Rat Man said, patting the computer confidently.

"I'll be here," Leandro said. There was nothing else to be done at this stage, of course. They had to keep stringing the guy along, no matter what they decided afterward.

"Not you—her. Just her," Rat Man said. "I like her."

He smiled, showcasing his yellowed and prominent canines. Leandro opened his mouth to protest, but Claudia's hand clamped down on his thigh beneath the table.

"Done. I'll see you on Friday," she said.

She didn't look at Rat Man again as she slid from the booth and strode for the door. Leandro wanted very badly to wrap his hand around the skinny guy's throat and shake him until the videotape and all the copies the little creep had no doubt already made came tumbling out.

But he knew that wasn't the smart way to play it, so he followed Claudia out the door and up the street.

He could tell by the way she walked that she was angry. Amazing how quickly a person could learn to read another person. He'd only ever seen Claudia at a handful of organizing committee meetings prior to the actual convention, but he could read her like a book. And right now she was steaming.

"What a sleazy loser," she vented once she'd reached a silver Porsche Cayenne SUV. "Exactly how dumb does he think we are? The moment we give him his five hundred grand, that footage is going to every downloadable porn site on the Net. Even if only a small percentage of people actually pay to see it, he'll still make a fortune."

"Yep," Leandro said, digging his hands into his jeans pockets as Claudia paced back and forth in front of him, her high-heeled boots clicking on the pavement. She was wearing tight black jeans that hugged her legs like a second skin, and even though most of his brain was busy trying to find a way out of the mess their two stars had landed them in, a small, primitive part of his mind was noticing that she had the pertest, perkiest damn butt he'd ever seen.

"No wonder Alicia was crying. That tape will ruin her career," Claudia fretted, running a hand through her silky bob. "All because that…rat got his hands on something private and personal."

She'd been right about the footage, about Alicia's part in the taping. Alicia had been knowing, aggressive, a real vixen. And if it went public, she was going to be labelled a porn slut by the media no matter what spin was put on it. Rob Lowe might have lived his escapades down, but the only way Alicia could recover anything from this situation would be if she went the Pamela Anderson, Paris Hilton route. He didn't have to know Alicia to guess it wasn't exactly the career trajectory she'd had planned.

"What do you think?" Claudia asked, stopping in front of him and tucking her hands into the back pockets of her jeans.

The action thrust her breasts out, and he allowed himself one lingering, appreciative look before responding.

"We don't have a choice. We have to bring the police in," he said.

"I agree. Then we have to hope they can wrap this thing up nice and tight. Poor Alicia and Wes."

Leandro checked his watch. It was just past ten.

"Want to head over to the nearest station now and get the ball rolling?" he suggested.

She nodded and fished in her pocket for her car keys.

"My car's just around the corner," he said. "Might as well go together."

She clicked the button on her remote locking and the SUV behind her beeped to life.

"My ride's here. Hop in," she said.

Leandro frowned. "I'll follow you over."

She eyed him wryly. "Don't tell me—you hate women drivers?" she asked.

"No, I hate this neighborhood. I figure my car will be safer outside the police station than in a dark street off the Strip," he said.

She took a step closer, head cocked to one side.

"Liar. You can't stand someone else having the last word. Like last night when you kissed me and walked away."

He snorted his exasperation.

"You really think that's why I kissed you?" he asked.

She shrugged. "Why else? I kicked you in the shin, I won the award. You had to score somewhere. You figured walking away made you a winner."

"Did I? Wouldn't hanging around have made me an even bigger winner?" he said.

Her dark eyes glittered dangerously and she stepped closer again. She had her pointing finger extended and ready to jab at his chest again—but this time he was ready for her.

"You weren't about to score, if that's what you're thinking. You were minutes away from a knee in your privates, buddy," she said.

He caught her finger as it moved toward his chest, his hand enveloping her much smaller one.

"Hey," she protested.

"Didn't your mother teach you that it's rude to point?" he asked mockingly.

She tugged on her hand, trying to pull it from his grip.

"Give me my hand back," she growled.

"If that's what you want," Leandro said, but not before he'd pulled her closer. Only a foot separated them as he placed her palm flat on his chest.

He held her eye, very aware of how hot her hand felt, even through the shirt he was wearing.

A beat of taut silence, then the side of her mouth quirked up into a quick smile.

"You think you're so smart," she said, then she fisted her hand into the fabric of his shirt and jerked his body toward hers.

Her other hand snaked up and around his neck, guiding his head down, and then his lips were on hers again. She tasted like coffee and chocolate and desire, and he invaded her mouth the way he wanted to invade her body. His hands found her back, sliding down to cup her great little butt and hauling her close. She gyrated her hips against his hard-on and made a needy sound in the back of her throat.

She was liquid fire, and he wanted to be inside her. Angling her head back, he deepened their kiss, wanting to own all of her. His right hand slid around her torso and up her rib cage until he found the swell of her breasts. They were soft yet firm, and he could feel how hard her nipples were through the fabric of her top.

She gasped and pressed herself closer as he gently pinched a nipple between thumb and forefinger. He gave a groan of satisfaction as her hand slid between their bodies to find the aching length of his erection. She smoothed her palm flat along the length of him, again and again, and the one remaining functional brain cell in his head remembered that he'd seen a motel just a few minutes up the road. Sure, it wasn't ideal, but neither was dropping to the sidewalk on the very public Strip and taking her the way he wanted to right now.

"There's a place up the road," he said, breaking their kiss and staring down into her dark brown eyes. Her cheekbones were flushed and her mouth wet and swollen from his kisses. His boner throbbed. He wanted this woman like nothing on the planet right now.

She nodded her head. "Yes. It's called the police station," she said. Then her lips curled into a triumphant little smile as she stepped away from him.

Her gaze dropped to his crotch, and she raised an eyebrow.

"You might want to wait a few minutes before you walk into the station," she said.

Then she opened her car door and slid behind the wheel of her expensive SUV.

He spread his hands wide as she lowered the driver's window.

"Come on, Claudia—tit for tat? Aren't we a little too old for these kind of games?" he said.

"Don't be too long," she said, giving him a cheeky finger wave goodbye.

He was still standing there looking—and feeling—like a dick when she pulled away from the curb and out into the traffic.

Running a hand through his hair, he let out a pent-up sigh of frustration and glanced down at the significant bulge in his jeans.

She was a minx, a conniving seductress, a master tactician.

And now he wanted her more than ever. Competitor be damned. Wife hunt be damned.

Grinning, he turned toward the street where his car was parked. He'd always enjoyed the thrill of the chase.

3

CLAUDIA HAD BEEN waiting at the police station for a full ten minutes before Leandro strolled in. In a perfect world, she would have been well and truly ensconced with detectives from the Major Crimes Unit by the time he'd arrived, but a woman couldn't have everything. Leaving him with a giant boner on the Strip had just about made up for any embarrassment she'd felt after he'd left her floundering like a landed fish at the awards ceremony last night. Just about.

If only her own pulse wasn't still pounding in her ears. Closing her eyes, she smoothed her palm down her thigh as she remembered how big and hard he'd felt beneath her hand. It definitely hadn't been easy to walk away from all that throbbing masculinity. But it had been worth it, even if her own frustration levels were at an all-time high. He needed to be taught a lesson, cut down to size. And since no one else was volunteering for the job, it looked like the task had fallen to her.

When she opened her eyes again, Leandro was walking through the automatic doors into the foyer of the West Hollywood police station. She was powerless to control the kick in her belly as she caught sight of his tall, strong body. She wasn't the kind of woman who lied to herself about what she wanted, and it was becoming pretty damned obvious that, sensible or not, she wanted Leandro Mandalor.

She liked the way he challenged her. And she'd have to be dead from the waist down not to want to go to bed with him. He had an amazing body, and she'd just had a sneak preview of the highlight, albeit through the fabric of his jeans. She couldn't stop her gaze from dropping to his crotch as he walked toward her now. What if she'd taken him up on his offer and gone to that motel up the road…?

"What's happening?" he asked as he dropped into the seat beside her.

As usual, he was too broad for the space allocated for ordinary mortals, and she felt the warm press of his body against hers.

It should have been annoying, but it wasn't.

"They're calling in two detectives from the Major Crimes Unit. They were on a dinner break," she said.

Leandro raised an eyebrow and looked at his watch. "Nice life. Maybe being a producer isn't so bad after all," he said.

She stared at him. "Being a producer is the best job in the world," she said.

He looked amused. "Maybe you ought to meet my boss. And my cast. And my writing team, for that matter. Bet they'd change your mind in a pinch."

She frowned. Was he serious? Sometimes she couldn't tell with him. Okay—most of the time she couldn't tell with him. It was one of his most intriguing and annoying aspects.

"You hate your job. Are you serious?" she asked.

He shrugged. "I've been doing it for five years now, so obviously I don't hate it. Let's just say the challenge has faded. Until recently."

He gave her a significant look. She sat up a little straighter.

"I get it," she said, crossing her arms over her chest. "You were bored—until we started giving you a run for your money."

He shrugged. "I love a challenge, what can I say?"

She narrowed her eyes at him. "Glad to be of service. When you're consistently running second in the ratings, you'll feel even more challenged, no doubt," she said.

"You're not going to steal our viewers, Claudia. Just like we're not going to win over yours. Our core fans are loyal, obsessive even. But I'm going to fight you for the floaters, tooth and nail."

She realized she was grinning. "Give it your best shot, big boy."

"Big boy? I'm going to take that as a compliment," he said, matching her grin.

"Size isn't everything," she said archly.

"You'll have to let me know."

"I beg your pardon?"

"You heard me."

She glared at him. "That's it—you are officially the most arrogant man I know."

"Yeah? I'm going to take that as a compliment, too," he said.

"It wasn't meant as one," she said repressively.

He leaned close so that only she could hear him.

"If we can get this hot with just words, imagine what it'll be like once we're both naked," he said.

She ought to feel outraged at his absolute self-assurance, the way he was taking it for granted that they'd sleep with each other. She ought to ice him down and send him home with a flea in his ear.

But she didn't. She didn't do anything except lock eyes

with him. She saw a million sensual promises in his dark gaze. Her breathing increased, almost became a pant. She leaned toward him, completely forgetting where they were.

"Ms. Dostis?"

She started in her chair and jerked away from Leandro as though she'd been busted with her hand in the cookie jar.

A middle-aged man in faded jeans and a nondescript T-shirt was standing in front of her. He held out his hand.

"Detective Arnold. This is my partner, Detective Wilkes," he said, indicating a tall woman in her mid-thirties standing beyond his shoulder.

Right. They were at the police station. Here to report the very serious extortion attempt by Rat Man.

She felt a dull flush warm her chest and face as she clued into how unprofessional she was being. She *never* mixed business and pleasure. She *always* put work first. But somehow, whenever she was with Leandro, other things seemed to get in the way.

"Pleased to meet you. This is Leandro Mandalor, producer of *Heartlands*," she said. At least her voice sounded relatively normal, even if her body was still burning with embarrassment.

"Hey, I love that show," Detective Wilkes said, smiling broadly and stepping forward to shake Leandro's hand. Claudia frowned as the other woman tossed her long red hair over her shoulder and smiled in a distinctly friendly way.

"You want to come through this way? You can fill us in on your situation," Detective Arnold suggested.

Claudia stood, Leandro following suit. It wasn't until they were all walking that she noted that the redheaded Detective Wilkes could almost see eye to eye with him. For some reason that she couldn't name, it really pissed

Claudia off. That, and the frankly assessing look the female detective sent Leandro's way.

Geez, have a bit of dignity, woman, Claudia thought. She wondered how Leandro felt, being eyed-up like a hunk of prime meat so blatantly. Then she caught him checking out Detective Wilkes's ass as they turned into the meeting room, and her mouth hardened.

He obviously welcomed any and all female attention. Not that this should surprise her, given the way he'd behaved around her to date. The biggest, most stupid mistake she could make was to take his flirting seriously. Or, worse, to follow through on it. She wasn't adverse to no-strings sex by a long shot, but she didn't relish being just a notch on any man's bedpost.

The scrape of metal chair legs on concrete brought her focus back to the matter at hand as she and Leandro sat facing the two detectives.

Detective Arnold had his notepad out and a pen poised. "Why don't you take us through the first contact you had with this individual," he said.

To her surprise, Leandro looked to her before answering. "I'll handle this bit, since he contacted me first, yeah?" he suggested.

She shrugged coolly. What did she care? He could run the whole show if he liked.

Leandro frowned slightly at her ready capitulation before turning back to face the detectives.

"My assistant put the call through at about ten today," he said.

Claudia listened as Leandro outlined Rat Man's first contact and their subsequent discussions to arrange a meeting. When he got to the actual meeting itself, he glanced across at her again, obviously willing to relinquish the role of chief informer, but she just made a keep-going gesture with her hand.

The two detectives questioned them both closely over the man's description, asking for the address of the break-in, and what they both knew about Alicia and Wes's private lives.

"Look, we're their employers, not their mothers," Leandro said when Detective Wilkes asked him if Wes had any gambling or substance abuse problems. "The guy shows up on set, does a good job and attends all his publicity obligations. I try to keep tabs on my team, but there's no way I can know for sure about any of this stuff."

Claudia eyed the other woman shrewdly.

"You think our actors might have set this up themselves?" she asked.

The two detectives exchanged loaded looks, as though they were trying to work out how honest they could be.

"It's something we need to consider. People get desperate when they need money," said Detective Arnold.

Claudia shook her head firmly. "Alicia would never risk that footage getting out," she said unequivocally. "It would destroy her career."

"Or make it," Detective Wilkes said cynically.

Claudia shook her head again. "No. This girl can act, and she knows it. If she wanted to be a porn star, she would already be one. Plus she's got a Disney movie lined up when we break for the holidays. There's no way she'd endanger that."

Leandro nodded beside her. "I agree. And Wes has been with the show for seven years now. He's one of our highest paid actors. He does a made-for-TV movie now and then.

I never got the sense he was ambitious for anything else. He has a pretty nice life."

Detective Arnold nodded. "We'll keep all that in mind. Now, this next meeting. We're going to have to put a wire on you, Ms. Dostis, so we can keep tabs on the situation. The goal here is damage control. We want to trace your contact back to his base and jump on him before he gets a chance to flick that footage on to anyone else."

"For what it's worth, this guy sounds strictly amateur-hour. My bet is he's a break-and-enter monkey who got lucky and scored that tape. He's already made the major mistake of letting you two see him. Unless he suddenly gets an IQ injection between now and Friday night, I'm pretty confident we can nip this little escapade in the bud," Detective Wilkes said.

Claudia felt Leandro shift in his chair beside her.

Here we go, she thought.

"I think I should do the drop," he said predictably.

"But he specifically asked for me," Claudia reminded him.

"He wants the money. As long as he gets it, he's not going to care who the delivery man is," Leandro argued.

Claudia could feel her temper flaring. She knew what he was doing—trying to protect her. It was so damned Greek of him, it made her want to spit.

"I can take care of myself," she said.

"No offence, Claudia, but if things turn bad and this guy grabs you, you don't stand a chance in hell," Leandro said. "I don't want you to get hurt."

"Well, guess what? Not your choice. Last time I looked, you didn't own me and I had a mind of my own." She turned back toward the detectives who were watching their interplay with unashamed interest.

"So, I wear a wire. What else?" Claudia said.

Leandro sat back and crossed his big arms over his chest, radiating disapproval. Claudia ignored him. When hell froze over, he could call the shots for her.

Over the next hour, they outlined their plan of attack. Claudia agreed to arrive at the station at six on the evening of the drop in order to be wired and go over any last-minute instructions. The overall plan was simple—meet the contact, hand over the money, trail him back to his bolt-hole. Once the police were confident they had him bottled up, they would raid the place and seize both the money and the footage.

"What about when this goes to trial? Can we keep the footage under wraps?" Leandro asked.

"Your lawyers can take care of that end. You should be able to keep the content quiet. It's the extortion itself that we're interested in," Detective Arnold said.

It was midnight by the time they exited the police station. Claudia stood in the cool night air and circled her stiff shoulders. Meeting with a blackmailer and spending hours with the cops was not exactly her idea of a rockin' Tuesday night in Hollywood.

"Okay, I'll see you on Friday. Call me if you think of anything else we need to cover. I'll talk to Alicia, reassure her," she said, fishing her car keys from her pocket and turning away.

"Not so fast," Leandro said, grabbing her arm.

She glared at his big hand wrapped around her forearm, her message clear: *back off.* Typically, he didn't.

"I don't want you doing the drop," he said firmly.

"Well, when you're wearing the magical ruby slippers, you can close your eyes, click your heels and make that happen. Until then, I get to make my own decisions," she said sweetly.

He narrowed his gaze at her. "I bet you used to drive your parents crazy when you were a kid," he said.

"They survived," she said shortly, not liking the rush of unexpected hurt that washed over her at the mention of her parents. Twice now in two days they'd crept into her thoughts out of nowhere. She didn't like it. They'd all made their choices years ago. She'd lived with hers this long, and was satisfied that she could continue doing so.

He was staring down at her, concern written on his handsome face. Releasing her arm, he cuffed her gently on the shoulder, a gentle chastisement.

"You're an idiot. Is it so awful that someone cares if you get hurt?" he asked quietly.

She blinked, thrown. Flirting she could handle. Arrogance and egotism, too. But tenderness, sincerity—she'd never been good with either of those.

"You sure it's not just because you want to be in charge?" she said.

He frowned. "Yeah, I am."

"I can handle it," she said firmly.

He nodded slowly. "Okay. Fine. I won't say another word—on one condition."

"This'll be good," she said, hand on hip.

"You have dinner with me."

It wasn't what she'd been expecting, and she shifted uneasily.

"Leandro, be serious. Sure, we're both curious about each other, about what it would be like. But it's our job to beat each other at what we do for a living. It's actually written into my employment contract. Under the circumstances, sleeping together would be pretty stupid."

He just held her eye. "Dinner. Restaurant of my choice."

Shaking her head, she turned toward her car. "You're a hot kisser, but not that hot," she said, deliberately echoing the words he'd used earlier on the phone.

Only she would ever know how much her hands were shaking when she got into her car. For good or for ill, she was terribly, terribly attracted to this man. She remembered her recent jealousy over the tall police detective with a wince. The sooner this whole extortion matter was dealt with and gone, the sooner she could go back to competing with Leandro from a distance. A nice, safe, long distance.

THE THING WAS, Leandro concluded on Thursday evening, he was used to being in charge of his world. He called the shots at *Heartlands,* he was respected in the industry, even his father listened to him these days. It had been a long time since things hadn't gone his way. Now, in the space of a few months, Claudia Dostis had challenged his status quo on several fronts. First, she'd beaten his wedding special in the ratings—even if only by a few points, technically she'd bested him. Then she'd won that damned award. And now he could not get her out of his mind.

Every night, as soon as he loosened his grip on his mind and drifted toward sleep, she crept into his bed. Her smell, the feel of her curvy body pressed up against his, the glint in her eyes as she defied him—his dreams became an elaborate series of cock-teases. Just when he'd get her where he wanted her, she'd slip from his grasp and disappear, only for him to chase her and the same thing happen again and again. Every morning he woke with a hard-on that would not quit. He was starting to feel like a fifteen year old, the amount of times he'd had to resort to hand relief in the shower before he was fit to go into work.

Somehow he had to get her into bed. Deliberately he gave no thought to what would happen after he'd satisfied his curiosity. What was the point? It wasn't as though they were talking hearts and flowers here—they were simply hot for each other. And with a bit of luck they'd put each other out of their mutual misery in the very near future. End of story.

Now, if he could get the ridiculous urge to protect her from her own folly out of his system as easily. She'd stated unequivocally that she was delivering the money to Rat Man. As far as she was concerned, that was the end of the discussion. But Leandro simply could not reconcile himself to the thought of her taking all the risk to save both their heinies. Maybe he was just a male chauvinist at heart, but surely it was okay for men and women to admit they were better at certain things, even in these enlightened times? For example, he was willing to admit that she would probably have a leg up when it came to counseling an upset employee. Maybe she'd even have him whipped in casting to suit a female-based audience. So what was so wrong about both of them acknowledging that when it came to matters of brute force, he had about a hundred pounds and over a foot in height on her?

The worse thing was, he knew he was going to have to suck it up. Short of kidnapping her and keeping her tied up in the trunk of his car until the exchange was complete, there was no way he could stop her from putting herself in danger. Which left him feeling both horny and worried as he paced the polished floorboards in his West Hollywood condo.

Shaking his head at his one-track mind, he padded barefoot into the kitchen and filled a tumbler with an inch of the single malt Scotch he kept for such occasions. His mail sat unopened on the kitchen counter, neatly stacked there by his housekeeper. Savoring the burn of good liquor finding its way to his belly, Leandro leafed through the envelopes. He recognized Peta's handwriting on the last letter—a large, flat legal envelope—and he tore it open with more vigor than finesse.

She'd signed the divorce papers. He stared at their two signatures sitting side by side—two large, flamboyant, sprawling monikers that spoke volumes about each of them individually and the two of them as a couple.

He was a free man. Again. It was only as he registered the fact that he understood it was the last thing he wanted. It wasn't about Peta, about missing her. He'd fallen out of love with her long ago. It was that he liked being in a relationship. He liked the routine, the companionship, the private jokes and small moments of silent communion that peppered any good relationship. He wanted to share his life with someone. Work was not enough anymore. Sex with women he didn't care for wasn't enough, either. He wanted more.

Tossing back the last of his Scotch, Leandro made his way to the living room and threw himself down on the sleek leather couch lining one wall. The television offered no solace and he switched it off after sixty seconds of fruitless channel surfing.

Finally, after a pointless ten minutes of internal struggle that had been destined to fail from the very beginning, he picked up his cell phone and punched in Claudia's number.

She answered on the third ring.

"Leandro," she said.

She sounded sleepy and surprised.

"Hi," he said, settling back onto the couch and closing his eyes. She had a great voice—a rich contralto with a husk in the lower register.

"Has something come up?" she asked. He heard the sound of water slapping against something on her end of the phone.

"No. You're in the bath, aren't you?" he guessed.

She hesitated a moment. "Yes."

He groaned. "Do you have any idea what you're doing to me?"

"Some. If it's anything like what you're doing to me," she said.

He smiled. What was it about the phone that allowed people to say things they'd never say in person? He could never imagine Claudia making herself so vulnerable, admitting so much if she were standing in front of him. Still, now that she had...

"I could come over there and do it in person," he said.

"I've got an early start," she said after a significant pause.

He sat up straight. He'd expected an outright no, but obviously the few days since they'd last spoken had been as tough for her as they had been for him.

"Okay," he said slowly, "maybe we should book that dinner, then."

"Okay."

One word, and he was as hard as titanium. Harder.

"Jesus," he swore under his breath.

She laughed, the sound low and knowing. "You okay there?"

"Barely."

"I've been thinking about you."

"Yeah?"

"I was thinking about you just before you called, actually," she purred.

He swallowed. "Yeah? Any particular part of me you

were thinking about?" he asked, shifting to ease the pressure caused by his raging hard-on.

"Oh yeah. Your nose," she said.

He was so surprised he barked out a laugh. "You're kidding."

"It's a very sexy nose. A nice, big strong nose," she said.

He shifted again. "Claudia, you're killing me here," he said.

"Tomorrow night. Let's do dinner tomorrow night," she said.

"After the drop? Done," he said.

"I have to go now. I don't want to get the phone wet," she said.

He closed his eyes and prayed for patience.

"You're a super vixen, did you know that?" he said.

"Yeah, I knew that," she said. Then she laughed and ended the call.

Leandro stared at the dead phone for a second, then dropped focus to the ridge of his erection that would not quit. Tomorrow night. Tomorrow night he would touch her and taste her and rid himself of what was fast becoming an obsessive need to know her inside and out.

But first he had to get through tonight.

Sighing, he went into the bathroom to have a cold shower.

CLAUDIA HELD STILL as a female technician taped a tiny mike into the valley between her breasts. The lead ran along the edge of her bra around to her back, where it followed the hollow of her lower spine. A slim-lined transmitter was strapped to the small of her back, discreet and hidden beneath her jeans and the T-shirt and jacket she was wearing. Instead of her usual high-heeled boots, she wore a pair of sneakers with her jeans, her one concession to tonight's mission. If something went wrong, she wanted to be able to hustle.

"Okay, we're done," the tech said, stepping back and letting Claudia drop her T-shirt in place. "Let's just test this thing. Say something for me, Claudia."

"Hi. Does my ass look fat in this concealed mike?"

The woman smirked. "Levels are great. You're good to go."

Claudia smiled her thanks and exited to the main office of the West Hollywood station where Detectives Arnold and Wilkes were waiting with Leandro. She noted that Wilkes had taken advantage of her absence to get in some one-on-one time with Leandro. She was seated opposite him, her long legs propped on the desk, her body sema-phoring every go signal known to womankind.

Leandro glanced up as Claudia entered, and the expression on his face switched from polite to smoky in no seconds flat. Claudia smiled a little smugly as her jealousy turned to dust. Ms. Long Legs might have a few inches on her, but right now the only woman Leandro was interested in was her. And tonight, at long last, she was going to lay hands on his hard, hot body. They were going to tangle themselves into delicious knots, explore each other, tease and soothe and satisfy each other.

Just the thought of it sent a wave of desire pulsing through her. Ever since she'd ended the call with Leandro last night she'd been at fever pitch, nervous about the drop, excited about getting him naked, and not sure where one feeling ended and the other began.

Perhaps that was why they were so hot for each other, she speculated as she ran her eyes over his broad chest as he lazed in the chair. This weird combination of sexual attraction and the novelty and stress and challenge of the blackmail threat.

He was wearing a dark gray T-shirt, the fabric outlining his muscular pecs and shoulders and skimming over his taut abdomen. Her gaze traveled to his hips and then his legs, admiring the firm musculature of his thighs and the latent power of his big body.

Grrrrr, as Grace would no doubt say. And tonight he was all hers.

She just had to survive the drop first.

"We ready to go?" Arnold asked.

"I'm officially wired for sound," Claudia said, even as the tech gave a thumbs-up.

"Let's roll," Arnold said, pushing himself to his feet and grabbing his coat.

Claudia met Leandro's eye as he stood. He looked as though he was biting his tongue for all he was worth, and she smiled at him. She bet he was gagging to offer to swap places with her yet again.

"You're very quiet," she said.

"I'm saving myself," he said shortly. He ate her up with his eyes and she fought the urge to squirm. Thank God the hidden mike wasn't sensitive enough to hear her heart galloping in her chest.

In case Rat Man was smart enough to watch the bar, she and Leandro arrived together with no sign of their police escort. Claudia was seriously impressed by how invisible they were, until it occurred to her that perhaps they simply weren't there. Maybe they were sitting in a van somewhere remote, listening in on her mike. Maybe when she went in to meet Rat Man, she'd be all alone, her ass flapping in the breeze…

"Nervous?" Leandro asked as they pulled up outside the bar.

They'd been mostly silent on the drive over, both of them very aware of the mike recording their conversation.

"No," she lied.

He gave her a wry look. "Sure you're not, Ace," he said. He shot a look toward the entrance of the bar, a frown forming between his eyebrows. He looked concerned when he turned back to her.

For a second she wished she'd let him do the drop, as he'd asked. He was right—if Rat Man got nasty, she didn't have a chance in hell of standing up to him.

But she'd made her bed. It was time to lie in it.

"I'm going in," she said, unclipping her seat belt.

Leandro nodded, then reached into the back seat of his car where he'd stowed the case full of cash. She'd been a bit surprised by his red Honda when he'd picked her up from the office that afternoon. She'd been expecting something sporty and sexy—a penis car. She'd gotten a Honda Insight hybrid, with slightly goofy covered rear wheels and zero sex appeal. He'd correctly interpreted her surprised look and responded with a shrug.

"I have nieces and nephews. I figure they should have a planet to enjoy, too."

Leandro Mandalor was environmentally sound. She still couldn't quite reconcile the idea with what she knew of him.

"Don't worry about the money," he said as he handed it to her. "It's insured, if it disappears it gets replaced. You're the important part of the equation. I'm pretty sure they broke the mold when they made you."

She forced a smile to cover the fact that her stomach was doing loop-the-loops.

"Come on, think of those rating points you'd score if I disappeared, Leandro. Where's your competitive spirit?"

He tucked a strand of hair behind her ear.

"Don't be a dick," he said.

She stared at him, her mouth drying as she imagined having this sexy, smart man all to herself in the privacy of a bedroom.

"Okay, here I go," she said for everyone's benefit.

Shooting Leandro a small nervous smile, she exited the car and strode toward the entrance to the bar. The moment she pushed through the scarred wooden door, she felt very, very alone. She'd forgotten how dim it was inside, and she blinked her eyes a few times before moving toward the booth she'd occupied on her previous visit. To her consternation, it was full, as were the next two booths.

The only empty booth was the one against the farthest wall—about as far from the front entrance as possible.

Great.

Her knees feeling distinctly wobbly, she slid into the booth, her back to the wall, her eyes glued to the front door. Intellectually she knew the place was under intense observation, that the mike taped to her breast offered her additional protection, even that there might be undercover police in the bar with her. None of it stopped her from bitterly regretting her bravado.

Idiot, she chastised herself. Why did she always have to bite off more than she could chew? She'd always fought above her weight. As a kid, she'd insisted on playing ball with her brothers, even though they were taller and faster than her. She'd practiced her pitching until her arm ached so she could give them a run for their money. At university, she'd taken double subjects to fast-track her degree.

And she'd produced three student films while working a full-time job as an assistant in her first year out, she'd been so determined to move up the ladder.

It had all paid off. She had a house in West Hollywood, a great career. She just couldn't quite work out where insisting on handling this drop alone would get her. Maybe she needed to learn to back off every now and then. Work smarter, not harder. Choose her battles.

She was still anxiously dissecting her need to achieve when Rat Man slid into the booth opposite her. He hadn't come in the front door, and she figured there must be a back entrance. For a second she wondered if the police knew about it, then mentally rolled her eyes at her own stupidity. Of course they did. It was probably in the police training manual on page one—check for rear exits.

"You got my money?" Rat Man asked.

"You got my tape?" Claudia responded.

Rat Man tipped his baseball cap back a little, revealing pale blue eyes and a thin, blade-like nose. His teeth were still yellow, and he was sporting a scraggly three-day growth that did nothing for his sallow skin.

"You're pretty mouthy for a little chick, aren't you?"

"Yep. Let me see the tape," Claudia said.

"I call the shots, remember? This is my deal. Show me the money," he said. His gaze darted nervously over his shoulder.

"Fine."

Her heart hammering against her ribs, Claudia lay the briefcase on the table. Angling it toward the wall, she cracked it to give him a glimpse of the money stacked inside.

"Jesus," Rat Man said, his eyes lighting up. He pulled the case toward himself, preparing to flip the lid wide open.

"You might want to be careful who gets an eyeful of that in here," Claudia warned him before he had a chance to flash the money to the whole bar. The guy was seriously running on minimum brain cells. She could only imagine what the bruisers at the bar would do to get their hands on five hundred grand of easy cash.

Rat Man blinked nervously, then nodded his agreement.

"Yeah, I knew that," he said. Angling the case some more, he allowed himself a quick glimpse of the neat rows of notes before snapping the case shut.

"Okay. Now I want the tape," she said.

Euphoria had kicked in, she could see. Rat Man was mentally spending his five hundred thousand, no doubt decking himself out in a bad suit and putting himself behind the wheel of a pimped-up sports car.

"Sure." He laid a videotape on the table and slid it across to her.

She picked it up and noted the brand name on the label. Wes had told Leandro the original recording was on a Sony tape; this was also a Sony. It didn't mean anything, of course, since they'd already digitized the footage, but it was something.

"What about what we saw the other night—has it been erased?" she asked.

"Done," he assured her, sliding his way out of his seat.

"We hear from you again, we're going straight to the cops, understand?" she said. "Five hundred thousand buys us silence. But we're not spending another cent. You got that?"

Rat Man grinned widely.

"I hear you. Chill, lady. We did a deal. We did a good deal. Let it ride," he said.

Then, still grinning like the fool he was, he disappeared into the darkened doorway leading to the pool tables and the washrooms.

"He's gone out the back," she said as soon as he was gone.

It was over. She could barely process the fact as she beat a retreat toward the front entrance. The smoggy night air of the Strip had never smelled so good as she emerged from the bar. Leandro was still in his car on the next block, and she repressed the need to run to him, keeping her pace measured just in case Rat Man was watching her.

Leandro exited the car to greet her, wrapping his hands around her forearms and peering down into her face.

"You okay? Nothing happened?" he asked.

"All good," she said.

He smiled, and she could feel his relief. It was stupid, but she was touched. It didn't mean anything, but still.

"We should head back to the station," she said.

He nodded his agreement, and they climbed into his car.

Now that the adventure was over, she felt free to register a whole host of sensations that had been crowded from her consciousness by anxiety and fear.

The tape from the mike was pinching her skin, and the transmitter was digging into her back. The armpits of her T-shirt were damp with sweat, and her stomach rumbled with hunger.

"God, I'm starving," she said.

"Me, too."

She caught the flash of his dark eyes as he glanced at her, and she knew he was talking about more than food. A hot bolt of need surged through her, strong and undeniable, unadulterated by anything else now that the nasty business of the exchange was done.

Now, tonight was just about her and Leandro.

Back at the police station, the tech removed the mike and informed them that detectives Arnold and Wilkes and the team had followed the blackmailer to a house in the valley. She and Leandro waited to hear news of the raid, sharing pizza with the other on-duty officers. Finally, an hour after they'd arrived, a call came through and the techie handed it to Claudia.

"We got him," Detective Arnold said. He sounded pleased with himself. "Him and his little buddy were sitting on a stash of DVDs, churning out a hundred an hour. Guess he wasn't planning on sticking to his deal with you guys."

"Gee, why am I not surprised. Have they sold any online yet?" she asked, tension banding her shoulders as she waited for the answer to this all-important question. All of their careful handling would be for nothing if the footage had been passed on already.

"There are no guarantees. We'll bring them downtown and talk to them for a few hours. I suspect we'll get a straight answer out of them pretty soon."

"Great. Thanks, Detective," Claudia said.

"No problems. You can pick up your money from our evidence lockup sometime tomorrow."

Ending the call, Claudia repeated the conversation to Leandro. He nodded his understanding, then flicked his wrist over to check the time.

"It's nearly eleven. Bit late for our dinner," he said.

He was watching her, waiting for her to make the call. But she'd been waiting for this all week, ever since he'd cornered her in the foyer at the awards ceremony and kissed her till her toes curled.

"I know a place that's open late," she said. "But I need to shower first. Can we swing by my place?"

His eyelids dropped a notch. "Sure we can," he said.

They were both silent as he drove to her home. She was acutely aware of the bulk of him, his height and his breadth as he followed her to her front door.

"Make yourself comfortable," she said, gesturing for him to take a seat on her low-line modern white leather couch. "I won't be long."

She could feel him watching her as she left the room. In her en suite, she shed her clothes and stepped beneath the steamy heat of the shower. The brush of her hands, the caress of the water, the slide of the soap—every touch heightened her anticipation of his touch, his hands, his body against hers.

Stepping out of the shower, she paused only long enough to blot the bulk of the water from her body. She'd planned on taking him to an all-night restaurant she knew, drawing it out, teasing him and herself some more. But she couldn't stand not having him a minute longer.

Dropping the towel behind her, she walked naked into the hallway. She was comfortable with her body—her frenetic working life kept her slim, and regular gym workouts kept her firm. Tonight, desire gilded her confidence. She wanted him, and she knew he wanted her. She felt like the sexiest woman in the world.

Her dark hair whispering against her neck with each step, she made her way to the living room.

He was sitting on her couch, flicking through the latest issue of *Variety*.

"I was thinking we could skip dinner and go straight to dessert. What do you think?" she asked, pausing in the doorway.

His head came up and she saw his jaw tense as he registered her nakedness.

"You are full of good ideas tonight," he said.

Holding his eye, she walked slowly toward him, loving the way his eyes followed the bounce of her breasts.

"You have no idea," she said as she pushed him farther back onto the couch and climbed on board to straddle him. She could feel the firmness of his thighs beneath hers, the rasp of his denim against her skin.

His hands found her torso on either side, sliding up until they were resting just beneath her breasts. They both watched as her nipples pebbled into jutting peaks.

Then, his gaze holding hers, Leandro leaned forward and sucked a nipple into the hot, wet heaven of his mouth.

At last.

Her head fell back as sensation rioted through her. Closing her eyes, she gave herself up to the moment.

4

HER NIPPLES WERE a delicious dusky latte, small and tightly erect and demanding in his mouth. Her skin was silky smooth, her body firm and soft in all the right places. He couldn't get enough of her, couldn't decide which part of her to taste or touch first—her breasts, her smooth stomach, the heat at the juncture of her thighs, the perky curves of her butt. As his hands roamed from site to site, he switched his attention from her right breast to her left, and she clamped her knees hard around his hips and groaned inarticulately. Her head was thrown back, her hair an ebony fall down her shoulders, her eyes closed. She seemed utterly lost in desire and need, and he was so hard for her he was in serious danger of losing it before he even got his clothes off.

"You keep that up and this isn't going to last long," he warned her.

She lifted her head and he found himself gazing into slitted, glittering eyes filled with need.

"Maybe I want it hard and fast," she said.

Hard and fast. Just the words were enough to nearly push him over the edge. His whole body tensed with desire. He'd been thinking about her, wanting her, dreaming about her all week. For months she'd been challenging and teasing him. And now she was naked in his lap, telling him she didn't care about finesse and foreplay and sophistication.

"You're sure?" he asked through gritted teeth. He'd been told numerous times that he was a good lover. He considered it a badge of honor that his bed partners always found their climax before he even thought about sliding inside them. But she was too hot, and he was too hard, and he wanted to bury himself inside her and sprint toward completion.

Holding his eye, she grabbed his hand from her butt and slid it around her hip and down her lower belly. He felt her stomach muscles quiver with anticipation as she guided his fingers into the neatly trimmed thatch of curls between her legs. His fingers slid into slick, steamy heat, sliding over the plump, swollen petals of her desire.

She was more than ready for him, the hiccup in her breathing and the involuntary jerk of her hips giving away how close she was.

It was too much for his self-control. Sliding his hands up her back, he grasped her securely beneath her arms and simultaneously leaned forward. With one explosive move he was on his feet, and she instinctively wrapped her legs around his hips and reached for his shoulders.

Swiveling, he placed her butt on the wide, padded arm of her leather couch, even as his hand was sliding into his back pocket to find the condoms he always carried in his wallet.

Her butt supporting her weight now, she loosened her legs and reached for his fly. She had him out of his jeans and boxer briefs in seconds, and her eyes widened flatteringly as she took in his arousal.

"Wow. You really are a big boy," she said.

"A wise woman once told me size wasn't everything," he said as he sheathed himself.

"She was a damned fool," she said, her gaze glued avariciously to his erection as he spread her legs wider still.

Her breasts jerked as she took a deep, involuntary breath as he probed the heat between her legs, and he held on to his self control long enough to ease himself into her inch by inch, allowing her time to adjust to the length of him. Three inches in, she growled with frustration, grabbed his hips, lifted her own and drove him the rest of the way home.

"*Yessss,*" she hissed.

He lost it completely then. He'd tried to be considerate. Even when she'd given him permission to go for it, he'd tried to hold back. But now he was inside her, and she was tight and hot around him, and her evident arousal and hunger pushed him into crazy land.

Lowering his head to pull a nipple roughly into his mouth, he began to pump into her, his eyes closing as he reveled in the erotic friction between their bodies. She lifted her hips to meet him thrust for thrust, her breathing erratic and desperate, her hands clenched into his hips as she urged him on.

Mindless, lost, he buried himself inside her again and again, his hands curled possessively into her butt, his mouth suckling urgently on first one breast and then the other.

"Faster," she panted as he felt himself nearing the peak. "Harder."

Because it was exactly what he wanted, he abandoned her breasts and obeyed her, pounding into her with a single-minded intensity, his eyes never leaving her passion-flushed face as he soared toward his climax.

"Claudia," he gasped, just as she dropped her head back

and bucked her hips, her eyes closing as she clenched again and again around him.

His body tensed, and he exploded at last, sensation flooding him as he came.

It was so intense, so mind-blowing that he nearly staggered as he fell back down to earth. Still panting, Claudia eased herself away from him and tumbled off the arm onto the seat of the couch, her body flopping back onto the cushions, her very bonelessness screaming satisfaction.

Taking care of essentials, he walked through her house until he found the bathroom and disposed of the condom. She was still lying limp and spent when he returned, and he stared down at her.

"Move over."

She smiled sleepily without opening her eyes and curled her legs up into her chest. He slid onto the couch and she lowered her legs onto his lap. For a long beat he stared down at her body, still rosy with desire, the faint redness around her nipples testament to how urgent his need had been.

She was the sexiest woman he'd ever been with. He loved her utter lack of self-awareness, the way she didn't seem to give a fig for the fact that she was stark naked and he was still fully clothed. He loved how responsive she was, how she'd known what she wanted and hadn't hesitated to ask for it.

Most of all he loved the fact that just looking at her got him hot all over again, despite having lost his mind inside her mere minutes ago. Unable to resist touching her again, he smoothed a hand up her thigh and onto her stomach, reveling in the weight of her breast in his hand as he cupped her again. Her nipple hardened beneath his palm, and her eyes flickered open.

A slow smile curled her lips as she registered the need in him again.

"This time, we take it slow," he said.

"What did you have in mind?"

CLAUDIA REVELED IN the buzz of satisfaction vibrating through her body. As she'd instinctively known, Leandro was dynamite in the sack. And if the speculative, hungry look in his eye was anything to go by, she was in for another round of passion at his hands. Her body tightened just thinking about it, and like that she was ready to go again, the dozy satiety of a few minutes ago fading into oblivion as he slid his big hand from one breast to the other, toying with her nipples almost absentmindedly.

"What do you like?" he asked as he squeezed a nipple between thumb and forefinger.

"Everything that feels good. I'm not into pain, and I'm not into degradation," she said honestly.

"That makes two of us. What I'd really like to do, Claudia, is get you so hot you can't remember your own name. I want to make you come so hard you can't speak or think or talk. How does that sound?"

She shivered, loving the threat/promise in his deep voice.

"Like something I could get used to," she said.

"Show me what you like, what turns you on the most," he said, eyelids at half-mast, his pupils so dilated with desire they almost swallowed his irises.

The throb-throb of desire started up its tattoo between her legs, just from his hot words and his even hotter eyes. He wanted to watch her touch herself. He wanted to learn from her. Her heart kicked against her ribs and she was suddenly short of breath.

"You have to take your clothes off first," she said.

"Deal."

She watched as he stripped his shirt off, exposing the broadest, sexiest chest she'd ever seen. She squirmed on the warm leather of her couch as he tugged his jeans and boxer briefs down, revealing his already-straining erection.

"Maybe we should skip to the good bit…" she hinted, her eyes gobbling him up all over again. Looking at him brought back the memory of how hard, how long, how right he'd felt inside her.

He smiled and batted her greedy hands away. "Patience is a virtue."

"No one ever called me virtuous before." She pouted.

He grinned, crossing to the armchair opposite the couch and sitting down in all his naked glory.

"You asked for it," she warned him.

Maintaining eye contact, she rearranged herself on the couch, sitting upright more conventionally and then draping one leg over the arm so that he had a box seat on her performance, so to speak.

She shivered at the look on his face—pure hunger and absolute focus on the slick heart of her.

She'd touched herself in front of men before, but never like this. Never so…blatantly. As she slid a hand onto her own breast and caressed her nipple, she fought a surge of self-consciousness. He wanted to see the way she touched herself when she was alone, she understood that. But by definition, she wasn't alone. She felt very…exposed all of a sudden. Even vulnerable.

He seemed to sense it.

"The other night, in the bath. You were thinking of me?" he said, his voice a deep, low purr.

"Yes," she said. Closing her eyes, she remembered the warm embrace of the water, and the way she'd pleasured herself as she fantasized about Leandro.

Her hand slid from her breast and down her belly into the curls on her mound. She shifted her hips a little, feeling how wet and swollen she was for him. Tracing her outer lips, she began a slow, torturous journey, teasing herself and him, building herself to a fever pitch. It was almost as though he were touching her, as though he knew exactly where she gained the most pleasure, what drove her wild.

She forgot he was there as desire spiraled inside her. She shifted her hips again, instinctively seeking fulfillment. Increasingly desperate, she ran her free hand over her breasts, sliding from one straining peak to the other.

She didn't hear him move, just felt the warmth of his hands on her thighs. She opened her eyes and he was kneeling in front of her, lifting the leg she'd left on the floor so that it rest on his big shoulder but leaving the other where it was on the arm of the couch.

"Yes," she begged as his dark head moved toward her thighs. "Please."

Her whole body quivered with anticipation as she waited for his mouth to touch her. But he didn't give her the all-encompassing wet heat she wanted. Instead, he began to tease her with quick, darting flicks of his tongue. First on her clitoris, then lower, on her outer lips, then ducking quickly inside her, then her clitoris again. There was no pattern, no rhyme or reason, and she held her breath as she waited for each touch, trying to anticipate where he would tease her next. Her hands slid into his thick, dark hair and she curled her fingers through it, holding him in place and silently urging him to give her what she needed.

She was almost screaming with desire and frustration when he finally opened his mouth wide and began to feast on her with no holds barred. She was instantly boneless with need as he laved her with the flat of his tongue, a delicious combination of pressure and texture and heat that quickly sent her soaring toward orgasm.

Because he'd watched her, studied her, he knew what she needed now and she sobbed with relief when he slid a finger inside her, and then another. As he worked his fingers in and out, he sucked her clitoris into his mouth and flicked it repeatedly with his tongue. Taken by surprise, she arched her hips up as sensation exploded within her, her hands clenching as her climax hit her like a tsunami.

She was so far gone she almost missed the crinkle of another foil packet, but she definitely didn't miss the hard probing of his erection at her entrance, and then he was inside her, filling her utterly, stretching her.

She was reduced to sheer mindless instinct. Nothing existed but his body and hers and the place they were joined and the restive, pleasurable pain of the need they created in one another. Arching her back, she murmured her appreciation as he nuzzled her breasts, his face damp from his work between her thighs. By the time he reached her throat, she was grabbing at his ass and hanging on for life as he pounded into her. His tongue trailed up her neck and into her ear, the wet invasion a shocking, sensual pleasure. And then he was kissing her, deep, wet, openmouthed kisses that smelled of sex and need and want.

She was coming again in seconds, her body vibrating around his as he played her masterfully. Then she felt his body tense, and his chest expanded as he sucked in a great breath and he shuddered into her.

"Claudia," he said, his face pressed into her hair. "Claudia."

Sliding to the floor beside him, she stared blindly at the ceiling as her body began the slow descent back to earth.

Somehow, some way, it felt as though the planet had shifted on its axis. She had the distinct, unsettling feeling that Leandro Mandalor had just ruined her for any other man.

THE NEXT MORNING, Claudia woke to a world of regret and self-recrimination. As a general rule, she didn't believe in regrets. Life was full of experiences, some good, some bad—a roller coaster ride with peaks and troughs. She dealt with it all as it came, and she moved on. In her opinion, there was no other way to stay sane.

But regret was waiting for her when she woke the day after her sex-fest with Leandro. It didn't descend immediately. For the first precious five minutes of her weekend morning she stretched languorously in bed, the fine cotton of her sheets creating pleasant friction on her naked body— her highly satisfied, well kissed, licked, caressed naked body.

She purred contentedly as she remembered the magic she and Leandro had made in this very bed after they'd showered late last night. Some time in the very early hours, he'd dressed and gone home. She'd bid him a drowsy goodbye and rolled over into deep, contented sleep.

He was an amazing lover. Attentive. Generous. Earthy in the best possible way. The way he'd tasted her, as though he couldn't get enough. The look in his eyes as he caressed her body. The barely repressed passion in his big, hard body. Thinking about him made her stir restlessly in the bed.

Even though she knew it was crazy, she fantasized about calling him. As she slipped on her silk robe and padded out into the kitchen, she imagined what she would say to him to get him hot, where they might meet, what they might do to each other.

Then she saw her open satchel on the kitchen counter.

The leather flap lay open, the four scripts inside displayed for anyone to see. Anyone who was interested in taking a peek, that was.

Beside her satchel was a lone water glass. Just in case she had any doubt as to whether Leandro had had the opportunity to take full advantage of her folly last night.

That quickly, her memories soured in her stomach. Was it possible he'd looked through the scripts? There was no way of knowing if he'd pulled them out for a quick look, then carefully slid them back into place. Tugging them free from her bag, she stared at them nonetheless, searching desperately for any sign that he'd looked through them even as part of her railed against the suspicion that Leandro would take advantage of her like that.

He'd buried himself inside her time after time. He'd pressed his face, his mouth into her most intimate places. He'd been generous and fun and gentle and passionate. Surely he couldn't be all those things as well as a ruthless exploiter of other people's weaknesses? Or, in this case, her carelessness?

Then she remembered what he'd said to her at the conference. *What would you have done if the same opportunity fell into your lap?*

She didn't need to flip through the scripts to know that if Leandro *had* taken advantage of her stupidity, he was now privy to one of the biggest secrets the show had— namely, the write-out of Mac Harrison's long-term character, Kirk, in an extensive, ratings-grabbing ten-week story arc that was designed to dazzle, grip and torture their audience. Mac was at last leaving the show to take up directing full-time, having more than proved himself as a dazzling talent with the feature-length special. Between them, the four scripts in her bag made up the climax of his write-out story. If Leandro had so much as taken a peek, he'd know that *Heartlands* was going to be battling for every ratings point in three months' time.

The question was, had Leandro considered her leaving her satchel around while they were having rampant animal sex an *opportunity* that he couldn't pass up?

She honestly didn't know. She'd had sex with him four times. She'd groaned and moaned his name, taken him in her mouth, clawed at his back and begged him to satisfy her.

But she really didn't know him at all.

She guessed he was around thirty-five, but she really had no idea how old he was. She knew he was Greek, but knew nothing about his family except that he had nieces and nephews. She knew he cared about the environment—enough to drive a geeky car, anyway. But that was it.

Sliding the scripts back into her bag, she slammed the glass down into her sink and gripped the edge of the counter. It was very clear to her all of a sudden. Last night had been a mistake. A big, stupid, red-letter mistake.

She'd spent nearly fifteen years building her career in the entertainment industry. She'd worked two jobs at the same time, she'd kissed ass, she'd eaten more than her fair share of shit sandwiches. She'd worked for insulting wages, she'd swallowed other people stealing her credits, she'd pushed when she'd had to, and stepped back when she deemed it necessary. And all the while she'd felt the scrutiny and judgment of her male colleagues, peers and rivals. If she lost her temper at work, she was a bitch, not hotheaded. If she stuck up for herself, she was aggressive, not assertive. If she was passionate about something, she was emotional, not committed. She'd learned a long time ago that female executives were measured by different rules than their male colleagues, and she'd sucked it up and played the game because she'd been determined to prove herself.

Now she'd made a rookie's mistake—her head had been turned by a cute ass and some well-rounded pecs, and she'd made herself vulnerable.

She took a deep breath, then let it out on a long sigh. If Leandro had taken advantage of her, she'd soon know about it. If he hadn't, she'd had a valuable wake-up call. Sleeping with the enemy had been a bad, bad idea.

HIS LEGS POUNDING the ground, his heartbeat a steady thump in his chest, Leandro ran to the top of the hill. Beside him, his younger brother, Dom, wheezed and gasped for air.

"Jesus, Leandro," Dom choked when they reached the peak.

"You want a break, just say so," Leandro said, knowing his brother would hate conceding defeat, a hangover from their childhood battles for supremacy.

"Asshole," Dom said, slowing to a walk and then stopping altogether to hunch over, his arms braced on his knees.

Leandro stretched out his hamstrings and calves, taking in the view of Hollywood spread out below them. They were running through Griffith Park on a wide, well-maintained fire trail, and the white letters of the Hollywood sign were visible on the hillside to the west.

"I need to get back to the gym," Dom said after a few minutes of heavy breathing and brow wiping.

"No kidding," Leandro said, patting his brother's burgeoning beer belly. "You look like you're about four months along there."

"I'm growing out in sympathy with Betty," Dom said, shaking his head. "Man, I still can't believe we're having twins. What were we thinking going back for a third kid?"

Dom and Betty already had two small children, Alexandra and Stephen, both of them under three.

"You guys love it. The lack of sleep, the screaming, the scratched furniture, the smelly diapers," Leandro said.

Dom grinned, then cuffed Leandro lightly on the shoulder.

"Don't forget the good stuff. The good-night cuddles. Reading them books. Hearing them run up the hallway when you walk in the door at night."

"Hey, you don't have to convert me. As soon as I find a woman who'll stick, I plan on adding to the family album myself," Leandro said.

Dom eased the backpack from his shoulders and handed over a bottle of water to his brother.

"Not getting any younger, bro," he said.

"No shit. Thanks for reminding me," Leandro said dryly.

"I might be getting fat, but you're old—and I can diet," Dom said, rubbing salt into the wound now that he'd found a point of weakness.

"Yeah, but you're not going to. My bet is, you'll have a big belly like Pa's by the time you're forty," Leandro said.

Dom shrugged a shoulder philosophically. "Stored happiness. That's all it is."

Leandro laughed and took another swig of water.

"So, any prospects for the second Mrs. Mandalor?" Dom asked.

Immediately—insanely—he had a flash of Claudia

from last night, spread-eagled on her couch, one leg over the arm as she touched herself.

"Nope," Leandro said firmly, as much to himself as to his brother.

If Peta had been a bad prospect for happily ever after, Claudia was doubly doomed. She was ferociously ambitious and competitive and she struck him as being absolutely committed to her single state. Everything in her home screamed single career woman—the modern, clean lines of her furniture, the lack of family photos and sentimental knickknacks. There wasn't a single frill, flower or furbelow in her house, and he suspected her mind was just as streamlined.

No, Claudia Dostis was not a viable prospect for "'til death do us part" fantasies.

Which meant he really shouldn't have had such a hard time resisting calling her all weekend. One of the reasons he and Dom were running through the Hollywood Hills right now was because his fingers had itched to dial her number on more than one occasion. He'd figured some good honest sweat and some friendly rivalry with his brother would bring him back down to earth.

If only Friday night hadn't been so hot. She'd been so tight and wet and ready for him, so abandoned to her own desire, so eager to explore anywhere he chose to take her. Before he'd lost himself inside her curvy, petite body, he'd imagined that stripping her bare and having her would more than satisfy his curiosity. But she was like fine chocolate, or freshly ground coffee—one hit and he only wanted more.

"Betty's got this friend," Dom said, waggling his eyebrows. "Nice Greek girl, works as a beautician, but she's studying at night school to be a teacher. Loves kids, great rack, even greater baklava."

Dom closed his eyes blissfully as he mentioned the honey and nut filled Greek pastry.

"No more blind dates. I can't handle them," Leandro said.

"What's your problem? This woman has been hand-chosen for you by people who care. Trust me, she's a hottie. And she wants kids big-time."

Leandro stared at his brother. He should say yes, he knew he should. But his mind kept sliding across to those memories from last night. Claudia clenching her thighs around him, urging him on with her hands on his butt. Claudia bucking her hips as he tasted her. Claudia taking him in her mouth and teasing him with her tongue and her lips and her hand.

"Give me her number," he growled. Maybe his mother and sisters were right—maybe he did have a self-destructive attraction to the wrong kind of woman.

"You won't regret this," Dom said, slapping him on the back. "Her name is Stella. You're going to love her."

Sure he was. She was going to be so hot, so absolutely right for him that he was going to forget Claudia's name, the feel of her body against his, the sound of her husky voice in his ear.

Silently cursing his own stupid libido, Leandro turned back to the trail.

"Think you can survive the run back to the car? It's mostly downhill," he asked his brother.

Dom gave him the finger and started off downhill at a punishing pace. Leandro hesitated a moment before following him.

No matter how much he wanted her, he had to put Claudia out of his mind.

Letting out a whooping war cry, he plunged down the trail after his brother.

"CLAUDIA, I HAVE Leandro Mandalor on line two for you." Gabby's voice was carefully disinterested, but Claudia knew her assistant well enough to know she was bristling with curiosity.

If her stomach hadn't suddenly dropped into her shoes, she might find it in herself to smile over Gabby's old-woman tendencies. Unfortunately, it had. And her heart had also started pounding at a disturbing rate, and her palms were moist and she had what felt like a big wad of cotton wool stuck in her throat.

Despite herself, despite her suspicions and fears, she'd dreamed about him all weekend. She'd come to work this morning, determined to push him from her mind with the help of her towering in tray. And now it was eleven in the morning and he'd called and she was awash with sensual memories from their few hours together.

Giving herself a mental slap, Claudia took a deep breath and picked up the phone.

"Claudia," he said. Instantly her nipples turned into two demanding peaks of arousal.

Eyeing them sternly, Claudia sat back in her chair and put her feet on her desk—anything to give herself the illusion that she was in control.

"Leandro."

"How was your weekend?" he asked.

"Over. How about yours?"

"Long. Boring. Lonely."

Between her legs, damp heat began to build.

"Was there something I can help you with?" she asked

coolly, angry with her body for being so easy. This man had potentially helped himself to one of her show's most precious secrets. Was she really such a cheap date?

There was a moment of silence, then he spoke again.

"Is there something wrong?" he asked.

"Should there be?" she countered.

"I don't know. When I left the other night, I got the definite impression that we'd both had a good time. So…did I make you sleep in the wet patch? Or maybe I used the good towels? Help me out here," he said.

He was awfully charming. And his voice was awfully sexy.

But she'd learned her lesson in those stomach-churning few minutes in her kitchen on Saturday morning.

"Look, Leandro, you're right. We both had a good time. But that's all it was. And it was definitely a one-off. I don't think we should fool ourselves about that," she said firmly.

"Why?"

"Because we're competitors. For starters. And I'm not interested in a relationship."

"But you are interested in sex, right?" he asked, his voice very low and intimate.

The way he said it, the meaning he injected into every word… She pressed her thighs together on a surge of desire, ignoring the fillip of unease that came hand-in-hand with the sensation as she recognized how much power this man could have over her. If she let him.

"Not with you. You're my rival. I worked too hard to get this job to jeopardize it," she said.

"We're both grown-ups. We can deal with the situation," he said confidently.

"No. I'm not interested," she said crisply, mostly

because parts of her body were already screaming "yes." God, she really was cheap.

"Now, that's a lie," Leandro said, his voice lowering an octave. "I bet that if I was in your office with you right now, I could slide my hand into your panties and you'd be wet and ready for me. I bet if I unbuttoned your shirt and touched her breasts, maybe sucked on your nipples…I bet you'd be more than interested."

She swallowed, hard. Just like that, her body was on fire. It was almost as though he *was* in her office with her, as though he really did have his hand between her legs. Squirming in her chair, she recrossed her legs and straightened her black shirt and tried to remember her name and all the reasons why Leandro Mandalor was a nightmare on legs.

"I don't trust you," she heard herself say. She winced. The thought had formed in her mind and found its way out her mouth before she could engage her mental editor.

"I beg your pardon?" he asked.

"Not sexually," she clarified, in case he'd misunderstood her. "I meant professionally."

"I see."

He sounded puzzled. And definitely offended. She felt driven to explain.

"There were scripts in my bag Friday night. On my kitchen counter," she said.

Nothing but silence from his end of the phone.

"I have no way of knowing if you looked at them or not," she said defensively.

More silence. Why was she feeling so thoroughly in the wrong here all of a sudden? It had felt like a legitimate concern on Saturday morning as she stood there staring at those scripts. But now she felt like a paranoid bitch.

"I didn't look at your scripts, Claudia," he finally said.

She let out the breath that she hadn't realized she'd been holding. She believed him. Maybe that made her an even bigger fool than she already was, but she believed him. To her knowledge, he hadn't lied to her yet. The band of tension that had bound her chest since Saturday loosened a notch.

"But you could have. If they'd been sitting there, outside of my bag, say. You might have been tempted to take a look at a scene or two. It would only be human nature. And who's to say the same thing wouldn't happen for me if we were at your place? We're busy people. Work invades all aspects of our lives. I don't want to be on guard all the time, and I bet you don't, either," she said.

"I think you're exaggerating. And I find that interesting. What are you really afraid of, Claudia?" he asked.

She rolled her eyes. "Spare me the analysis, Dr. Phil. It really is that simple."

"Yeah? You sure it's not because we were so good together? Because you couldn't stop thinking about me all weekend?"

"Wow. That ego of yours has got its own zip code, hasn't it?" she said, even as she recrossed her legs again restlessly.

"Admit you dreamed about me."

How does he know this stuff?

"No. No dreams all weekend. Slept like a baby," she said.

"Hmm. I thought you were braver than this, Claudia," he said.

"Excuse me?"

"I thought you were a big, bad, bold woman of the world. I thought you weren't ashamed of sex how you like it."

"This is where I'm supposed to say 'am not' and fall flat on my back for you, right?" she asked dryly.

"I'd settle for all fours. Or against the wall. Or maybe on your desk. You've got a nice, wide desk, right?" he asked.

A ridiculous thrill ripped through her and she caught herself eyeing her desk assessingly.

"You want me to put in it writing? I'm not interested," she said a little desperately.

"Chicken," he taunted.

"Look at that—the president is on line three. I'd better take it," she said, slamming the phone down before her baser instincts got the better of her.

Her body was thrumming with need, she was breathing fast, and she suspected she was currently more liquid than solid. If he walked in the door right now, she'd have him out of his pants and inside her in no seconds flat.

Thank God he wasn't there.

Never in her whole life had she been so tempted to take such a stupid risk. It was amazing what great sex could do to a woman, it really was.

Fortunately she'd had enough self-control to protect herself from making the same mistake twice.

LEANDRO SAT STARING at the phone for a full minute after she'd ended their call.

He'd fought himself and his need all weekend and most of the morning. But the truth was he wanted her. And until he was involved with another woman—his future wife—he didn't see any reason why he couldn't have her again. That was the conclusion he'd come to—the self-serving, incredibly convenient conclusion—at about one minute to eleven that morning. Thirty seconds later, he'd been on the phone with her.

And why not? They were obviously sexually compatible. If the ground rules were clear, what was to stop them from exploring the chemistry between them? According to her, though, there were plenty of roadblocks standing in their way.

He'd be lying if he didn't admit she'd surprised him with her suspicions regarding him and her scripts. He had never cut corners in his career. Television was an industry full of secrets, rumors, big egos and big money, but as much as he wanted to be a success, he'd never taken anything that he hadn't earned. Regardless of how it had looked, utilizing the information about *Ocean Boulevard*'s feature-length special had been good business sense. He hadn't gone trawling for the information, it had landed in his lap, and he'd have been a fool if he'd ignored it. Had he had a twinge of conscience at the time? Maybe. But since he hadn't been able to un-know what he'd been told, he'd had to act on it.

But if he'd been in her shoes, if she'd acted on confidential information to try to outmaneuver him, maybe he'd hesitate to trust her again. Especially after what had happened with Peta. So he wasn't entirely unsympathetic to her concerns. With another guy, at another time, they might be valid.

But now that they'd cleared the air, he figured it wasn't an insurmountable problem. She trusted him. He'd heard it in her voice when he'd offered her his reassurance. She trusted him, and she wanted him again, the way he wanted her. They could work around the confidentiality thing. As long as neither of them talked in their sleep, and they were discreet, he figured they were free to feast on each other for as long as their mutual lust lasted.

Except, of course, for the fact that she wasn't interested. Apparently.

He smiled to himself. She was a seasoned bullshitter, but he'd been inside her. He'd felt her shatter around him. He'd breathed in the scent of her desire.

Not interested, his ass.

Reaching for his mouse, he called up a search engine on his computer screen. At heart, all men were hunters. And Claudia was a worthy opponent.

His smile turning into an out-and-out grin, Leandro began to plan his campaign.

5

THE FIRST PACKAGE arrived the next day. Claudia left the Tuesday morning pitch meeting to find a small, exquisitely wrapped box on her desk. It wasn't too much of a stretch to guess who'd sent it—she wasn't exactly inundated with admirers at the moment, thanks to her hectic work schedule.

Reaching for her phone, she buzzed her assistant.

"Gabby, what's the deal with this thing on my desk?"

"It came by courier while you were in your meeting."

"Okay. Thanks."

Definitely from Leandro, then.

Claudia picked up the small glossy black box, toying for a second with the knot of ribbon on top. She really wanted to open it—simply out of curiosity, that was all—but she didn't want to be tempted. She was already very tempted—by his body, and his voice and the excitement they generated together. But it really would be sleeping with the enemy.

Dropping the box into the bottom drawer of her desk, she told herself it didn't matter what he'd sent her, her decision remained the same.

Her determination held until mid-afternoon. Every time her mind turned away from work, it reverted to the same loop of thought. What had he sent her? And was she really so weak-willed that she was worried she could be swayed by the contents of one small black box? Because she was afraid the answer to that last question was yes, she put off the inevitable until she literally couldn't go five minutes without her thoughts turning to the contents of her desk drawer.

"Damn you," she growled under her breath as she finally wrenched her drawer open and grabbed the box.

Eyeing it as though it was about to explode, she gave herself one last chance to be sensible. Then she unraveled the elaborate bow and eased the lid off.

"You smug bastard!" she swore as she saw what she'd been agonizing over all day.

Nestled in amongst a bed of artistically crinkled black tissue paper was a single, perfect white feather.

He thought she was a coward.

She was still staring in outrage at his provocative *gift* when Grace stopped in her doorway.

"Hey, you got a minute?" Grace asked.

Claudia dropped the stupid feather back into its stupid black box and pushed the whole mess away from herself.

"Yep. What's up?" she said, making an effort to focus her thoughts.

"I wanted to run the changes for next week's block past you."

"Sure thing. Fire away," Claudia said crisply.

Grace gave her a peculiar look before sitting down in Claudia's guest chair.

"Okay. Since we've had to write Rianna out for a week because of her morning sickness, we had to fiddle with the B story for all five episodes next week," Grace began.

Claudia tried very hard to concentrate on what her friend was saying about the changes to one of the subplots, but her eyes kept drifting toward the black box. Every time she thought about the white feather inside it, her hands clenched into fists and she imagined what she'd say to Leandro if she had him in her office.

For starters, she'd never walked away from a challenge in her life. Ever. She'd systematically conquered all her fears—from spiders to snakes to thunderstorms—and she prided herself on always being able to hold her own. He had no idea the kind of challenges she'd conquered in her life. Just because he didn't understand the ramifications of them continuing what they'd started the other night didn't mean she was a coward—it simply meant she was smarter than him.

"Claud, is something wrong?" Grace asked after five minutes.

"What? No," Claudia said, dragging her gaze away from Leandro's gift.

"You sure? You're not pissed with me about something?"

"No." Claudia really focused on her friend. "Why on earth would you think that?"

"Maybe because you're scowling at me," Grace said. "And you keep clenching and unclenching your hands. And I swear I just heard you growl."

Claudia felt the warmth of embarrassment creeping up her face.

"I'm fine. Just a little…preoccupied with something to do with *Heartlands*," she said, opting for a half-truth. Normally, she wouldn't hesitate to ask Grace or Sadie's advice regarding man trouble. But Leandro was no ordinary man—he was her avowed enemy. And she'd screwed his brains out on her living room couch. And in her bedroom. And in her shower. She'd made such a big deal out of what an asshole he was for stealing their special feature idea that she felt distinctly embarrassed over succumbing to their mutual desire. She might be passionate—she might even be impulsive sometimes—but she was never stupid. And sleeping with her rival had been very, very stupid.

"Mandalor again, huh?" Grace asked. "What's he done this time?"

Claudia's gaze automatically slid across to the black box. Before Claudia could stop her, Grace leaned forward and flipped the lid.

"A white feather?" Grace asked incredulously. "What the hell is that about?"

"He's trying to be clever," Claudia fudged. "He thinks he's funny."

Grace was still frowning. "But a white feather?"

Claudia bundled the box and feather up and swept it into the wastebasket.

"Just a stupid joke. From something I said at the convention," she fudged a little more.

"Hmph. He really is an asshole, isn't he?" Grace said. " And he doesn't know dick. You're the gutsiest woman I know."

"Thanks, Gracie," Claudia said, even as guilt made her want to squirm. She told herself that technically what she'd said wasn't a complete lie, but it was hard to fool your own conscience. Mentally, she added another misdemeanor to the growing list of crimes committed against her by Leandro Mandalor. First, he tormented her with his hot kisses, then he drove her crazy with his hot body, and now he was messing with her head so much that she couldn't admit to having slipped up to her friend.

"Next time I see him, I'm going to kick him in his other shin," Grace said firmly.

"Make sure you're wearing those metal-tipped stilettos of yours," Claudia said. "And get a good run up."

By the time they'd finished discussing the following week's script changes, Claudia had successfully pushed the white feather from her mind. Leandro had had his little joke. She wasn't going to give him the satisfaction of responding in any way. And she certainly wasn't going to waste any more time dwelling on it.

The next day, another parcel arrived. A glossy lime-green box this time, big enough to hold a pair of shoes. But she knew better than to think that there was a pair of killer heels inside. Lips pursed, she marched into the photocopy room and dumped it, unopened, into the recycle bin. Dusting her hands, her lips primmed into a satisfied smirk, she marched back to her desk.

He might think he could sit back and goad her from on high, but if she didn't play the game, he couldn't win.

She was still congratulating herself on her willpower and determination when Sadie popped her head into her office before lunch.

"This is so weird—guess what I found in the recycle bin?" she said, and Claudia's face froze as she saw a stuffed toy chicken in her friend's hand.

He'd sent her a chicken. First she was a coward, now she was a chicken. For a moment, she saw red.

"I was dumping a bunch of story lines from last year and I saw this gift box in there and this was inside. I can't believe anyone would throw out anything so cute," Sadie continued.

Claudia cleared her throat.

"I threw it out," she said. "But if you like it, it's yours."

Sadie looked perplexed. "Why'd you throw it out?"

"I hate chickens," Claudia improvised. "All poultry, in fact. They give me the creeps."

Sadie looked at the comically cute plush toy in her hand, and Claudia knew she wasn't buying.

"Okay…" Sadie said slowly. "Is this anything to do with the white feather thing from yesterday?"

Claudia closed her eyes for a long beat. She should have known Grace would tell Sadie. No matter what, eventually they always told each other everything. They worked with each other, they were women and they were friends—it was inevitable that they knew each other's lives inside out.

"All right. Okay. I slept with him. There, now you know," Claudia confessed in an impulsive blurt.

"You slept with Leandro Mandalor and he sent you a stuffed chicken?" Sadie asked.

"No. I mean, yes, I slept with him, but the chicken isn't about the sex. The chicken is about me saying no to more sex," Claudia said.

Sadie still looked perplexed, and Claudia sighed heavily.

"Maybe we should grab Gracie and go for an early lunch," she suggested.

Twenty minutes later, Claudia was surprised at how much lighter she felt after telling her friends the whole sordid story.

"I can't believe you did Leandro Mandalor," Grace kept saying, shaking her head in disbelief.

"I know, I know. It was dumb. My God, if Harvey ever finds out…" Claudia said, referring to her immediate boss at the production company.

"No, I mean, he's so *big,* Claud. I mean, he's huge. And you're so little," Grace said, her hands gesturing vividly to illustrate her point.

Claudia felt herself blushing. "We worked it out," she said.

Sadie smirked. "Are you blushing? I don't think I've ever seen you blush before."

"We *are* talking about possibly the stupidest thing I have ever done," Claudia said defensively. "Of course I'm embarrassed."

"Because of *Heartlands?*" Grace asked. She waved a hand dismissively. "It's no big deal. It's not like you're going to be telling each other secrets between orgasms or anything. You're both grown-ups, right?"

"Hell, no one would have sex with anyone in L.A. if they worried about conflict of interest," Sadie said.

Claudia stared at her friends.

"You really don't think it's a big deal? We're competitors. Rivals. Arch enemies," she insisted.

"Yeah…but none of that stuff's serious, is it? It's not fight-to-the-death material. It's just…fun, to keep us all on our toes," Sadie said.

Claudia blinked. Sadie and Grace didn't think her sleeping with Leandro was a big deal. Better still, they didn't think anyone else would think it was a big deal, either.

"Why am I the only one who sees that this is a big problem?" she asked. "There's no way I am going to risk years of hard work for great sex. It's not worth it."

"*Great* sex? Now you're talking," Grace said, rubbing her hands together salaciously.

"You guys didn't give me details, so you get none," Claudia said repressively.

"Fine. I'd just like to place a small wager on the table. Twenty bucks says you see him again," Grace said.

"What? Get out of here," Claudia said.

"I want in," Sadie said, reaching for her purse.

Claudia stared at her. "What is this, a conspiracy or something?"

"No. I just recognize the look," Sadie said.

"Definitely." Grace nodded.

"What look?" Claudia asked.

"The look I saw in my own bathroom mirror when Dylan came back into my life," Sadie said.

"Mac for me, but same deal," Grace said.

Claudia rolled her eyes. "Guys, it's not going to happen. Even if he wasn't the enemy, I'm not interested in a relationship and I don't have the time for anything else. I work seven days a week, remember?"

"Ask yourself—how long does great sex take?" Grace asked.

Sadie shot Grace a confused look. "I don't know about you, but great sex can chew up a bit of time for me."

Grace looked arrested, then nodded her agreement. "You're right. I withdraw the statement, your honor. How about this instead—how often does great sex come along?"

"Nice," Sadie said.

Claudia rolled her eyes again and collected her handbag. "Love your work, ladies, but I have a show to produce," she said, sliding out of the booth they were sharing.

THAT NIGHT, Claudia tore herself away from her desk to leave work early and stop in at the Third Street Promenade in Santa Monica to buy a birthday gift for her nephew, Nicco. He was turning five and was obsessed with pirates, according to her eldest brother, Cosmo. She selected a wooden pirate ship, complete with pint-size buccaneers, and tried not to notice how much the pirate captain looked like Leandro. She'd called him a pirate once, she remembered. Maybe she hadn't been that far off the mark, the way he kept hijacking her thoughts.

And she was doing it again—thinking about him! She frowned as she handed over her credit card to the teenager at the checkout. She'd made a deal with herself after her lunch with Grace and Sadie—she wasn't going to think about him anymore. For starters, that was exactly what he wanted her to do, with his little gifts and sly digs. He was counting on her making contact. And she'd be damned if she was giving in to his manipulation.

Annoyed with herself for wasting yet more time on something she'd consigned to the dustbin of history, she made the short drive to her brother's place in the Palisades.

"Auntie Claudia," Nicco yelled from up the hallway as her brother opened the door.

Claudia crouched down, her gift balanced in one arm, and returned his exuberant hug.

"Hey, my favorite monkey," she said, ruffling his hair. "How's the big birthday guy doing?"

"It's not my birthday yet, silly. Not till tomorrow," Nicco corrected her, his words lisping adorably through a new gap in his front teeth where his two baby incisors had dropped out.

Claudia gasped with laughter when she registered the profound change.

"Look at you! When did that happen? I bet the tooth fairy has been busy around here," she said.

"He brought me a whole dollar in quarters," Nicco said proudly.

Claudia raised an eyebrow at her brother. "When I was little, we only used to get a nickel per tooth," she said.

"Inflation," Cosmo said dryly.

"You want your present now or do you want to wait until tomorrow?" she asked Nicco.

His little face screwed up as he thought it through.

"I *want* to open it now, but it wouldn't be right because it's not my birthday yet," he finally said. She'd half-suspected this would be his answer—for an almost-five-year-old, he had some very rigid ideas about what was and what wasn't okay.

"Why can't you come to my party tomorrow night same as everyone else?" he asked, staring up at Claudia plaintively. "Grandma and Papa will be there, and Uncle George and my cousins and my friends. We're going to have red icing on a cake shaped like a big number five. I helped Mommy with it today."

"I can't make it tomorrow night, sweetie," she said. "But you save your present until then. I can call you later and you can tell me if you liked it or not."

"Okay. I'm going to go put it in my room so it will be there first thing when I wake up tomorrow," Nicco said. Sliding his arms around the big box, he tottered off down the hallway.

Claudia stared after him pensively, regretting that she wouldn't be there to witness the delight on his face when he saw the pirate ship.

"You could come, you know," Cosmo said as he led her into the kitchen.

"It would be a disaster, and you know it," Claudia said. "Papa would get angry all over again, and Mama would cry or worse… I don't want to ruin Nicco's special day."

It was the same rationale she'd used for the past three years, ever since she'd taken a stand against her mother's drinking and "detached with love," as the so-called experts called it. After a lifetime of watching her mother kill herself with drink, Claudia had had enough of the pain and disappointment. She'd given her mother an ultimatum—either she enter a residential rehabilitation program or Claudia would refuse to be a part of her life. Predictably, her mother had denied she had a problem, leaving Claudia with no choice but to carry through on her threat.

It was a move that had torn her family apart. For so many years, they'd all been in denial about Talia Dostis's drinking. When Claudia had been a teen, her mother's alcoholism had been explained away in so many ways— Talia was feeling emotional, or she was having a bad day or she had simply gotten carried away at a family celebration. But Claudia had walked up the garden path too many times after school and heard the clink of empty wine bottles being hidden in the garbage can. She'd smelled the sweet-sour stink of alcohol on her mother's breath, and endured the maudlin embraces and inevitable tears before her mother passed out more times than she cared to count. She'd cleaned up vomit and worse, changed sheets, helped trawl the streets when her mother went missing on one of her binges.

In her twenties, she'd hoped with the rest of her family when her mother had declared herself on the wagon time after time. It never lasted. For a few weeks they would have Talia back, clear-eyed and focused and almost her old self. And then the subterfuge would begin. The sneaking around. The hiding of bottles. The stealing of money. Talia had become a consummate liar, like all addicts. And not just about her drinking. By the time Claudia had made her stand, it had become impossible to tell where the truth ended and the lies began.

Detaching herself had not been a decision she'd taken lightly, but Claudia had been at her wit's end. She'd held on for so long, believed her mother's vows and promises so many times, been so disappointed and hurt and ashamed when her mother let her down again, again, again…. In the end, it had come down to doing what was right for herself, also. She couldn't force her mother to admit she was an alcoholic. But she could choose not to be part of the disaster area her mother created around herself. Once Claudia stepped back and stopped participating—stopped believing, and rescuing, and making excuses—she'd stopped being a part of the pretence.

Of course, it didn't mean she'd stopped caring. Or that there wasn't always a part of her mind that fretted. Talia was her mother; Claudia would always be connected to her fate.

The one thing she hadn't anticipated had been her father's rage at her decision. She'd broken the unspoken covenant of her family by putting a name to her mother's behavior. She'd made it impossible for them to all look the other way and pretend it didn't exist. All the anger and disappointment that had built up inside him over the years had been redirected toward his daughter. She had betrayed the family, disrespected her mother, shamed them all. Now, her father refused to look her in the eye, and she chose not to put herself, or her extended family, through the torture of hosting them both at the same time.

Which was why she was reduced to seeing her nephew the day before his birthday, rather than attending the party itself. And why she'd missed her cousin Zoe's wedding, and her uncle Costa's sixtieth, and a myriad of other family events and occasions.

Now, she accepted a coffee from her brother and greeted her sister-in-law, Yolanda, with a kiss.

"It's been a long time, Claudia," Yolanda said, picking up on their conversation.

"And nothing has changed," Claudia said firmly. She didn't want to talk about it. For the first year, she had questioned her decision every day. But she had stuck to her resolve because as painful as it was to be apart from her family, watching her mother's slow self-destruction was a million times worse.

Claudia could see that Yolanda wanted to argue some more—she wouldn't be Greek if she didn't—but she didn't want to go over old ground. She'd made her decision, it was done.

"We haven't had a chance to talk—how was Zoe's wedding?" she asked, deliberately changing the subject.

Yolanda and Cosmo exchanged speaking looks before Yolanda shrugged and sat down at the kitchen table beside Claudia.

"It was great. She was beautiful. I'll show you the pictures later…"

For the next few hours, Claudia listened as they updated her on the wedding and other recent family sagas—her uncle's battle with the police department over parking tickets, her aunt's upcoming eye surgery, her father's big win at bowling. Nicco peppered their conversation with questions of his own and repeated invitations for Claudia to come to his room so she could see his latest pet rock, and Claudia basked in the warmth of home and hearth. The loud voices, the talking over each other, the big hand gestures— she missed her family, knew that she would be missing out on so much fun and love by being absent tomorrow night.

When Yolanda dug out her cousin's wedding photos, Claudia found her gaze lingering on shots featuring her parents, almost as though she were looking for evidence that, despite what she'd said earlier to Yolanda, something had shifted, something that would allow her to come back into the family fold.

But what she saw only made her feel sadder and more determined. Her father looked older, smaller. Her mother was painfully thin and scrawny, her face caked with makeup to cover the damage alcohol had done to her skin over the years. Claudia paused over one particular shot, her stomach clenching with old, old pain as she saw the lopsided, vague smile on her mother's face and her father standing behind her, one hand on Talia's shoulder in a gesture Claudia knew so well. Even if she hadn't known that distant smile of her mother's so intimately, she'd have known Talia had been drinking because of that hand—that guiding, loyal, ever-patient hand on her mother's shoulder. Her father had been shepherding his broken wife for too many years to count.

But Claudia could not do the same.

"For what it's worth, everyone asked after you," Cosmo said when he noticed her lingering over certain photos.

"I'll catch up with Zoe when they're back from their honeymoon," Claudia said, shuffling the photos back together and sliding them into their envelope.

She stayed for a little while longer, read Nicco his bedtime story, then wished them all luck for the party tomorrow. Her house seemed very empty and quiet when she let herself in, and she was doubly annoyed with herself when her thoughts defaulted to thinking about Leandro Mandalor yet again.

What was wrong with her at the moment? For the first

time in a long time, she felt plagued by doubts. About her parents, about Leandro, about her life. And Claudia Dostis didn't do doubt.

Thoroughly out of sorts, she went to bed.

LEANDRO STARED OUT into the dark night sky, swirling the remnants of his whiskey around the bottom of his tumbler. He'd expected to hear from Claudia by now. It had been three days since his campaign had begun. On Tuesday he'd sent her the white feather, on Wednesday the toy chicken. Today, he'd sent her a rubbery, yellow-bellied frog—and still she hadn't responded to his goading.

Which probably meant she wasn't going to.

Swallowing the last of the whiskey, he made the decision he'd been putting off all week. Leaving the tumbler on the window ledge, he leaned across his couch to grab the phone. Pulling his brother's business card from his wallet, he tapped in the number jotted on the back.

A woman answered after the third ring.

"Hello?"

She had a pleasant voice, light and mellifluous.

"Is this Stella Diodorus?" he asked.

She sighed heavily. "Please don't tell me you're trying to sell me something because I've had a really shitty day and I don't want to be rude to you but I'm afraid that's what's going to happen if you start talking about life insurance or time-shares."

Leandro grinned. Maybe this wasn't such a bad idea after all.

"This is Leandro Mandalor calling—my brother Dom gave me your number."

There was a long silence on the other end of the phone.

"Hello? Stella?"

"I'm still here. I'm just wondering how long it's going to take for me to get my foot out of my mouth," she said.

He laughed. "Hey, if our positions had been reversed and I thought you were a telemarketer, I'd have been a hell of a lot ruder," he said.

"Betty was right—you are a nice guy," Stella said.

Leandro rested his head against the cool glass of his window and stared out into the night again.

"Betty's a little biased—and she has an ulterior motive. She wants cousins for her kids," he said.

"Family makes the world go around, Leandro," she said softly.

He wasn't deaf to her unspoken message. As his brother had said, she'd been handpicked by people who cared.

"When would you like to have dinner, Stella?" he asked, cutting to the chase.

"I've got exams the next two weeks. Did Dom tell you I'm getting my teaching degree at night school?"

"He mentioned it. How's it going?"

"I'm surviving. How does a week from Friday sound?"

Two weeks away. He felt oddly…relieved. What was that about?

"Suits me. Shall I pick you up or would you prefer to have an escape route?" he asked.

"*Oooh,* tough choice. Why don't we live dangerously?"

He jotted down her address and they agreed on a time.

"Looking forward to it, Stella," he said before he ended the call.

"Me, too," she said, her voice full of soft promise.

He poured himself another finger of whiskey and sank down into his well-worn armchair.

He had a date with a nice, baby-craving, family-oriented Greek girl. Exactly what he wanted, right?

So why was he still pondering what to send Claudia tomorrow?

CLAUDIA LIFTED HER HEAD slowly on Friday morning as Gabby slid a box onto her desk.

"Another parcel for you," her assistant said.

"So I see."

"Would you like me to throw this one away?" Gabby asked.

"That's fine. I can take care of it," Claudia said calmly.

She didn't feel calm. The frog yesterday had almost broken her. She'd taken one look into its bulging amphibian eyes and felt an overwhelming need to find a tender, vulnerable part of Leandro's anatomy and plant her fist in it. Why wouldn't the man take no for an answer?

But the last thing she was going to do was betray her feelings to her gossipy assistant. Lord only knew what Gabby thought was going on between Claudia and Leandro. No doubt there were scuttlebutt-laden rumors doing the rounds of the office already, thanks to this stupid campaign of his. Another thing she could thank Mr. Arrogant for. It wasn't enough that flashbacks to their night together had ruined every night's sleep she'd had so far this week. No, he also had to turn her into a laughing stock in her own place of work.

Having lingered for as long as she could without actually having an excuse, Gabby sighed heavily and retreated to her desk. A few seconds later, Sadie and Grace appeared in Claudia's office doorway.

"Hello, hello. What have we here?" Grace asked, sauntering forward to examine the bright aqua box on Claudia's desk.

Claudia realized they'd been on the lookout for Leandro's latest delivery. It was becoming a regular workplace occurrence, like the arrival of the mail or the morning coffee round.

"What do you think it is this time? I was thinking a yellow ribbon," Sadie suggested.

"Nah—that's for remembrance, not cowardice," Grace said, studying the box.

"Do you mind?" Claudia asked snappily. "Some of us are trying to work here."

"Can we open it?" Grace asked, ignoring Claudia's outburst.

"Yeah, can we, huh, huh?" Sadie asked, doing her best imitation of a kid on Christmas day.

"For Pete's sake," Claudia said, exasperated. She thrust the box toward them. "Take it away, do whatever you like with it. I'm not interested," she said.

"Sure you aren't. We'll just open it here," Grace said archly.

Sadie tugged on the big purple bow wrapping the box, and Grace removed the lid.

They both frowned down into the box for a long beat.

"What is it?" Sadie asked, frowning.

"I don't know. I mean, I get what it is, but what's it meant to symbolize?" Grace looked puzzled.

"Longevity? Because of the nine lives thing, do you think?" Sadie asked.

Claudia told herself to keep her eyes on her notepad, to keep writing, to ignore them. But she'd never been good at self-denial. Not knowing what was in the box was killing her.

Throwing her pen down, she pulled the box toward

herself. Sitting in the bottom amongst a nest of purple tissue paper was the most timid, beseeching, terrified looking toy cat she'd ever seen in her life.

"What do you think it's supposed to be?" Sadie prompted.

"It's a scaredy cat," Claudia said through gritted teeth.

"Of course it is! He's a real smarty-pants, isn't he?" Grace said admiringly. "I would never have thought of that."

"This is ridiculous," Claudia said. "It's getting out of hand."

"Then tell him to stop. Have you called him yet?" Sadie asked.

"No. That's exactly what he wants," Claudia said, hands on hips. "I'm not giving him what he wants—he'll think he's won."

Grace gave her a look. "That's one way of looking at it. Or…you could just let the man know he's barking up the wrong tree."

"Look, I don't want to speak to him, okay?" Claudia snapped. She could still remember the smoky bass of his voice curling around her from their last phone conversation. "You have no idea how persuasive he is, how sexy his voice is. I can't stop thinking about him, and I don't like it and—" She broke off as Sadie and Grace stared at her. Realization dawned, and Claudia sat back in her office chair, profoundly shocked.

"My God. He's right," she said, forcing herself to face a painful truth. "I *am* a scaredy cat! I'm afraid to call him. I'm afraid of how much power he has over me."

There was a stunned silence for a long beat, then, good friends that they were, Sadie and Grace stepped into the breach.

"I totally understand. You're really into your career right

now, you don't want to be distracted," Sadie said. "Your contract is up for renewal soon, you want to put your best foot forward. Being producer is a big job."

"Just because you know what you want doesn't mean you're afraid," Grace said.

Claudia made a rude sound in the back of her throat. It was bull, and they all knew it. She'd been using work and the contest of wills between her and Leandro and the conflict of interest issue as convenient excuses to mask her true feelings. When she was with him, she felt on fire, out of control. And she was a woman who prided herself on being in control of herself and her life. She had a five-year plan, a ten-year plan. She knew what she wanted to be— and Leandro had no place in any of it.

Standing, she reached for her car keys. She'd never backed down from a challenge in her life. She might be scared of the intensity of her reaction to him, but that didn't mean she couldn't conquer it, control it, the way she had everything else life had ever thrown at her.

"What are you doing, Claud?" Sadie asked as Claudia snatched up her handbag as well.

"I'm not a chicken," she said through gritted teeth, already on her way out the door.

"Claud," Grace called urgently.

Despite the fact that every cell in her body was focused on proving something to herself and Leandro, Claudia forced herself to pivot on her heel.

"Yep?"

"You might need this," Grace said, pulling out something she had tucked inside her bra.

Claudia automatically caught the shiny silver packet: a single condom, still warm from Grace's body heat.

"Just in case," Grace said.

"Why do you have a condom in your bra?" Sadie asked dryly, cocking her head at her friend.

"Just in case," Grace repeated, deadpan.

CLAUDIA PURPOSELY DIDN'T think as she drove across town to where *Heartlands* was filmed. She certainly didn't acknowledge the tremble of trepidation in the pit of her stomach.

As she'd said to her friends, she was no chicken, and she'd do whatever it took to prove it.

Including giving in to her secret desire to have Leandro Mandalor again, no matter how much that challenged her view of her life and her future.

She didn't bother waiting for the receptionist to buzz her through when she arrived. A long time ago she'd interviewed for an assistant's role on the show, and she had a rough idea of the office layout.

"I'll show myself through," she reassured the receptionist blithely as she sailed past.

It seemed only fair to ambush him, since he'd ambushed her every day so far.

She paused on the other side of reception and scanned the office area quickly. She spotted his office to her left, smiling a feline smile of satisfaction when she saw he was holding an open-door meeting with two of his staff.

They'd have an audience—perfect.

Chin high, she strode toward his office, her gaze pinned to his downturned head. He glanced up when she was still several paces from his doorway, and she saw the arrested expression in his eyes as he sat back in his chair.

She'd surprised him. Even more perfect.

"Claudia," he said when she arrived on the threshold.

But she didn't stop there. Ignoring the eye-popping stares of his staff, she rounded his desk, slid her hands around his neck and into his thick, dark hair, and lowered her mouth to his to deliver her best take-no-prisoners, tongue-till-Tuesday French kiss.

For a second he froze, and she felt an intense thrill of satisfaction. Scared, her ass! Then she lost her balance as he tugged her into his lap, taking control of the kiss now as he bent her back over his arm, completely disregarding the two members of his team who were probably taking notes on every nuance of their lip-lock.

He crushed her breasts to his chest, his tongue telling her in no uncertain terms what he'd like to do to the rest of her. Her body was more than up for it, already aching for his touch. Beneath her butt, she felt the distinct, arousing firmness of his burgeoning erection, and she gave a feminine murmur of approval.

He'd so successfully scrambled her brains and hijacked her purpose that she was about to slide her hand down onto his crotch when someone in the room cleared their throat. She stiffened as she remembered where she was, what she was doing, and who was watching her.

Leandro reluctantly broke their kiss, and she was eternally grateful for the fact that he slid a hand onto the nape of her neck and held her face against his shoulder, guarding her privacy, as he spoke to his people.

"I'm going to take an early lunch, guys," he said in an admirably deadpan tone. "I'll leave you to decide between the two actors on our short list, okay? I'm happy with either."

"Sure thing, boss," someone said, and then Claudia heard the scuff of feet and the shuffle of papers as they made themselves scarce.

"It's times like these I hate the interior designer who made these offices out of Plexiglas," Leandro murmured ruefully as he ran a hand over her hip.

"Do you really think I'm going to go at it with you in your office after that display we just put on?" Claudia asked, desperately trying to cover how good it felt to be in his arms again, how much she'd craved his taste, his touch.

"Thirty seconds ago, you were about to," he reminded her.

Aware that he was smiling like a particularly self-satisfied Cheshire cat, Claudia pushed against his arms, trying to win her way free of his lap. It was one thing to take up his challenge, and another thing to put herself entirely in his hands. Leandro just grinned and tipped his chair back, overbalancing her into his chest again.

"Let me up," she demanded.

"Not until you tell me why you're here," he said.

"You want me to draw a diagram?" she asked.

"I want to hear you admit I was right," he said, grinning down into her face.

Yeah, right, she was going to admit she'd been afraid of the powerful connection between them. She might be in his lap, but she wasn't brain-dead. She grinned right back at him.

"Not a chance in hell, pal." She slid a hand between their bodies, finding the undeniable evidence that his need was a powerful as hers. Confident that his desk and computer shielded them from the general office view, she rubbed him through his jeans.

"Now, are you going to do something with this or are we going to argue for the rest of my lunch break?"

6

He had her outside the production office and standing by the elevator bank in about five seconds flat. She smiled to herself as she noted the way he was holding his jacket draped in front of his body, conveniently masking the tent pole in his pants.

"Very discreet," she murmured as they both watched the floor indicator impatiently.

"Oh yeah. Discreet is my middle name," Leandro said. His gaze dropped below her neckline, caressing her breasts. She got hot all over again.

"Stop it," she said.

"Or what?"

"Or I won't be answerable for the consequences," she said.

"Maybe I like the sound of that."

He moved behind her, and she felt a warm pressure as he slid a hand down her back and onto her butt. Cupping a cheek, he squeezed her firmly through her slim-lined black skirt. They were alone for the present, but still she shot a nervous glance around.

"I bet you played with matches when you were a kid, too," she said over her shoulder.

"Couldn't stay away from them," he said. He was

standing so close, she felt the rumble of his voice through her body.

She pressed her thighs together as she willed the elevator to arrive. She couldn't remember the last time she'd been so turned on. Leandro Mandalor infuriated her, intrigued her, fascinated her. And she wanted him, bad. She was going to have him, too—on her terms.

She gave a grunt of impatience when she realized the elevator was still miles away. The damn thing was obviously stopping on every floor. Behind her, Leandro slid his hand to her other butt cheek, his fingers curling in toward her inner thighs in a delicious intimation of things to come.

"Okay, this is ridiculous," she said.

A red door to the left of the elevator bank indicated a stairwell, and she turned to grab Leandro by his waistband and belt buckle. Yanking him forward, she dragged him toward the door.

"Hey!" he protested, but he went willingly enough.

Once the door had closed behind them, Claudia backed him against the wall and pressed herself against him.

"Don't tease me like that again," she said.

He felt very hard and very ready. She rubbed herself against him and pressed her breasts to his chest, itching to feel his skin against hers.

"I don't know. I kind of like the results," he said, big hands sliding down to cup her butt.

Lowering his head, he kissed her, and quickly she was lost in the passion that flared between them.

The things this man could do with his tongue! The thrust of it in her mouth reminded her of the way he'd feasted on her, the intense pleasure he'd brought her. Running her hands up his back, she measured the width of his broad shoulders, then wove her fingers into his hair to deepen their kiss further still.

He gave a grunt of satisfaction and she felt a tug at the waistband of her skirt as he pulled her shirt free. Then his warm hand was gliding up her rib cage and taking possession of her breasts.

"Yes," she murmured into his mouth, racing her own hands around to find the ridge of his erection through his jeans.

For a few seconds more they tortured each other, then they broke apart by mutual unspoken consent, both panting like they'd run a mile.

"Let's go," Leandro said, grabbing her hand.

As he led her down four flights, she calculated how long it would take for them to get in his car, exit the parking garage and find someplace private.

Too long. *Waaaay* too long.

"Here we are," he said as they left the stairwell and stepped into the dim coolness of the underground parking garage. "My car's over there."

She waited until they were both inside and he was reaching for the ignition before making her move.

"Don't bother. I can't wait," she said.

He gave a startled bark of laughter as she climbed over the hand brake and gearshift and into his lap.

"What if someone comes?" he asked as she laved his neck and slipped her tongue into his ear.

"Someone is definitely going to come," she said.

He laughed again as his hands once again slid up on to her breasts.

"You know what I mean," he said.

"It's dark. We're in the corner. Good luck to them," she said as she began unbuckling his belt.

"Where have you been all my life?" he asked, his fingers plucking at her nipples.

"Waiting for this," she panted, sliding his fly down and gripping his erection with firm, knowing hands.

His whole body shuddered as she worked his shaft, caressing the sensitive head with her thumb. He was so big and hard. Parts of her shivered in anticipation. She was so wet and hot for him, so ready to go, she pushed his hands away from her breasts so she could concentrate on getting her underwear off. He sucked in a breath as she accidentally elbowed him in the ribs.

"Sorry."

"Never apologize for taking your underwear off," he said, his breath coming fast as he watched her slide her black lace panties over her stiletto heel.

Instantly his hands were pushing her skirt up. She gave a small yelp of surprise as he adjusted something and they both tumbled back with the seat as it dropped flat, then he was pushing her thighs wide so she straddled his lap and racing his hands up legs to where she craved his touch the most.

"Claudia," he said as his fingers discovered her slick center. "Man, you drive me crazy."

"Ditto. *Ohhh!*" she gasped as he found her clitoris and began to massage it with his thumb while the rest of his fingers teased her mercilessly.

It was so good, so intense, so exactly what she needed. She grabbed on to his shoulders as her climax thundered toward her, shaking with the intensity of it as his clever hands pleased her and pushed her over the edge.

"Leandro," she gasped. "Leandro."

"I know baby, believe me, I know," he said. She was vibrating with aftershocks when she felt him trying to lever his body up so he could get at his wallet, and suddenly she remembered Grace's parting gift. Sliding it from her skirt pocket, she dropped the condom on his chest.

"Goddess," he breathed gratefully when he saw what it was.

"Hurry," was her response.

His answer was the rip of the foil packet opening, and within seconds he was lifting her hips as he guided her down onto him. She bit her lip as she felt the first delicious inch of him slide inside her, and then he thrust his hips upward and she shuddered as he filled her to overflowing.

"Have I told you lately that you have the best, most amazing body in the world?" she said as she began to ride him.

"No. But keep talking," he said, his eyes narrowed to slits as he gazed up at her from his near-prone position. Pushing her shirt and bra up, he covered her breasts with his hands and began to tease her nipples.

But she was beyond words. Panting, straining, her hips moving to a primitive, needful rhythm that he seemed to know and match instinctively, she climbed toward another orgasm. His hands found her butt as she began to tighten around him, his fingers digging in as he strained toward his own climax.

"Yes," he said, even as she writhed on top of him, pleasure exploding inside her, rippling through her body in hot, liquid waves. She felt the urgent shudder as he reached his own peak, and looked down into his handsome face as his features tightened with desire.

He was incredible. She couldn't get enough of him.

Still breathing hard in the aftermath of his climax, he

flopped flat on the seat, threw his head back, closed his eyes and let out a low belly laugh.

"Please tell me this is real," he said, opening his eyes to gaze up at her.

"Why wouldn't it be?" she asked, bracing herself on one elbow.

"Because you have just stepped straight out of my fantasies," he murmured, his dark gaze dropping to catalogue her breasts, her belly, her widespread thighs.

She grinned down at him, something deep inside her responding to the possessive, hungry masculinity in his eyes.

"Something else we have in common."

His expression became more serious as he smoothed a hand over her hip.

"Spend the night with me?" he asked.

There were a million reasons to say no. But lying astride him, her everything bared to him, she couldn't deny him or herself anymore. She'd taken the plunge into uncharted territory when she'd barreled into his office fifteen minutes ago, but she was confident she could ride out the storm.

"Yes," she said.

LATER THAT NIGHT, they sat naked and cross-legged in Leandro's bed and ate pizza straight from the box.

"I am *starving*," Claudia said, stuffing her face with yet another piece of super supreme.

Leandro watched her lick a drop of tomato sauce off her bottom lip and felt his body respond like clockwork. He didn't know what it was—her perfect petite body, her deep brown eyes, her smart mouth—but she did it for him, every time, big-time.

As though she sensed the direction his thoughts were going in, Claudia's gaze fixated on his crotch.

"Look who wants in on the conversation," she said, arching an eyebrow.

"He can wait. For about another five minutes," Leandro said, his gaze zeroing in on a piece of pepper that had dropped onto the upper curve of her breast.

"The joys of eating naked," she said, following his gaze. "If I was dressed, that would have just ruined a perfectly good shirt."

She lifted a hand to rescue the pepper, but Leandro spoke up first.

"I'll get it," he volunteered.

She laughed as he leaned across and licked it off her breast, managing to include a hell of a lot of nipple along the way. She tasted amazing, and he instantly wanted more.

"Maybe we should make it two minutes," Claudia said as he nuzzled closer and tugged her other nipple into his mouth.

"I really like cold pizza, I don't know about you," Leandro said, pushing her back onto the bed, his eyes devouring her erect, glistening nipples all the while.

She was still holding a crust in her hand and she tossed it over his shoulder, back into the pizza box.

"Not enough hot salami on it for me, anyway," she said wickedly.

He laughed at her double entendre. "You like hot salami, do you?"

"The hotter the better," she said, grabbing on to his erection and sliding her hand up and down his shaft.

"Let's see how hot we can get it," he murmured as his hand moved between her thighs and into her warm, silky folds.

They didn't talk much after that, communicating via grunts and murmurs and moans. When she came, he watched the flush of pleasure color her face, savoring the far-off look in her eyes, the small, inarticulate cry she made. Her fulfillment pushed him over the edge, spurring him to his own climax, and he wrapped his hands around her hips and buried himself to the hilt in her sweet tightness as he spent himself inside her.

Afterwards, they lay spread-eagled on the bed in silence for several minutes.

"You're looking very pleased with yourself," she said.

"Am I? I'm feeling pretty good, too," he said, stretching his arms over his head.

She rolled onto her side and propped her head on her hand, her gaze travelling from the boxes of books in the corner to the stack of papers piled up on his bedside table.

"How long have you lived here?" she asked.

He grimaced. "Four months. Looks it, huh?" he said. "I was renting for a while, but I finally bit the bullet and bought this place."

Half his stuff was still stacked in boxes, and furniture was fairly thin on the ground since he'd only taken the stuff Peta didn't want and hadn't gotten around to buying anything of his own. The result was an apartment that looked thrown together, a typical bachelor pad.

"It does feel a little…temporary," she said.

"You're being very kind," he said, noting the sparkle of amusement in her eyes.

"I thought so. How long ago was the divorce?" she asked shrewdly.

"I signed the papers last week, but we've been separated for over a year. Is it that obvious?" he asked.

"Only to the trained eye," she said. "How long were you married?"

"Six months."

"Ouch. Who cheated?" she asked.

He raised an eyebrow at the assumption. She shrugged.

"Come on, something pretty big had to happen," she said.

"No one cheated. We just realized we wanted different things."

She nodded, and didn't pry any further. He decided it was time to turn the tables. Apart from the fact that she drove him wild, he knew damn all about her.

"What about you? Ever been married?"

"Nope. Not even close," she said, pulling over the pizza box to inspect the remaining cold slices.

"Not interested?"

"Marriage is for men," she said, biting into a small slice of pizza.

"Really? That must be why we get to wear the big dresses and play princess for a day," he said dryly.

She waggled a finger under his nose.

"The wedding is for women, I won't disagree there. But marriage only benefits men. Single women live longer than married women, you know."

"And married men live longer than single men. I know the stats," he said.

"There you go then."

He frowned, even though she was essentially confirming his assumptions about her—that she was a career woman through and through.

"So what happens when Mr. Right comes along and sweeps you off your feet?" he asked. "Or don't you believe in love, either?"

She regarded him over her slice of pizza, a serious light in her eye.

"Sure I do. I just don't think it's worth sacrificing my whole life for," she said.

His frown deepened. In his book, love did not equal sacrifice. He opened his mouth to probe further, but was interrupted by the ring of a cell phone.

"That's me," she said, sliding to the edge of the bed to rummage in her coat pocket on the floor.

Checking the display, she threw him an apologetic look. "I need to take this—it's my brother," she said. "We've been missing each other's calls for the past two days."

He shrugged his lack of concern, dragging a pillow under his shoulders to support them while he studied her, trying to define for himself what it was that he found so compelling about her.

She had a great little body, that was a given. He particularly liked her pouty, dusky nipples, and the pertness of her butt. Which was, coincidentally, looking particularly excellent as she rolled onto her belly to take her phone call.

But he'd been out with women with great bodies before, and none of them had exercised the same fascination for him. Of course, she had plenty of personality to go with her hot bod. She was savvy, funny. Bold, too. Definitely brave. He shook his head in admiration as he recalled how she'd sassed Rat Man, despite the fact that the guy had had them both over a barrel. She was good at what she did, too, which had always been a turn-on for him.

Still, none of it quite explained the surge of attraction he felt when she glanced up from her phone call and caught him watching her. Her big, dark eyes sparkled with repressed humor and speculation as she met his gaze, and she cocked an eyebrow at him challengingly.

There was no explaining or defining it. He just found her…irresistible.

She broke eye contact with him and he belatedly tuned into what she was saying. He frowned, confused for a moment as he registered the tone of the conversation.

"Wow. That sounds amazing. And did you blow out all your candles at once?" she asked in the bright, cheerful tone usually reserved for children or the mentally challenged.

Hadn't she said it was her brother calling?

She laughed at the response her comment garnered. "Well, maybe next year you'll get them all. Five is a lot of candles, my little monkey man," she said warmly.

His brow cleared. She had a nephew—a five-year-old nephew, if his powers of deduction weren't failing him in his old age.

She laughed again. "No, you're right. Six will be even more candles. Maybe you can practice on my birthday cake—I've got a lot more than six, I promise you," she said.

She listened some more, a small smile on her face. "No, I understand, off you go, sweetie. I'm glad you liked your pirate ship," she said. "Nighty-night, don't let the bed bugs bite."

She still had a slightly goofy smile on her face when she ended the call.

"Nephew?" he asked, fascinated by the soft expression in her eyes.

"Nicco. He just had his birthday, in case you couldn't tell. He's so funny. He just lost two of his front teeth, and he has this adorable lisp."

A tension he hadn't even been aware of eased from his

shoulders. He told himself it was ridiculous to read anything into her obvious love for her nephew. But somehow, it made him feel not quite so reckless to be plunging headfirst into a hot and heavy affair with a woman who, to all intents and purposes, was totally wrong for him.

"Come here," he said, beckoning her with his hand.

"Nope," she said, sliding off his bed. "I'm going to have a bath in that big old tub you've got in there."

She sauntered toward the bathroom, stopping on the threshold to throw a saucy look over her shoulder.

"You need a written invitation or something?" she asked.

He laughed as he levered himself up off the bed. Where she was concerned, he definitely did not.

A WEEK LATER, CLAUDIA swept up the pile of scripts she was taking home for the weekend and scooped up her coat. She was turning toward her office door before she realized Sadie and Grace were blocking it.

"Leaving early *again?*" Grace said significantly.

"It's six forty-five on a Friday night. It's not early," Claudia said a little defensively.

"It's early for you," Sadie said. "So, where are you and Leandro going?"

"How do you know I'm going somewhere with Leandro?" Claudia countered.

"It was tough, but the fact that you've seen him every night this week, added to the fact that he's been leaning against his car out the front of the building for the past ten minutes was something of a giveaway," Grace said.

"Busted," Claudia said dryly.

"Oh yeah, big time. So spill," Sadie said. "Where are you guys going?"

"Didn't you say he's been waiting for ten minutes already?" Claudia said evasively.

It wasn't that she didn't want to talk with her friends. Normally, she liked nothing more than a good session with her two best buddies. But right now, right this minute, she was a little preoccupied with a certain six-foot, four-inch hunk of man. Plus—and probably more importantly, if she was being scrupulously honest with herself—she had the feeling Grace and Sadie were about to ask her questions that she didn't know the answers to.

"He can wait. Think of it as his personal atonement for all the centuries women didn't have the vote," Grace said.

"I'll be sure to mention that to him," Claudia said. "I know he'll feel warm and fuzzy about doing his bit to address the power imbalance."

"You really like him, huh?" Sadie asked, a smile hovering around her mouth.

Claudia frowned, aware that Sadie had been viewing the world through rose-colored glasses since she and Dylan found one another. She and Leandro were not rose-colored material, however, and the sooner she made that clear and nipped any romantic fantasies in the bud, the better.

"I really like his penis," Claudia said. "The rest of him I tolerate."

Grace snickered. "Nice."

Sadie just crossed her arms and cocked her head to one side, clearly waiting for a serious answer to her question.

"What? What do you want me to say? We have sex with each other. The man is really, really, really good in bed. That's pretty much it."

"Right. And does he know this?" Sadie asked.

"I think he's got some idea. He's a pretty confident guy. I suppose I *could* throw a few compliments his way…"

"That's not what I meant and you know it. The man has been waiting patiently out the front for ten—no, fifteen minutes now. No phone calls, no horn honking. And Gabby said he's got a bottle of champagne and a picnic hamper in the back of his car."

Claudia gasped with outrage. "How in the hell does she know that?"

"The woman has eyes on stalks, and a team of invisible ninja informants." Grace shrugged.

Sadie just made a low growling noise in the back of her throat, clearly growing irritated with Claudia's avoidance of a direct answer.

"Okay, all right—we're staying overnight on a yacht. Leandro's friend offered it to him for the night. It's no big deal."

"Again, I ask you, does Leandro know that it's not a big deal?" Sadie asked.

Claudia felt a pang of unease as she met Sadie's serious gaze. For the past week, she'd spent every night in Leandro's arms, mapping every inch of his beautiful body, discovering new levels of pleasure and fulfillment under his attentive hands.

She'd laughed at his jokes, shared his toothbrush, melted under the best nonprofessional massage she'd ever had, and had more orgasms than she could count. It had been…amazing. But not once had either of them ever referred to the future. They hadn't made plans beyond the weekend, and they'd never talked about their feelings.

"We're having a fling. I told him I wasn't interested in a relationship. He said, and I'm quoting here so you might want to take this down, 'But you *are* interested in sex, right?' I figure we're both on the same page," she said carefully.

Sadie looked disappointed, and Claudia regarded her fondly.

"Sorry, sweetie, but I'm just not looking for the kind of commitment that you and Dylan have. You know that."

"I know. I just thought that since you and Leandro seem to get on so well, and things seem so intense…would it be absolutely hideous if you fell in love?"

Claudia frowned, even as a surge of panic slid down her spine. Falling in love with Leandro was the last thing she wanted. In fact, falling in love with Leandro was exactly what she'd been worried about when she'd resisted his invitation to explore the attraction between them in the first place. He was a very, very charismatic man. If she wasn't very careful, she could find herself in deep waters indeed with him. Which was why she'd been doing her level best to keep things light and breezy between them.

"I'm not wife material, Sade," she said bluntly. "I don't want marriage, I don't want kids. There's nowhere for a relationship with Leandro to go, even if I was stupid enough to fall in love with him."

"Never say never, Claud," Grace said. Claudia knew she was talking from personal experience.

"The man's just signed his divorce papers. The last thing he wants is to get tied down again," Claudia said, tackling the issue from the other side.

Sadie and Grace looked distinctly disgruntled, and Claudia paused to hug them both on the way out the door.

"Don't worry—I'm having a very nice time. There's nothing for anyone to worry about," she said.

Her words echoed hollowly in her ears when she exited the building and saw Leandro leaning against his car, arms crossed over his chest.

Her stomach dropped like an elevator in free fall, and she found herself exhaling an abrupt puff of air.

Man, but he was gorgeous. She paused for a moment to simply appreciate him—the length of his muscular legs displayed to perfection in well-worn dark denim, the breadth of his shoulders showcased in a classic white T-shirt. His arms were tanned bronze from all his running, and the last rays of sunlight glinted in his springy black hair. Then there were his eyes—those killer, dark brown eyes that seemed to reach out toward her and strip her bare, even from a distance of twenty feet.

She cleared her throat round a lump of lust as she forced her legs into motion again.

"Sorry. I got held up," she said.

"No problem."

She flashed him an appreciative smile. Another thing she liked about him—he understood the demands and stresses of her job. She'd kept him waiting more than once this week—although he'd returned the favor a few times, too—but they both knew the deal. Being a producer was the equivalent of playing mom and dad to the entire cast, crew and writing team of a soap, and the job was never done, the hours never neat and tidy.

"I have it on good authority I have champagne to look forward to. And a picnic hamper," she said, quizzing him with her eyes.

He huffed out a surprised laugh.

"Someone's got good intelligence."

"Nosy assistant. I think she's part bat," Claudia said.

He laughed outright as she stood on tiptoes to kiss him. His arms wrapped around her, and she leaned into the warm, solid strength of him. Before the kiss got too out of control—a definite hazard where Leandro was concerned—she broke away.

"Hold that thought," she said.

He opened the passenger door for her and she dumped her work bag on the back seat before getting in.

"Shouldn't take us too long to get there," he said as he started up his Honda.

She knew his friend's yacht was moored in Marina Del Rey, and she settled back in her seat for the short ride. Inevitably, once her body had acclimatized to being in Leandro's presence again, her thoughts turned to what Grace and Sadie had said.

She sneaked a peek at him out of the corner of her eye, but she found it impossible to read his expression beyond knowing that he was pleased to be with her. Generally speaking, she found him hard to read. Oh, she knew when he was horny. And she knew when she frustrated him by not allowing him to have everything his way. Each and every one of their encounters so far had involved some contest of wills. She figured it came from them both being used to being in charge—and neither of them being willing to concede the helm to the other.

But beyond that, she often had no idea what he was thinking. She hoped that, like her, he took what was happening between them at face value. They enjoyed each other's company, and the sex was…well, the sex deserved a whole goddamned thesis devoted to it, it was so good. The way she saw it, there was no need to make it any more complicated than that.

She turned her face toward the side window, aware that there was more than a hint of desperation in her thinking.

"Here we go. We're looking for parking bay five-one-six," Leandro said as he turned into the marina.

Claudia spotted the number on their second pass of the aisles, and they were soon walking along the wind-whipped dock looking for the *Foam Dancer*.

"He wanted to rename the boat when he bought it," Leandro explained, "but apparently it's bad luck."

"*Foam Dancer*'s not so bad. It could be worse," Claudia said.

He obviously didn't think so and he cocked an eyebrow at her. Claudia just pointed to a yacht they'd just passed, the *Wetdream*.

"Point taken," he said.

They hadn't gone ten steps before they'd spotted several more boats with cringe-worthy names—*It's A Moray, Pier Pressure*, and *Boobie Trap* being the pick of them. By the time they'd found *Foam Dancer*, they were in hysterics over *Sea My Johnson* and Claudia had to pause to wipe the tears from her eyes before she could safely clamber on board.

"Wow. Is your friend a mobster?" Claudia asked as she stepped into the upper cabin and surveyed the acres of shiny brass, polished wood and deep burgundy upholstery, all of it just a bit too flashy.

Leandro gave the cabin a single brief glance, but he was more intent on pulling her close. She gave herself up to a long, drugging kiss, her tongue dancing with his, her hands exploring the muscular planes of his back.

"I've been wanting to do that all day," he murmured, smiling down at her.

There was no mistaking the warmth in his eyes and she looked away, uncertainty dogging her after her recent conversation with Sadie and Grace.

He just wants sex, she assured herself. Then he lowered his head and nuzzled her neck.

"I love the way you smell," he said. He wrapped his arms around her and held her close. Before she knew it, they were swaying together, almost dancing, in fact.

"I got some of those organic strawberries you like," he said, "and some of that fancy ice cream you were raving about the other day."

He'd gone out and bought her favorite things? Suddenly their night on the yacht was beginning to feel like it was a lot more about intimacy than sex.

Don't ruin it, she pleaded silently. *It's been so good— don't ruin it yet.*

Because she couldn't say the words out loud, she did the only thing she could do, the only thing she was comfortable doing. Sliding her hand inside his jeans, she took a hold of his erection and held his eye.

"Do you mind if I borrow this if you're not using it?" she asked.

For a moment, she was sure she saw a flash of something—disappointment?—in his eyes. Then he reached for the buttons on her shirt.

"As long as we can work out some kind of reciprocal arrangement with these breasts of yours…"

As he lowered his head to her breasts and licked and sucked and gently bit her nipples, the rest of the world fell away and there was only his body and hers. Closing her eyes, she pushed everything else away.

"AT LAST, YOUTH TRIUMPHS over experience," Dom crowed as he reached the peak ahead of Leandro. At least, he tried to crow, but the fact that he was gasping for air ruined the effect somewhat.

Leandro didn't bother responding to his brother's goad—they both knew Dom had enjoyed a substantial head start since he'd taken off while Leandro was still tying his shoelaces at the bottom of the hill.

It was Saturday on the week following his Marina Del Rey sojourn with Claudia, and the sun was high in the sky as they once more ran the fire trails in the Hollywood Hills. Below them, the L.A. basin basked in heat and haze, and a warm breeze dried the sweat on Leandro's face. He felt the press of something cold against his arm and saw that Dom was offering him a water bottle.

"Thanks," he said, turning away from the view and swallowing half the bottle in three big glugs.

Dom also made short work of his water, then he mopped the sweat from his face with the hem of his T-shirt.

"I definitely did better this time," he said.

Leandro just smiled to himself, and Dom nudged him.

"Don't you think?" he said.

"Well, you don't look like you need a cardiac team on standby. That's a good start," Leandro said.

Dom laughed and squirted the last of his water at Leandro's chest.

"Smart-ass."

Leandro returned the favor, and once they'd stopped laughing they stood and stared out at the view together.

After a moment, Dom broke the silence.

"Hey, I've got a bone to pick with you, Mr. Big Shot.

Why'd you pull out on your date with Stella? Betty is seriously pissed. She thinks you don't trust her taste."

"How could I doubt her? She married you, didn't she?"

"Very funny. Seriously, what happened to your big date?"

Leandro shrugged uncomfortably. "It didn't feel right. She seems like a great woman, but my head's not in the right place right now."

Dom gave him a cut-the-bullshit look.

"What's her name?"

"Why does there have to be another woman?"

"Because last time we came up here, you attacked this mountain like it had done you a personal wrong, and today you were happy to let me lead the way. Me thinks you are getting laid, brother o'mine."

Leandro shrugged a shoulder. Why did he feel so…uncertain about mentioning Claudia to his brother?

"Her name's Claudia," he said, just to prove to himself it wasn't an issue. "I've been seeing her a few weeks now."

Two weeks, to be exact, if he counted from the day she'd barged into his office and taken up his challenge.

"Is she Greek?" Dom asked.

Leandro did a mock double take.

"My God, for a moment there I thought I was standing next to Mom," he said.

"It's relevant! It doesn't matter one way or the other, but it's relevant," Dom said, hands gesticulating defensively.

"Yeah, she's Greek."

Dom gave him a searching look. "Why are you being so cagey? What's the big secret?"

"There's no big secret."

"So is it serious?"

Leandro frowned. "Have you been taking hormones or something? What's with the twenty questions?"

"Just answer the question, asshole," Dom said good-naturedly.

Leandro peered up at the sun for a few seconds before answering. "Yeah. I think it might be."

"You think?"

"She's…complex," Leandro said.

"She's a woman. It comes with the territory."

Leandro tried to explain.

"She's smart, successful. Really into her career. She plays her cards pretty close to her chest."

Dom made a disgusted sound. "Let's just call her Peta mark two and sign the divorce papers now," he said. "Why do you keep going after these career chicks, man?"

"She's not like Peta," Leandro said firmly. And she wasn't. She was warmer, and more vulnerable, despite her bravado. He laughed with her more. When they were together, time was irrelevant.

"Sounds like Peta to me. Another power-hungry bitch more interested in picking out the upholstery in her Audi than having a life."

Leandro swung around to glare at his brother. "You haven't even met her, okay? Back off."

Dom held up a hand. "Whoa there, Slugger. No need to go *loco*."

Leandro saw that his brother was trying not to smirk, and he realized that he'd snapped at Dom's bait like a greenhorn.

"You're a dick," he said.

Dom nudged him. "So you really like her, huh?"

Leandro shoved his brother back.

"Yeah, I really like her."

"You should bring her to Grandma's party next weekend," Dom suggested. "Introduce her to everyone. Ease her in."

"Ease her in? The whole family will be there."

"She's got to meet them sometime, right? If you guys are serious?"

Leandro squinted up at the sun again. His instincts told him it was too early to do the family thing with Claudia. The truth was, he didn't know where he stood with her. She liked the sex. She enjoyed his company. But he could never get a read on her. And the more he saw of her, the more he got to know her, the more he knew he wanted things to work out between them.

"I'll think about it," he said after a long silence.

"Way to go, really decisive. I love that captain of industry thing you do," Dom said, ragging on him mercilessly.

He shut his brother up with the simple expedient of giving him an atomic wedgie, Mandalor-family style.

"You son of a bitch! I think you just ruptured a testicle," Dom howled.

"I thought you'd given up balls for Lent," Leandro said.

Then he took off, his brother hot on his heels.

7

A WEEK LATER, CLAUDIA checked her lipstick in her hall mirror one more time and smoothed a hand over her hair. It was as perfect as it had been thirty seconds ago, but at least it gave her a break from checking her watch and pacing.

Leandro was late. He'd been away on business in New York for the past three days, and she had missed him so much it scared her. She hadn't been able to sleep, food had tasted like sawdust in her mouth, and she felt about as stupid as she'd ever felt in her life. How could sex be so powerful?

The sound of a car door shutting jolted her from her thoughts, and she opened her front door just as Leandro stepped up onto the step. Without pausing to think how it might look, she launched herself into his arms, her body going crazy just at the sight of him.

His arms closed around her, and his head lowered toward hers, and she gave a sigh of pure relief as they kissed. His smell, the size of him, his strength—she'd craved him like a drug, and she pressed herself closer and closer, her hands clutching at his shoulders.

His caresses were equally as fervent, and they moved into her house without breaking their kiss. Kicking the door shut, Leandro pressed her against it and ran a hand up the inside of her thigh. She felt the muscles of his arms bunch for a second as he discovered she was sans underwear, and then he groaned low in his throat.

"I swear, you're my dream woman," he said as he slid his fingers into her ready wetness.

She gasped as he slipped a finger inside her, then two. She'd needed this so badly, and she whimpered with need when he withdrew his hand. But he was just kneeling at her feet, pushing the skirt of her black sundress up around her waist and pressing his face into the neat curls at the apex of her thighs. He inhaled deeply, his hands sliding around the back of her thighs, his fingers caressing the lower curve of her butt.

"You've kept me awake every night, you know that, don't you?" he said, glancing up at her. She could feel the warmth of his breath between her legs, and she bit her lip. She didn't think she could stand any more teasing, any more waiting.

"I want—" she said, but she was unable to articulate how much she needed him right now.

He just pressed his face more closely between her thighs and began to stroke her with his tongue.

"Yes," she moaned. "Yes, please, Leandro."

He nuzzled deeper again, his tongue laving from her inner lips up to her clitoris, his fingers reaching between her legs from behind to tease her hot center.

"Oh!" she gasped, her orgasm already building.

Then he sucked her clitoris into his mouth, flicking his tongue over and over the tight bud. Her hips rocked forward of their own accord and she clutched at his shoulders as she climaxed powerfully, her inner muscles spasming again and again.

Her knees wouldn't hold her in the aftermath, and she slid to the ground, boneless with sensation. He cupped the side of her face and kissed her deeply, and the scent of her sex surrounded them with an earthy perfume.

Pushing him onto his back, she fumbled with his belt buckle and fly and finally had him in her hands. She slid onto him with one shift of her hips. Throwing her head back, she shivered with pure wanton pleasure at how good he felt inside her. Leandro's hands roamed up her thighs to find her hips, and he began to move inside her, pumping up into her with strong strokes, lifting her hips to increase the friction between them. Desire tightened inside her, and she found his rhythm, tilting her hips as she rode him. After an intense, breathless few minutes, his hands tightened on her hips and he stilled. She opened her eyes to find him staring up at her.

"Condom," he said reluctantly.

She shook her head. "I'm safe," she said, starting to ride again.

He hesitated a moment longer, then he gave into the need gripping them both. She began to pant as pleasure gathered within her, and she stared down into his face, loving the flush of desire along his cheekbones, and the wicked glint in his eyes. His teeth were slightly bared, and the muscles of his neck tensed as he climaxed. Her own orgasm swept her away, and she threw back her head and gave a cry of absolute abandonment.

She collapsed onto his chest and listened to the thundering of his heart as he, too, returned to reality.

His hand came up to caress the back of her neck, and she pressed her face into his neck, enjoying the small moment of satisfaction and peace.

"It's good to see you, too," he said dryly after a few long minutes.

She smiled as she slid off him, even though a part of her was reeling at the rawness of what had occurred between them.

"That'll teach you to go away again," she said, but her voice wavered uncertainly.

He reached out and caught her hand when she started to stand.

"I missed you," he said, his eyes serious.

"I believe the feeling was mutual," she said lightly, her gesturing hand reminding him that they hadn't even made it past the foyer of her house.

He just held her eye, not saying anything, and she felt faintly ashamed of her flippant answer. Before she could stop herself, she lifted his hand to her mouth and kissed his knuckles. He curled his hand into her cheek, his thumb caressing her cheekbone as he stared into her eyes.

She had to look away from what she saw in his face. She didn't want this—did she? She didn't want to lose herself in a relationship, to feel the pull of all the obligations and concerns that love brought with it.

Pushing herself to her feet, she left him behind as she made her way to her en suite and shucked her dress. She was beneath the shower and lathering up when he joined her.

"We're going to be late," he said.

"Where exactly are we going again?" she asked.

He'd been very cagey about what he had planned for their Saturday afternoon together.

"Don't tell me—you don't like surprises? Typical control freak behavior," he said as he soaped her back.

"I'm a control freak, am I? Who was it who insisted on

knowing where the cashews in his salad came from the other day when we were out?" she asked archly, pleased that he wasn't about to bring up what had just happened between them.

She'd been sure that he was going to push things, but it seemed she could enjoy what they had for a little while longer before it self-destructed.

"Cashews from Vietnam might have been exposed to Agent Orange," he said pedantically.

"Spoken like a true control freak," Claudia said.

He swatted her backside and moved in for a kiss. "Takes one to know one."

They were in the car and on the way to God knows where when he casually fished a small, flat parcel from his door pocket and passed it to her.

"Saw this and thought of you," he said casually.

She stared down at the elegant paper for a beat, taken off guard.

"Thank you. You shouldn't have," she said.

"Too late," he said.

She sensed that he was being very careful after their earlier moment, and she slipped a finger beneath the tape and unfolded the gift wrap. A slim, deep red silk scarf lay inside, and she instinctively ran it through her fingers. It felt as soft as a cloud against her skin, and she admired the rich ruby color.

"It's beautiful," she said sincerely. "Thank you, Leandro."

She leaned across and pressed a kiss onto his neck, not wanting to disturb him while he was driving.

"I know you like black, but red seemed like the right choice," he said. "I thought it would look good with your dark hair."

Flipping down the visor mirror, Claudia impulsively tied the scarf in a jaunty knot around her neck. It contrasted beautifully with her sleeveless sundress made from black Broderie Anglaise, and she preened happily.

"I should wear color more, I know," she said ruefully. "Black is the lazy woman's escape clause."

He flashed a smile at her, and for the first time it occurred to her that he was behaving a little oddly. It wasn't the gift, or the crazy foyer-sex. He seemed…nervous. A little uncertain, even. Both were so foreign to the way she thought of him that she peered at him through narrowed eyes.

"So, where are we going again?" she asked.

"We're here already," he said, pulling into a parking space.

She glanced up and saw they were out the front of a Greek restaurant in downtown L.A., a place she'd driven past a million times and always meant to try.

The tension went out of her as she realized he was simply taking her out for lunch, Greek style.

"They make great dolmades here," he said as they exited the car.

It had been a while since she'd had Greek food. Her mouth watered as she thought of bean salads, fresh fish, lemon and garlic.

The restaurant was cool after the warmth of the sun, and surprisingly empty. Claudia looked around at the whitewashed walls and red-and-white checked tablecloths and wondered if she should be worried about food poisoning. Where were all the other customers?

"There's a courtyard out the back," Leandro said, obviously sensing her confusion.

"Oh, right," she said.

He led the way up a terra-cotta tiled hallway, and then

he pushed open a door and they were outside, surrounded by the buzz of people, the twang of bazouki music and the savory smells of cooking meat and fresh baked bread.

For a second she clutched at Leandro's shirt, thinking they'd accidentally walked into the middle of someone else's party and readying herself to make a graceful exit. Then a nut-brown, gray-haired man just a shade shorter than Leandro spotted them and sent up a cry.

"Leandro! Finally you come!"

Every head seemed to swivel toward them, and Claudia felt a hundred pairs of eyes scan her from head to toe, taking in her cherry-red nail polish, her strappy high heels, the tight, low-cut bodice of her sundress, the jaunty scarf at her neck and the fact that Leandro had rested a proprietorial hand on her shoulder.

"This must be Claudia," the man said, stretching both hands out toward her as he approached. "We are so pleased you could come with Leandro today to celebrate my mama's birthday," he said.

She submitted meekly to being kissed on both cheeks as she realized that she'd just met Leandro's father.

"Claudia, this is my father, Stavros Mandalor," Leandro confirmed. "Dad, this is Claudia Dostis."

She was still trying to come to terms with the fact that Leandro had thrown her into the midst of a family party— an extended *Greek* family party—when the rest of the hordes descended. She found herself kissing cheek after cheek and subjected to hearty embrace after hearty embrace as the Mandalors welcomed her with flashing white teeth and good cheer.

Leandro's mother was smaller than Claudia with gray-streaked black hair confined in a tight bun and she touched

Claudia's cheek approvingly as she stepped away from their greeting kiss.

"So beautiful. Leandro did not say you were so beautiful," she said.

Leandro rolled his eyes.

"Ma, stop trying to get me into trouble," he said.

She met his two brothers and two sisters, their wives and husbands, their children. She met cousins, uncles, aunts, family friends. She met the guest of honor, Mrs. Mandalor, a formidable gray-haired old lady who cast more than one disapproving glance at Claudia's cleavage.

And she felt utterly overwhelmed and ambushed. The noise, the laughter, the aroma of the cooking food, the vines climbing the walls—it was all too familiar, too dear, but also *not hers*.

She hadn't been with her family like this for three years. She'd missed christenings, weddings, birthdays. And all of a sudden Leandro had thrown her into the middle of his grandmother's birthday and all the grief, the memories, the sadness of missing out, of being an outsider when she'd grown up with all this love and warmth came rushing up at her.

She needed air. She needed silence. She needed to *think*, to get a grip.

Leandro was talking to one of his brothers nearby, and Claudia leaned toward the brother's heavily pregnant wife, hoping she'd remembered the woman's name right.

"Betty, could you tell me where the ladies' is?" Claudia asked.

"Go back the way you came, but turn left just before you step into the dining room," Betty supplied readily.

Claudia smiled her thanks and struck out for the door. She was stopped twice by Leandro's cousins, all of whom seemed to know that she worked on *Ocean Boulevard* and who wanted to tell her how much they loved the show.

She filed away the fact that Leandro had obviously been talking about her with his family, made what she hoped were coherent responses to their comments, and dove for the door again.

The door closing behind her cut the ambient sound in half, and she fought the sudden sting of tears as she made her way to the bathroom.

Shutting herself in a cubicle, she leaned against the door and willed herself not to cry. She hadn't been prepared, that was all it was. She told herself the same thing over and over, but she couldn't stop the wellspring of grief bubbling up. A single tear rolled down her cheek, and she clamped her jaws shut.

She would not cry.

Yes, she missed her family. Perhaps more than she'd ever admitted to herself. Yes, she felt lost, very alone, very isolated without them, and the last twenty minutes had brought that home to her. But life was full of tough decisions, and she'd made hers, and missing out had been the price she paid for removing herself from her mother's orbit.

Gradually the emotion filling her chest subsided, and she unclenched her fists from around her handbag. Exiting the cubicle, she washed her hands and checked her hair. She looked absolutely normal, completely unaffected, she was pleased to see. Tweaking the scarf at her neck so that the knot sat more to one side, she headed back out to join the Mandalors.

It wasn't until she stepped through the door and spotted Leandro that the full import of what he'd done—and what it meant—came home to her. She'd known that he cared, of course. The intense looks. The thoughtfulness. The tender caresses, the warmth. He wanted a relationship with her. He wanted to turn their sex-only fling into something much more substantial.

And she was going to have to break up with him.

A leaden weight settled in her belly at the thought. The past three weeks had been so good, so rich, so right. But she was about to come up against the wall of Leandro's expectations—and there was no way she could meet them.

"I got you some punch," he said when she'd made her way back to his side.

"Thanks."

She took a sip of something cold and tart and delicious. She could feel him watching her.

"You okay? Not too freaked out?" he asked.

His expression was sheepish when she glanced up at him.

"Would it matter?"

He sighed. "I'm sorry. I didn't want to do it like this, but I wanted you to be here, and I figured you wouldn't have come if I'd asked you up front."

"You're right, I wouldn't," she said. "And you know why—this isn't part of the agreement, Leandro."

He frowned. "We have an agreement?"

"Yeah, we do, and you know it." She could feel her voice rising, and she pushed her emotions back down. For starters, this was not the place to end things with him. And she was already feeling emotional. It was silly to tempt fate.

"Look, I just wanted you to meet my family. They're important to me," he said.

He left the rest of his sentence unspoken—that she was important to him, too, but he didn't need to say it. Suddenly she was filled with a great sadness.

If she were a different woman. If she'd had a different life. But she wasn't, she hadn't.

"There you are. Alexandra wants to show you her woogie," Leandro's sister-in-law, Betty, said from behind them.

Leandro looked frustrated for a split second, but he quickly hid it. They both knew this was not the time or place to talk.

"First of all, I want to know what a *woogie* is," he said as Betty led forward a dark-haired little girl with long curly hair. Claudia guessed she was about three years old.

"This is a woogie," Alexandra said, holding up a scrap of old blanket.

"Oh, you mean a *wuggie*," Leandro said, crouching down so that Alexandra wouldn't have to crane her neck to see him. "That's what we used to call them when I was little. You know, your dad used to have a wuggie. He took it everywhere."

Betty snorted her amusement. "Something he neglected to tell me. No wonder he's so keen to stop her from carrying the damn thing around."

"Cried when it got washed accidentally, too," Leandro said.

Claudia suspected he was slandering his brother shamelessly, and despite herself she laughed. Betty looked from one to the other of them.

"Is he pulling my leg?" she asked Claudia.

"Yep," Claudia readily confirmed.

"Where's your sense of loyalty?" Leandro asked her.

"Where's yours, calling Dom a big sook? Lucky he didn't hear you," Betty said.

"Feel free to tell him if you want," Leandro suggested.

Betty slapped his arm.

"You'd like that, wouldn't you?" she said, but she laughed.

Turning to Claudia, she indicated Leandro with her thumb. "You'll have to tell me how you know he's lying. I never know when he's pulling my leg or not."

"It's the eyes. He was laughing on the inside," Claudia said.

"Hmph," Betty said, rocking back on her heels to study Leandro narrowly. "Better watch out, Leo—I'm on to you now."

Dom joined them, and as the conversation moved on to the rose garden the family had arranged to have planted for their grandmother's birthday, Alexandra tugged on the leg of Leandro's jeans.

"Want to go up," Alexandra said, arms held over her head imperatively. "Please, Uncle Leo."

Without breaking his conversation with his brother, Leandro ducked down to scoop up his niece and place her on his shoulders. Claudia couldn't help but note his ease with the little girl, or the care with which he handled her. A gentle giant in every sense of the word. Despite all her deeply held beliefs about herself and children, she felt a definite twinge from her ovaries. What was it about big, masculine men and little kids? It was like catnip for female hormones, and even she was not immune. Shaking off the stupid moment, she tuned back into the conversation.

The sun moved across the sky, and before long she was holding a plate and standing in line with the rest of the family, waiting to help herself to the buffet laid out along one side of the courtyard. Leandro stood behind her, talking to one of his uncles, and she automatically plucked his plate from his hand when it became clear he was too absorbed to focus on serving himself. Making sure she gave him plenty of the spit-roasted meat, she loaded his plate up with salads and topped the lot with some fresh pita rounds. Leandro patted her backside in thanks, and Claudia became aware of the sensation that she was being watched. Glancing around, she locked eyes with Leandro's mother. The older woman smiled warmly, and Claudia frowned. She felt like such a fraud, being here with Leandro. Not only did he think they had a future, but his family did, too. And they were all wrong.

Filling her own plate, she joined Leandro at a trestle table and got sucked into a raucous, laughter-filled discussion about the latest World Cup soccer match. She surprised several of Leandro's male cousins with her wide ranging knowledge of the players and stats, and Leandro sat smiling at her goofily as if she were a prize poodle he'd brought along to do tricks. Ignoring the fact that his approval, ridiculous as it was, made her hum with pleasure, she concentrated on the flavors of the meal in front of her.

They were the flavors of her childhood, familiar and beloved—tender slices of roast lamb, spicy dolmades, salty taramasalata, olives, feta cheese and crispy calamari with fresh lemon juice and pepper. As the meal wore on, and the laughs kept coming, Claudia forgot about the difficult conversation she was yet to have with Leandro. She forgot about feeling like a fraud, about being there under false pretenses.

She laughed, she teased Leandro and his cousins and was teased in return, she gossiped about Hollywood stars with the women, and promised to do her level best to increase the quota of shirtless scenes on *Ocean Boulevard* to make their daytime viewing a little spicier. When the tables were pushed to one side and the bazoukis brought out, she clapped along with everyone else and even allowed herself to be drawn into the dancing. She knew the steps—

of course she knew the steps—and she was soon regretting her high heels. Seeing her dilemma, Leandro dropped to his knees and undid the delicate buckles on her sandals, and everyone howled with approval.

As the sun began its slow slide toward the horizon, the sweet trays appeared with the traditional honey-sweet baklava, loukamades, custards, chocolate-covered almonds and more. She drank strong Greek coffee, listened as Leandro's mother read the coffee grounds and prophesied good luck in love in her future, and entertained Betty's young son while Betty cleaned up Alexandra's honey-smeared face and dress.

But mostly Claudia watched Leandro. She had a hard time keeping her eyes off him at the best of times, and seeing him in his element only made him more charismatic. It wasn't because he was the tallest man there, although a few of his cousins rivaled him for height. It was everything about him—his laugh, deep and contagious, the mischievous sparkle in his eye, the careless grace of his big body. Slowly she realized she wasn't the only one drawn to him. His cousins applied to him to resolve disputes, his brothers and sisters deferred to him, his mother gazed at him with adoring eyes. He was like the unofficial king of the family, and they all wanted to bask in his reflected glory.

She was sitting to one side, her sandals lying beside her chair, when Leandro's mother joined her. Suddenly all the ease of the last few hours evaporated and she braced herself for the typical Greek mother's interrogation.

"Are you having a nice time, Claudia?" Alethea Mandalor asked.

"I'm having a great time. Everyone's been very welcoming," she said.

Leandro's laugh rang across the courtyard, drawing both their gazes.

"It is hard not to smile when Leandro smiles," Alethea said.

"He's very charming," Claudia agreed.

This seemed to please Alethea.

"I wanted to talk to you, Claudia," Alethea said, turning to regard her with eyes that were uncannily like Leandro's.

Here we go, Claudia thought.

"Okay," she said. She'd give the woman two minutes, then she was making a bolt for the bathroom.

"There is a woman on your show—a gray-haired actress," Alethea surprised her by saying.

Claudia frowned, having trouble switching gears mentally. This wasn't quite the opening gambit she'd been expecting. "There are a couple of older women characters. Do you mean the actress who plays Leona, or Priscilla?" she asked.

"Priscilla—that's her name." Alethea leaned toward Claudia confidingly. "Do you think her haircut would suit me, Claudia?"

Claudia blinked as Alethea tugged the pins loose from her bun and shook out her hair. It fell to just below her shoulders in a thick curtain.

Leandro's mother wanted beauty advice. Claudia almost laughed she was so relieved.

"My husband, he loves it like this, but I want something shorter, more stylish. I saw that actress the other day as I was switching channels, and I wondered…" Alethea elaborated.

Claudia smiled to herself. One by one, all of Leandro's female relatives had confessed they watched both *Ocean Boulevard* and *Heartlands,* taping one while they watched the other. They'd all begged her not to tell Leandro, not wanting him to think they were disloyal. And now, Mrs.

Mandalor was admitting in a roundabout way that she, too, followed the fortunes of the *Ocean Boulevard* characters.

"It's much shorter than what you have now," Claudia said, tilting her head to one side and seriously assessing Leandro's mother's face.

She guessed Alethea was in her late fifties-early sixties, and she had the kind of strong facial structure that had aged well.

"You've got the cheekbones to pull it off. And a nice high forehead. I think it would really suit you," Claudia said.

"Thank you!" Alethea said, touching Claudia's arm gratefully. "The rest of the family—they're used to me looking a certain way. This face, this hair is what they think of when they think of Alethea Mandalor. But it's time for a change, and I'm going to do it. I'm going to make an appointment tomorrow."

"You know, if you'd like, I could ask Priscilla's stylist to take a look at you," Claudia heard herself saying.

Before she could regret the impulsive offer, Alethea's face lit up with such genuine gratitude that Claudia was touched to the heart.

"Oh, Claudia," Alethea said. "I cannot tell you what that would mean to me. I would know I was in such safe hands. Priscilla always looks so elegant, so refined."

Suddenly realizing that she'd just admitted to actually watching the show, Alethea lifted a hand to her mouth and turned wide eyes to Claudia, looking for all the world like a naughty schoolgirl.

"Don't worry—your secret's safe with me," Claudia said.

A shadow fell over them, and Claudia knew before she looked up that it was Leandro.

"How's it going over here?" he asked warily.

"Oh, relax, Leandro, I'm not grilling your friend. What do you think I am, some prehistoric cultural cliché?" Alethea said, waving her hand at him dismissively as she relinquished her chair.

Leandro stared after his mother in bemusement, then he looked down at Claudia.

"She really wasn't giving you the third degree?" he asked.

"Nope."

He raised his eyebrows as if to say "go figure."

"You ready to go home?" he asked her.

"If you are," she said.

She was surprised at her own answer. If anyone had told her when she first arrived that she'd be reluctant to go home, she'd have laughed in their face then shimmied over the nearest wall and made a run for it.

"I had a nice time," she said to Leandro as they made their way out to the car. The sidewalk was warm beneath her bare feet despite the fact that the sun had almost set.

"Good," he said. The gaze he shot her was cautious, assessing.

It reminded her of what she had to do now. Having held her peace all afternoon, she couldn't bite her tongue any longer.

"Leandro, we need to talk," she said.

"Yes, we do. But not this close to a million flapping Mandalor ears," he said.

She nodded her agreement, and slid into his car. She grew more and more tense as they neared her house and she ran over the words she'd convinced herself she needed to say.

He helped her out of his car, and as she looked up to thank him she put her foot down on something cold and sharp.

"Ow!"

She lifted her foot to find a shard from a broken soda bottle on the sidewalk and blood welling from a cut in her foot.

"Here," Leandro said, bending down to scoop her into his arms.

Sliding a hand around his neck, she winced with pain as he strode up her garden path to her front door. Within seconds they were in her house and he had placed her on the kitchen counter and was examining her grubby sole.

"I don't think there's any glass in there still," he said.

"No, it was just that one big piece," she agreed.

He disappeared into the hallway then, and she heard him rummaging in her bathroom. He returned with her first aid kit, along with a washcloth. Pulling one of her kitchen chairs in front of her, he took her foot in hand again.

"It's a bit dirty," she apologized.

Shrugging his lack of concern, he reached across to run the washcloth under the tap, then gently wiped her foot clean.

"Not hurting?" he asked as he dabbed gently near the cut itself.

She shook her head, something inside her expanding warmly at the great care he was exerting to mend her hurt.

"I'm going to put some antiseptic on now—that bit might sting," he said, unscrewing a small bottle from her kit.

"I'm tough," she said, and he squeezed her ankle in response.

She hissed out a breath, however, when he dabbed the cut, jerking her leg back instinctively. He maintained his warm, firm grip on her ankle until he'd put a bandage on the cut, but the glance he gave her afterward was full of regret.

"Sorry," he said simply.

She stared at him, getting lost in his eyes, admitting to herself a truth that had been growing inside her for weeks.

She was in love with Leandro.

So much for flings and fun and light and breezy. So much for conquering her fear and taking what she wanted and doing it her way.

"I was going to break up with you tonight," she said.

"I know," he said.

They stared at each other for a beat, tension crackling between them.

"I didn't mean for this to happen," she said.

"Me, either. But it did. And I'm glad." He slid his hand farther up her calf, his palm hot against her skin.

"What do you want from me?" she whispered, her hands gripping the edge of the counter as though her life depended on it.

"This. What we have now, and to know that we have a future," he said. "To have the right to come home to you. To plan with you. All the usual stuff."

She closed her eyes. *All the usual stuff.*

All the stuff that scared the living shit out of her. Routine and domesticity and expectations and obligations.

When she opened her eyes again, he was waiting patiently, his gaze unwavering.

"I don't know if I can do all that, Leandro," she said faintly. "I know that this is about more than sex, that we've moved beyond that and there's more between us now. But I don't know where it can go."

"It's not something we have to decide right now," he said quickly. "Can't we just keep doing what we've been doing? Except that I'm allowed to buy you gifts and show that I care about you without you freaking out?"

She managed a wry little smile.

"You can read me like a book, is that it?" she said.

"Something like that."

He stood, moving close to take her in his arms. She spread her thighs wide so he could stand within their embrace.

"This is a good thing," he said as he framed her face with his hands. "Only a fool would throw it away."

"And I'm not a fool?" she asked, drowning in his eyes.

"You're the smartest woman I know," he said.

He kissed her, and for the first time she allowed herself to feel the full magic of being treasured by such a special man. She realized with a rush of panic that she was going to do this—she was going to throw all her caution to the winds and allow this thing between them to have its head and rampage its way through her life.

For a moment she was awash in fear, but then the flick of his tongue against hers and the slide of his hand over her breast and the growing heat between her thighs pushed everything else away.

He carried her to the bedroom and they made slow, languorous love on her bed, staring into each other's eyes, caressing each other with new intensity. Afterward, she lay wrapped in his arms and marveled that after all her years of careful planning, she'd slipped up so spectacularly.

Somehow, though, in the aftermath of her day with his family, it didn't feel like such a disaster.

She didn't see the light blinking on her answering machine until after he'd left, explaining he had an early-morning location scout the next day despite it being a Sunday. She pressed the message button absently, her fingers rising to her lips as she remembered Leandro's kisses.

"Claudia," Cosmo said over the speaker. He sounded

serious, and instantly she tensed, her gaze zeroing in on the answering machine. "Mom has gone missing. Dad and I have been out looking, but she's not in any of the usual places. She might turn up at your place. Call me."

The message ended with a clatter, as though her brother had dropped the phone before returning it to its cradle.

Snatching up her own phone, she shot a glance at the wall clock. It was past ten, but this was important and she dialed a number that she hadn't needed for nearly three years.

"Papa, it's me," she said when he picked it up on the first ring. He would be sitting by the phone, she knew, waiting for news.

There was a long pause before he spoke.

"I don't want to tie up the phone. There's been no news."

She stopped him before he could hang up on her.

"When did she go? How long has she been gone?"

"This morning. I went out for a while, and when I came back she was gone. She never came home."

His tone was cold, abrupt. As though he begrudged telling her anything.

"Have you called—"

"I've called everyone. We're handling things. I only let your brother call you because she might come to you."

"Papa, I want to help," she said.

"You gave up that right when you turned your back on your mother," he said, and then he did hang up on her.

Claudia stared at the phone. Her mother was missing, no doubt on a drinking binge that could last a day, or even a week, and might well end up with her father receiving a call from the hospital. Or worse.

She'd gone missing before, but this was the first time it

had happened since Claudia had distanced herself from the family. And her father wouldn't let her help.

You chose this, she reminded herself.

But it didn't make her feel any better.

8

"THERE'S SOMEONE OVER there, near the wall," Claudia said, squinting into the darker shadows.

She quickened her step, not even bothering to see if Sadie and Grace were following her as she moved across the garbage-strewn tarmac of a downtown L.A. parking lot. Her flashlight beam cut through the murky shadows and picked out the huddled shape of a body curled up against the wall. Claudia's steps slowed as she saw the piles of collapsed cardboard boxes nearby and the shopping trolley groaning with "treasures" gleaned from the street. This person had clearly been living rough for a while. There was no way it could be her mother.

Shoulders sagging, she turned back toward the street. It was three in the morning, and the three of them had been combing the fifty-block area of downtown L.A. not-so-affectionately known as Skid Row since midnight. Claudia's feet were sore, her shoulders aching with tension.

"Where to next?" Grace asked. Like the rest of them, she was wearing jeans and running shoes and carrying a flashlight.

"I don't know. The last time she dropped out like this was eight years ago, and we found her at a soup kitchen down here," Claudia said.

She didn't explain that her mother had fought them tooth and nail as they dragged her into the car. Left to her own devices, Talia had devolved to a state where finding the next drink was the only objective. She'd been missing for four days when they found her that time, and her face had been bruised and scratched from an accident or fight she'd had on the streets. Claudia would never forget the smell of her mother's unwashed body, or the feral, desperate light in her eyes, or the way she'd twisted and writhed to get away from them, knowing that at home she would not have ready access to the drink she craved.

But Skid Row had moved on in eight years, even if her mother had not. Developers had moved in, and many of the makeshift shantytowns were gone, replaced by shiny new apartment blocks and office buildings. The numbers of homeless sleeping in doorways, camping out in parking lots and against walls were far fewer.

"She's probably still cruising the bars," Claudia said, her gaze roaming aimlessly up and down the silent, dark street.

Her mother's patterns were fairly predictable; she would stay in the bars for as long as her money lasted and as long as they'd have her. Once she'd worn out her welcome— vomiting, passing out or picking a fight with another patron—she'd be reduced to drinking on the streets. It would take a few days for her to form friends with other drunks and vagrants, and Claudia knew that their current search was probably futile, but she wasn't ready to give up yet.

They'd already trawled through all the old bars her mother used to frequent. No one had seen her, or if they had, she hadn't made enough of an impression to be remembered. Claudia didn't know what her mother had been wearing, or how she had her hair these days. She didn't know if her father and brother had already searched the same places she was searching. She was on the outside, locked out, unable to help. Frustration welled up inside her as she tried to order her thoughts.

"The man from the shelter said a lot of the homeless have been pushed down to the river now," Sadie said. "We could go down there, take a look around."

Even though Sadie's voice was filled with determination, it was impossible for her to hide how tired she was. She was in the first trimester of her pregnancy still, and Claudia knew she'd been feeling low on energy lately. She was looking very pale, her fine-boned face fragile in the hazy street light.

"You need to go home, Sade," Claudia said. "You look exhausted."

"I'm fine. I want to do this with you," Sadie said staunchly.

"Claud's right, Sadie. You're gray. We'll drop you home and Claudia and I will keep looking," Grace said.

"I'm not leaving, so get over it. I'm pregnant, not dying," Sadie said.

"Dylan will kill us if we take you home looking like something the cat dragged in," Grace said.

Claudia tuned out of their bickering, her gaze gravitating toward the huddled figure at the rear of the parking lot. Somewhere in this big city, her mother was doing her best to drown herself in a bottle. Claudia shivered to think of the dangers Talia Dostis had exposed herself to. When she drank, her mother often became aggressive and confrontational, despite the fact that she was a meek, accepting woman when sober. Claudia had often wondered if the drunk Talia was the truer woman—the one who honestly shouted her feelings and thoughts to the world. Or perhaps her rages were simply the flip side to the quiet domestic martyr her mother had turned herself into, the inevitable consequence of being so good, so dutiful, so ready to please most of the time.

Last time she'd gone missing, Claudia had been the one to shepherd her mother into the shower and wash away the smell of sweat and alcohol and dirt. She was the one who saw that her mother's underwear was inside out. Drunks did many things they wouldn't do when sober, Claudia knew. Sex with strangers was one of them.

She closed her eyes against the images flashing across her mind. If she thought about any of it too much, she'd go mad.

"Claud," Grace said, and Claudia felt an arm slide around her shoulders.

"Don't, Claud. We'll keep looking, we won't give up," Sadie said earnestly, drawing close to embrace Claudia from the other side.

It was only then that Claudia realized she was crying, great big heaving sobs that seemed to come up from the soles of her feet. Unable to staunch the flow, she rested her head on Grace's shoulder and let her friends hold her.

"Why does she have to be like this?" she said brokenly. "Why?"

It was the lament of her childhood, and she knew there was no real answer.

Her mother never talked about her childhood in Greece, but Claudia knew it had not been a happy one. There was no one left to ask, but Claudia had pieced together enough to guess that Talia's own mother had been a drinker, and it was no secret that alcoholism ran in families.

But it didn't change the fact that Talia Dostis had every reason in the world to stay sober—a husband who adored her,

children who loved her—but didn't. Maybe she just couldn't.
It was something Claudia had considered—that maybe her
mother simply had no control over her own behavior.

It was such a bleak, despairing thought. Claudia pressed
her face into Grace's neck and sobbed her heart out. She
may have detached from her mother, but she hadn't given
up on her, not really. Accepting that Talia was not answerable for her own actions and was therefore unable to
change them would be the ultimate defeat.

"Come on, let's go," Sadie said when Claudia's sobs
had quietened.

They led her back to her car, and Claudia didn't object
when Grace got behind the wheel and drove them to an all-
night diner. Sitting in the car for privacy, they sipped at hot
chocolates and ate dry, day-old donuts while Sadie and
Grace offered their comfort.

"She'll be okay, Claud," Grace said. "She'll turn up, or
we'll find her, or someone will."

Claudia nodded, staring down into her paper cup.

"Your brother will keep you in the loop, right?" Sadie
asked.

"Yes. He's the one who called me tonight. Dad didn't
even want to talk to me," Claudia said dully.

"Come on, let's go home," Grace said.

Claudia nodded. She was bone weary. Briefly she
thought of how heavenly it would be to go home and be
able to curl up tight in Leandro's arms, to seek solace and
comfort against his big broad chest.

But he'd gone home. And, anyway, she didn't want to
rely on him for comfort. She'd always looked after
herself. Always.

Grace and Mac's place was the first drop-off, and

Claudia slid out of the back of the car to take the wheel when Grace pulled into the driveway.

"Try to sleep. She might turn up tomorrow, you never know," Grace said as she hugged Claudia goodbye.

"She might," Claudia agreed.

Sadie yawned hugely all the way to the house she shared with Dylan in the Hollywood Hills. As soon as they pulled up, a light switched on. Dylan had been up waiting, Claudia guessed.

"Why don't you stay the night with us?" Sadie said. "I don't like the idea of you going home alone."

"I'll be fine. Honestly. Before I was just…worn-out, I guess. I'm fine."

"What about Leandro? You could go to his place," Sadie suggested.

Claudia could see Sadie wasn't going to let this go.

"I'll give him a call if it will make you feel better," she lied.

The last thing she wanted to do was to drag Leandro into all of this. It was such a private, personal shame. She didn't want to see the distaste on his face, the condemnation. As crazy as it seemed, she didn't want him to think badly of her mother, a woman he was never likely to meet.

Sadie seemed to buy her lie, however, and she gave Claudia a fierce hug goodbye before running up the path to where Dylan waited by the open door. Claudia watched for a moment as they kissed, Dylan frowning down into Sadie's tired face with concern. Then she reversed down the driveway and back into the street and drove home to her empty house.

There were no messages on her answering machine when she got home, and she sank down onto the couch and rested her head in her hands. She was so tired, but she didn't know how she was going to sleep. What she wanted more than anything was to still the worried thoughts wearing a track in her mind. What if her mother ran into traffic? What if she screamed at the wrong person? What if she fell asleep in the wrong place, or hooked up with the wrong people?

Pushing herself to her feet, she went into the bedroom and toed off her shoes. Feeling pathetic, she crossed to her en suite and rummaged in the dirty clothes hamper until she found a T-shirt Leandro had left behind during the week. Shucking her own clothes, she pulled it over her head.

Surrounded by his smell, she curled up in bed. Perhaps her mother really would turn up tomorrow.

But it was hard to hope after so many years of disappointment.

WORKING AS A PRODUCER, Leandro had honed his people-reading skills to a fine art. It helped to know when people were lying, or uncomfortable, or unhappy when you were negotiating with creatives all the time and dealing with big egos and lots of money.

He didn't need any of his hard-won skill to know that Claudia was troubled, however. It was as though a light had gone out inside her. She was distracted, forgetful. She only picked at her meal when they went out for dinner on Tuesday night. And in bed, she made love to him with an intensity that was almost desperate. She'd been too busy to see him Wednesday night, and now, Thursday, she was looking hollow-eyed and tired and strung out.

"You want dessert?" he asked as she toyed with the salt and pepper shakers, her gaze unfocused, her thoughts clearly someplace else.

"No. But you have some if you want," she said, offering him a small smile that made it nowhere near her eyes.

Was this because of what they'd talked about after his grandmother's party? Was she freaking out over the acknowledgment they'd both made that what was happening between them was real and worth pursuing?

He studied her, noting the fretful way she pleated and unpleated her linen napkin, and the way she kept pulling her cell phone from her bag to check that it was on. His instincts told him that this wasn't about them. But something was clearly wrong, and he wanted her to tell him what it was.

Problem was, she was stubborn. She was also proud, and smart. She was used to being the boss, the person people turned to for solutions. He knew what that was like, and he knew that it was hard for him to ask for help when he needed it. Which meant maybe he had to offer it.

"Claudia," he said, only to be interrupted by her cell phone ringing.

She pounced on it as if she were expecting a call from God, and he frowned when he saw the profound disappointment in her face when she answered and the call clearly wasn't who or what she'd been hoping for.

"Okay. Yeah, no, thanks. I appreciate the update," she said.

She took an unnecessarily long time putting her phone back in her handbag, then she glanced up at him.

"Actually, if you don't mind, I think I'd like to go. It's been a long day," she said.

He stared at her, wanting to call her on her bull. But she *was* tired, he could see that. Tired and very worried about something. For the first time it occurred to him that it might be a work issue, something she didn't feel able to discuss with him.

"How's the show going?" he asked while Claudia signaled to the waiter that they wanted their bill.

She shrugged a shoulder, busy fishing in her handbag for her wallet.

"Fine. Good."

It was hard to wring much meaning out of two words, but she didn't look like she was covering. So, not work then. Something personal.

He waited until they were in the car on the way home before trying again.

"So, when do you think you're going to talk to me about what's going on?" he asked as they stopped at a red light.

She shot a look at him, startled.

"Sorry?"

"Come on, Claudia—you're clearly upset about something. Talk to me," he said. "You never know, I might actually be able to help."

Her lips quirked into a bitter little smile. "I doubt it."

"Try me," he said as he pulled into her driveway.

She toyed with the strap on her handbag, and after a long moment, she lifted her head.

"It's a long story," she said, then her focus shifted to something over his shoulder and she stiffened with shock.

Before he could react, she was scrambling out of the car and racing around the front of the car toward her front porch.

"What the hell?" he muttered, wrenching his door open to follow her.

She was huddled over something when he joined her, and it was only when she shifted that he saw it was a person, a woman lying crumpled at the top of the steps.

Claudia was slapping the woman's cheeks, to apparently no effect.

"She won't wake up," she said, looking up at him, her eyes huge in her pale face. "Leandro, she won't wake up."

Crouching down beside her, he searched the woman's neck to find a pulse, and relaxed a notch when he felt it, slow and steady beneath his fingers.

"Her pulse seems okay. Is she bleeding or anything?" he asked, trying to remember the first aid course he'd done in his teens.

"No, I don't think so, it's hard to see."

His words seemed to ground her, and she sat back on her heels and pulled out her phone.

"I need an ambulance, please," she said when her call was connected. While she gave her address and details, he shrugged out of his coat and lay it across the woman's body.

She was small and fine boned, and his coat covered her nearly to the knees.

Claudia made another phone call as soon as she'd finished the last, the conversation short and sweet.

"She's here, at my place," was all she said.

Then she glanced up at him.

"I don't want to move her, in case she damaged something when she fell down, but can you go in and turn on the outside light?"

She handed him her key and he squeezed past her to get to the door. Flicking the lights on, he turned back and froze as he got a good look at the woman's face for the first time.

There was no hiding the family resemblance—the nose, the hairline, the cheekbones. This woman could only be Claudia's mother or some other close female relative. As he watched, Claudia curled her hand into a fist and pressed her knuckles firmly into the woman's sternum. It was a move he'd employed when wrestling with his brothers, and one he knew doctors used to ascertain levels of consciousness in patients.

The woman flinched slightly, then moved her head from side to side.

"No," she whispered. "Don't want to."

She thrashed a hand out, nearly connecting with Claudia's face. Instinctively he ducked down to protect Claudia, and for the first time he registered the woman's smell—alcohol and sweat and unwashed body.

He shot a look at Claudia and she bit her lip.

"This is my mother," she said stiffly. "She's...she hasn't been well. She gets confused sometimes and goes wandering."

"Does she have Alzheimer's?" he asked.

"Something like that," she said, her hand smoothing the hair back from her mother's forehead.

"She's been missing all week? That's why you were so worried?" he asked.

Claudia nodded, still not meeting his eye. "Yes."

He frowned. She was lying to him. He didn't understand why, but she was lying to him.

The wail of an ambulance siren sounded in the distance, and he stood.

"I'll go flag them down," he said, resting a hand on her shoulder.

Striding to the sidewalk and out into the road itself, he spotted the flashing lights at the end of the street. Glancing back at the house, he watched as Claudia bent over her mother and pressed a kiss to her forehead.

Headlights loomed closer and he waved his arms, then stepped out of the way as the ambulance veered to the curb.

Within seconds, two paramedics were out the doors and grabbing gear from the back of the van.

"She's on the front porch," Leandro said, hanging back so as not to crowd the small space.

He couldn't hear what Claudia was saying to them as they checked her mother's vitals, but he saw one of the paramedics nod and reach for something from his kit. Clearly feeling she was in the way, Claudia stood and stepped back a few paces, wrapping her arms around herself as she kept an anxious eye on the action.

Wordlessly he moved to stand behind her, drawing her back against his body and wrapping his arms over hers. Her body was stiff with tension and fear, and he dropped a kiss onto the crown of her head.

She was so fierce, yet so small and fragile at the same time. He felt an overwhelming need to wrap her up and cocoon her from the world. But he was painfully aware that he could only do that if she let him—and at the moment, that wasn't looking likely.

THE DINNER SHE'D just eaten churned in her stomach as she watched the paramedics work on her mother. She kept telling herself that Talia was alive, that was the important thing, but inside she was resounding with shock over how thin her mother was, how wretched she'd looked when Claudia found her huddled on the steps.

"We're going to take her in," one of the paramedics said as he crossed back to the ambulance.

"Which hospital?" she asked, forcing herself to think. There were things to do, people to notify.

"Cedars Sinai."

She nodded, then wriggled free from Leandro's arms.

She couldn't look at him. She hated lying to him, but she also couldn't bring herself to explain that her mother was a chronic alcoholic, that the smell of urine and sweat and God knows what else on her was because she'd been living on the streets in pursuit of oblivion via the bottle for the past week.

Pulling her cell from her handbag, Claudia dialed her brother again, aware that he was with her father and that they were both on their way to her place.

"They're taking her to Sinai," she said when her brother picked up.

"Okay. How is she?" Cosmo asked.

"Unconscious, but she's responding to pain. I guess they won't know anything else until they run some tests."

Alcoholics were prone to a number of illnesses—liver problems, heart disease, pancreatic problems, and were far more likely to develop breast cancer than the general population. There was no knowing the extent to which Talia's binge had damaged her body.

"You okay?" Cosmo asked.

"I'm fine."

"I'll let George know and we'll see you over there, okay?" Cosmo said.

She ended the call and watched as her mother was strapped onto the stretcher, an IV line taped to her forearm.

"I'll lock up, then we can follow them," Leandro said from behind her.

She took a deep breath and turned to face him.

"You don't need to come. My father and brothers are meeting us at the hospital," she said, trying to inject as much cool strength into the words as possible.

"I'm coming," he said unequivocally.

Hunching her shoulders, she turned toward his car. Short

of snatching her keys from him, she knew she had no hope of discouraging him. She'd seen that stubborn light in his eye before.

They drove to the hospital in silence. On one level, she was aware that it was only a matter of time before he realized the truth—that her mother didn't have early-onset Alzheimer's or some other medical condition that could explain her current state. But she couldn't bring herself to say anything.

She was ashamed of her mother. An ugly, terrible truth. Sometimes she felt she'd been ashamed of her mother all her life. As a child, she'd never been able to have friends over to play like the other girls. There was never any knowing what state her mother would be in when she came home—happy, maudlin, angry, sober. It had been a lottery, one that Claudia had quickly learned not to play. At family gatherings, she or one of her brothers had always kept constant surveillance over their mother, waiting for her to have one ouzo too many, trying to steer off the slide into slurred speech and inappropriate laughter and unexpected anger. Having Leandro see her mother like this, her family like this—she felt weak and exposed.

Cosmo, George and her father were already waiting in the E.R. when they arrived, hovering amidst a sea of other worried people. Stretching out in front of them were rows of curtained cubicles, all of them apparently occupied. George hugged her in greeting, and Cosmo slid an arm around her shoulder, but their father barely met her eye. He was bristling with anger; she could feel it coming off him in waves. She squared her shoulders. None of this was her fault—she was the one who had tried to jolt her family out of its head-in-the-sand attitude to Talia's behavior.

"They brought her in five minutes ago," George said. "She's in the third cubicle there. Did she say anything when you found her?"

"Nothing coherent. She's pretty out of it," Claudia said, burningly aware of Leandro standing just behind her.

Slowly, reluctantly, she turned to introduce him.

"Leandro, these are my brothers, Cosmo and George, and my father, Spiro," she said.

Cosmo and George shook Leandro's hand, but her father just nodded his head once in acknowledgment.

The crash of a trolley being overturned in one of the treatment cubicles drew their attention, and Claudia stiffened as she heard her mother crying out.

A nurse and two orderlies rushed into Talia's cubicle, and Claudia wrapped her arms across her middle and gripped her elbows tensely as her mother's cries grew louder and louder.

"Get off me, get off me, let me go," Talia hollered shrilly, then she started with the four-letter words, and the people around them in the waiting area shifted in their seats and murmured amongst themselves.

Claudia imagined the scene in the cubicle—her mother rousing from her alcoholic stupor, angry to find herself in the control of others, disoriented, confused, scared. She'd be thrashing around, lashing out. When Claudia was fifteen, her mother had caught her unawares during just such a reaction and perforated Claudia's eardrum with a blow to the head.

She didn't dare look at Leandro as her mother's cries turned to despairing sobs.

"I want my girl," she began to wail. "Where's Claudia? I have to see Claudia."

A harried-looking nurse whipped open the cubicle as she exited, swiftly sliding it closed again behind her—but Claudia still caught a glimpse of one of the orderlies holding her mother's legs down. Tears pricked at the back of her eyes at the indignity of it all.

The nurse approached the waiting area with a brisk, no-nonsense step.

"Is anyone here with Talia Dostis?" she called over the low murmur of conversation in the waiting area.

Her father moved forward. "I am Spiro Dostis. Talia's husband," he said with firm dignity.

"Do you have any idea what your wife has been drinking? Does she use other drugs?" the nurse asked matter-of-factly.

"No. Never," Spiro said firmly. "She has been missing for six days. We…we have no idea where she has been."

The nurse nodded, obviously understanding how painful an admission it was for Spiro to make.

"She's very dehydrated, disoriented and aggressive. The doctor is reluctant to sedate her given her blood alcohol level. We'd like one of you to come sit with her. A familiar face might orient her."

"I'll go," Claudia said, stepping forward.

"No." Spiro did not even turn his head to look at her. "I am her husband."

"But she's calling for Claudia," Cosmo said. "And she wound up on Claudia's front doorstep. Maybe if she sees her she will calm down."

"No."

A high-pitched scream came from Talia's cubicle, and Claudia turned urgently to the nurse.

"Can I just go in?"

"I'll take you," the woman said, and Claudia turned to face Leandro for the first time.

There was no way he didn't know now—he'd overhead their whole conversation.

"You should go home," she said, forcing herself to meet his gaze.

Not waiting for his response, she followed the nurse.

Her stomach dipped as she saw that her mother had been tied down with restraints. Talia still fought, however, straining futilely against her bonds, arching her head off the bed, her mouth open in a plaintive wail.

"Mama, Mama—I'm here," Claudia said, hastening to her mother's side.

But Talia was lost in a haze of alcohol and confusion. Her head tossed from side to side as she wrenched her body violently, trying to free herself.

"Mama," Claudia said, leaning across the bed and grasping her mother's face in her hands to still her frantic movements. "I'm here. It's Claudia. I'm right here."

Talia froze, her mouth open in a silent wail. Slow recognition dawned in her bloodshot eyes, and all the fight seemed to drain out of her.

"My little girl. My baby girl," Talia said, the words slurred but still coherent.

"That's right. I'm here, so you have to stop hurting yourself, okay? You need to let the doctors and nurses look after you."

Big tears welled up in her mother's eyes as she stared at Claudia.

"You went away. You went away, but then I saw you in your pretty dress. So nice in red, always so nice in red," Talia said, her voice trailing into a whisper.

Claudia frowned, then she realized what her mother was referring to—the People's Vote Awards. Her mother had seen the televised ceremony after all.

A horrible thought occurred—was that why her mother had gone off on a binge? Because she'd seen Claudia on TV? Claudia closed her eyes for a brief moment, hating the thought that, however indirectly, she might have been responsible for what had happened.

"It's okay, I'm not going anywhere," she said, smoothing her mother's hair back from her forehead.

Talia's eyelids dropped shut, and Claudia saw the last of the tension ease from her mother's painfully thin body.

"Good work," the nurse said quietly, giving Claudia a thumbs-up.

Claudia could barely respond; she was too busy trying to swallow the enormous ball of grief lodged in her throat. With Talia's eyes closed and her body relaxed, it was possible to see the devastation that the past six days, and, indeed, the past three years had wrought. Always a small woman, she was nothing now, her collarbone poking sharply up from the tissue-like skin of her chest. Her cheeks were marked with a spiderweb tracery of red veins—angry against the pallor of the rest of her complexion. Like her chest, the bones of her face were scarily prominent, making Talia look much older than her fifty-nine years.

As Claudia reached for her mother's hand, Talia's mouth dropped open, and her head flopped to one side. Claudia stiffened and shot a worried glance toward the nurse.

"Is she okay? What's happening?" she asked.

The nurse checked Talia's pulse and other vital signs.

"She's sleeping," she finally said. "Hopefully she'll stay

that way—it's the best thing for her at this point. Apart from supporting the liver with IV fluids, we can't do much more for her until the alcohol is out of her system. Then it will be a matter of running tests to see if there has been any permanent damage."

Claudia nodded. So far, her mother had been remarkably lucky with her health. It would be foolish to think that her body could go on forever under such abuse, however.

She stayed with Talia for another half hour, holding her hand, watching her face, trying to reconcile her feelings of anger and guilt and shame and love. An impossible task. One that she'd thought she'd walked away from three years ago.

Finally she forced herself to her feet. Even though she'd told him to go, she knew Leandro would be waiting for her. He was that kind of man. Stomach tense, feet leaden, she exited the cubicle and crossed the shiny vinyl floor to where her brothers, father and Leandro sat grouped together.

"She's sleeping," Claudia said.

Her father ignored her, surging to his feet and brushing past her to go take her place by Talia's bedside.

"They're going to run more tests tomorrow," she told Cosmo and George, stupidly repeating the nurse's words just to avoid looking directly at Leandro again.

Cosmo nodded, scrubbing his face wearily. Glancing at the wall clock, she was surprised to see it was nearly midnight. With a small child and his own contracting business to run, her brother worked long hours.

"You should go home. You, too, George." She knew they'd been out looking for their mother most nights this week. "I'll stay here and let you know if anything changes."

For a moment Cosmo looked tempted, but he shook his head. "I wouldn't be able to sleep, anyway," he said.

"Yeah, pass," George agreed. "But thanks anyway."

Leandro stood, and her gaze skittered toward him and just as quickly ricocheted away.

"I'll go get some coffees for us all," he said. She felt his gaze on her. "You want to come?"

She didn't want to be alone with him, didn't want to have the conversation that had been looming since the moment they pulled up at her house earlier this evening. But it was inevitable, had been since the day they met.

9

GRABBING HER wallet from her handbag, Claudia followed Leandro through a maze of corridors till they found the cafeteria. At this time of night the vending machines ruled, and the bulk of the space was empty except for a handful of weary-looking medical staff and a couple of subdued family groups.

Fishing in her purse for coins for the machine, Claudia kept her head down, even though she could feel Leandro's steady regard. After a few seconds, he stepped forward and rested his warm hand on the nape of her neck.

"Are you okay?" he asked.

She shrugged a shoulder, still not looking at him. "I'm fine."

"It's okay to be upset, Claudia. Your mom's in hospital," Leandro said.

"It's not like we haven't been here before," she said before she could stop herself.

God, she sounded bitter and screwed up.

"How long has she been an alcoholic?" Leandro asked after a brief pause.

How like him to wade in and get to the point, asking the hard questions up front.

"I don't want to talk about this," she said, forcing herself to look up into his face.

"Why not?"

"Because I don't. It's irrelevant."

He shook his head as though he couldn't quite believe what she'd said.

"She's your mother," he said simply.

"Leandro—read my lips. I don't want to go over old ground," Claudia said.

He touched her arm. "How are we supposed to build a future together, have a family if you won't tell me what's going on in that head of yours?" he asked.

She let out a short, sharp bark of laughter.

"A family? Are you kidding?" she said, knowing even as she spoke that she was being a bitch, that all the things she should have said, should have told him last week were coming out the wrong way because she was terrified for her mother and she'd allowed her feelings for Leandro to get out of control.

He frowned. "I want a future with you, Claudia, you know that."

"I don't want children," she said bluntly. "Never have, never will."

"I know you're really into your career, but we can work around that. I'll share the load, we can do it together," Leandro said.

She shook her head.

"No. I told you right from the start that I wasn't interested in a relationship, but I wanted you so badly I kidded myself that maybe we could pull this off. But from the moment I saw you with your family, I knew I could never be the kind of woman you want me to be. I should have said this to you last week, except… Anyway, I'm sorry if you feel I led you on. I didn't mean to. But now we both know where we stand, and we can put this all behind us and move on."

It was hard to say the words, to finally draw a line under what had happened between them, but it had to be done.

He blinked. "What are you saying? That we're breaking up?"

"What's the point in carrying on when we're never going to be on the same page?" she asked.

"I don't believe this," he said incredulously. "Look me in the eye and tell me you don't love me."

"I love you. That's the problem. That's why I kidded myself that I could do this thing with you, that we could sleep together and I could control it. But deep down inside I knew we'd end up here. I won't give up my life for anyone, Leandro," she said.

He looked stunned, as though she'd whipped the rug out from beneath his feet. Guilt and sadness spurred her on.

"You knew. Right from the start. The reason you sprang your grandmother's party on me was because you knew I didn't want us to get serious," she said.

They'd both been complicit in this game of "look the other way."

"No, I just don't buy it. You were made to love people, Claudia. I've seen you with your friends, the way you look after your team, the way you talk to your nephew. You said when you saw me with my family last week that you knew you could never be the kind of woman I want—well, I had the exact opposite experience. I saw you laughing with my grandmother and dancing with my father and gossiping with my mother and I knew that you belonged, that we have the foundation for something great between us."

"You saw what you wanted to see," she said.

"No, I didn't. I saw you," he said.

Stepping closer, he pulled her into his arms and tilted her head up with a finger.

"I love you, Claudia," he said before lowering his head to kiss her.

He tasted familiar and precious and for a few stupid moments she let her body soften against his, let herself imagine what it would be like to have his comfort and strength to draw on, to know that she would always have him by her side.

It was too seductive, and way too terrifying. She had only to remember her mother's face to find the strength to resist him.

Sliding her hands between them, she pushed herself away from his chest.

"I think you should go now," she said quietly.

She felt him tense even though she was no longer touching him.

"I understand that you're upset about your mother," he said. She could see he was struggling to keep his emotions in check. "I don't want to lose you, Claudia. Let's just leave this for now and talk about it later."

"Nothing is going to change, Leandro."

"You don't know that."

"You want a family, I don't. One of these things is not like the other," she said.

He still looked stubbornly unconvinced.

She smiled sadly. "This is why your first marriage ended, isn't it?"

"Partly. But there were other reasons as well."

"Even if we did decide to look the other way for now, this would always be between us."

He looked stricken, disbelieving. She reached out and cupped her palm on his cheek.

"It's for the best," she said, dropping her hand and stepping away from him.

"I can't believe you'd give up on us so easily, that you won't even give this a chance," he said. He sounded angry, like she'd betrayed him. "What happened to the woman who kicked my shin for stealing her idea?"

"She's standing right in front of you," Claudia said, her voice calm even though inside her heart was breaking. The only way to stick with this, however, was to remind herself that worse pain lay ahead if she allowed herself to be drawn back into his arms.

"I hope it's worth it, this great career of yours. I hope those awards keep you warm at night," he said, his voice and face cold now.

"I know what I want," she said.

"And that's not me?" he asked stiffly.

Slowly she shook her head. "I don't have room for you in my life."

"Room for me?"

He stared at her as though he'd never seen her before. Then he walked away, back straight, head high.

That easily, it was over.

She stared after him, telling herself that she'd only done what had to be done. After a minute or two, the sick feeling in her stomach began to fade and she forced her mind to the matter at hand. Coffee for her brothers, her silent, condemning father and herself. Then conferences with the doctors as they began the inevitable fruitless rehabilitation discussions that would go nowhere because her mother refused to acknowledge her illness.

She managed a small, twisted little smile. She'd had her moment in the sun, her few days of glory. Now it was time to pay the price.

CLAUDIA WAS FEELING bone weary by the time she arrived at work the next morning. She'd texted Sadie and Grace to tell them about Talia's hospitalization last night, and they were waiting in her office with takeaway coffees and bagels when she arrived.

"How is she?" Sadie asked.

Claudia shrugged a shoulder. "Still sleeping."

She'd had no sleep herself, and had only made a pit stop at home to shower and change clothes.

"Do you have any idea where she's been?" Grace asked, pushing a bagel forward.

"She's filthy, so she's obviously been sleeping rough. God knows where, or with whom," Claudia said.

"Eat something," Sadie said, nodding toward the bagel. "You look exhausted."

Claudia picked up the bagel, but the warm scent of yeast and flour made her feel sick. Ever since Leandro had walked away from her, a heavy weight had been sitting in her stomach, and the thought of food was repellent.

"I had something at the hospital," she lied, putting the bagel down again.

"It must have been so horrible, coming home to find her on the doorstep like that," Grace said, rounding the desk to hug Claudia. "You should have called us, we would have come to be with you at the hospital."

"Leandro was with me," Claudia said flatly.

She felt rather than saw Grace and Sadie exchange glances.

"So he knows then, about your mom?" Sadie asked

hesitantly. Both her friends knew that she'd been holding
back on telling him about her mother's situation.

"He knows," Claudia said.

"How did he handle it?" Grace asked.

"Well. Leandro handles everything well," Claudia said.
She didn't want to tell them that she'd ended things with
Leandro last night. Not yet. They'd want to talk, and she
didn't want to. She felt as though one false move would
puncture the fragile bubble that held all her raw, aching hurt
inside her. And there was no point hashing it all over,
anyway—nothing was going to change the fact that she and
Leandro wanted two very different things out of life.

"So, what next?" Grace asked.

Even though she knew Grace was talking about Leandro,
Claudia chose to deliberately misunderstand her friend.

"Tests, a general checkup. They'll see if she's done any
permanent damage to herself. And then my father will take
her home, and everyone will go back to pretending that it
never happened. Just like the last time and the time before
that," Claudia said matter-of-factly.

"Maybe this time your mom will recognize she's got a
problem," Sadie said.

Claudia shook her head. "I can't believe in that, Sadie.
You know I can't. I've believed in too many second
chances over the years. She always lets us down. Always."

The heavy silence that fell between them was broken by
the ring of Claudia's phone.

Claudia snatched it up eagerly. For as long as she could
remember, work had been her solace, her safe house. She
drew confidence from her successes, and each step up the
ladder was another brick in the wall separating herself
from her mother's fate. Now, more than ever, she needed

to remind herself of that. She was not her mother's daughter, and last night she'd taken steps to ensure she never would be.

"Claudia Dostis," she said into the receiver.

"Claudia. You got a moment to look at those promo slots?"

It was Harvey, her immediate superior, calling to ask a question about the network's promotions schedule. Pulling the appropriate file folder toward herself, Claudia indicated to her friends that she had to take the call.

Sadie and Grace withdrew. Focusing on what her boss was saying, Claudia gave herself over to work.

THE FOLLOWING DAY, Leandro pulled up in front of Dom's house. His brother had signed up for another run along the fire trails, following through on his determination to lose his paunch. For his part, Leandro was hoping that a bit of physical punishment would give him some relief from the pointless circling of his thoughts.

Claudia had made her position very clear—she didn't have *room* for him in her life. And even if she had been able to slot him in, even if she had wanted to talk, he knew how immovable a committed career woman could be. He'd played this game before with Peta, after all. He knew all the angles, all the parries and thrusts. He knew exactly how irreconcilable two divergent life views could be.

He frowned with surprise when his mother opened the door to his knock.

"Ma. What are you doing here? And what have you done to your hair?" he asked, eyeing her new, elegant jaw-length cut.

Alethea put a hand to her newly cropped hair and preened. "Don't you love it? Claudia did it for me," she said.

His frown deepened.

"Claudia cut your hair?" he asked skeptically. He was used to his mother's roundabout ways of telling a story.

"She arranged for one of her show's stylists to cut it for me. So I could look like one of the characters. Not that I watch the show, of course. I was changing channels one day when I saw this woman's haircut."

"It's okay, I know you watch *Ocean Boulevard*. I watch it, too," he said dryly. Although that was probably about to change. There was no way he could watch a single frame anymore without thinking of Claudia.

"Really? You don't mind?" his mother asked as she led him into the kitchen.

He stopped short when he saw that his youngest brother, Theo, and his wife Isabella were there, as well as his father and his two sisters, Magda and Georgia, and their husbands Peter and Jack. Theo's two daughters, Alice and Chloe, were sitting under the kitchen table with Dom and Betty's Alexandra and Stephen, all of them coloring up a storm on scrap paper. Dom and Betty were the only absentees.

"What's going on?" he asked.

"Betty's gone into labor early," Isabella said. "Her water broke first thing this morning."

She sounded worried, and Leandro did some rapid calculations in his head.

"She's not due for another six weeks, right?" he said.

"Seven," Theo said tightly.

"It's all going to be fine," Alethea said firmly, filling the coffeemaker with water. "I refuse to believe anything different."

And there is the reason I let myself fall in love with a

woman I knew would make me miserable—genetic optimism, Leandro thought grimly.

As if she sensed the general lack of belief in her proclamation, Alethea began ticking off her arguments on her fingers.

"The babies are already a good size, we know that from the ultrasounds. And Betty has always come on early—Alex was two weeks early, and little Stephen was three. Plus, I read in Betty's coffee grounds that she will have four children."

His mother shrugged her shoulders as though this last "fact" sealed the deal.

Leandro ran a hand through his hair, his own problems receding for the moment.

If Betty and Dom lost the twins… He could only imagine the dark well of grief that would be waiting for them.

"We should go to the hospital," he said.

"Not with the children," Georgia said firmly. "Dom will call when they have news."

Leandro let it go. She was probably right, anyway. The kids would only get tired and bored at the hospital, and he knew from his night in the E.R. how difficult screaming children made it for everyone else.

Inevitably his thoughts clicked over to Claudia again as he remembered the events of Thursday night. He felt… Cheated was the only word that matched the emotion sitting on his chest like a dead weight. He'd fallen in love with her, and he knew in his bones that she loved him, too.

Without him consciously willing it, he had a memory flash of the anguish in Claudia's face as she'd listened to her mother's cries in the E.R. How he'd wanted to make the world right for her, but Talia Dostis's alcoholism was obviously a long-standing family issue. Just as obviously, there was a rift between Claudia and her father. And she'd never brought either subject up with him. All the while he'd imagined their relationship was progressing, that they were becoming closer and closer, she'd kept him firmly at arm's length.

Belatedly Leandro realized what he was doing: flogging a dead horse. Hadn't he learned his lesson? He and Claudia wanted different things. It was as simple as that.

Unless, of course, he changed what he wanted.

Could he give up his dream of a family of his own, children of his own, if it meant keeping Claudia in his life? It wasn't something he'd ever really considered with his exwife, but Claudia was different. He felt so connected to her, so complete when he was with her. Was it possible he could content himself with being an active uncle, channeling his frustrated parenting ambitions into his nieces and nephews?

Looking around the room, at his mother and father, his brother and sisters and their partners, at the four children lying sprawled beneath the table, he felt an expanding warmth in his chest. Family was important to him—the center of his universe. He found his career satisfying, but it was not his everything. These people were. It was part of who he was, part of his essential character.

The answer was no, he could not live without the love and laughter of children in his life.

"Uncle Leo, come and look at what I drawed," Chloe called from under the table.

Pulling his thoughts back to the here and now, Leandro crossed to the kitchen table and squatted down to peer under it.

"Look. This is you and the pretty lady from the other

day," Chloe said. "Mommy said you love each other, so I drawed a big heart for you to share, see?"

Isabella made an embarrassed noise as Leandro accepted the proffered drawing. Two stick figures filled the page, the only differentiating feature being the triangle of the woman's skirt. A big lopsided love heart encircled them both.

"That's great, Chloe," he said. "You got my hair just right." He went to give it back to her, but she shook her head.

"It's for you. For the fridge," she said firmly.

Thanking her, he stood and realized that the adult members of his family were all gazing at him speculatively.

"So, when are you going to ask her?" Alethea said, lining up coffee mugs on the counter.

"I beg your pardon?" Leandro said, even though he knew what she was getting at. This was the last thing he wanted to think about, let alone talk about. But he also knew it was easier for all of them to concentrate on his love life right now than on what might or might not be happening at the hospital.

"I can see you love her, Leandro. You couldn't take your eyes off her," Alethea said. "When are you going to ask her to marry you?"

"I don't think it's really the time—" Leandro stalled, but Theo cut him off.

"Might as well give, Leo. She's not going to stop until she hears what she wants to hear."

Leandro sighed and stared down at the two figures holding hands in Chloe's drawing. As much as he hated to say the words out loud, they needed to be said.

"Claudia and I decided not to see each other anymore," he said.

A stunned silence met this announcement.

"But we *liked* her," his father said.

Leandro felt a belated stab of sympathy for Peta, who had never been so unreservedly welcomed into the fold.

"She was perfect for you, Leo," his mother said. "Warm and smart and so pretty. Strong enough to match you, soft enough to love you. She was perfect."

"We wanted different things," was all he said. He wasn't about to go into the complexities of his and Claudia's relationship.

"I'm sorry, Leandro," Magda said quietly.

"Yeah, I really thought…" Theo said, trailing off when Isabella dug an elbow none-too-subtly into his ribs.

"Don't you like my drawing, Uncle Leo?" Chloe piped up from down on the floor.

Quickly Leandro squatted down to her level again.

"It's great. I especially like the colors. And how big my feet are," he said with a smile.

She smiled back, her dark Mandalor eyes sparkling up at him.

One day, I will have a little girl just like you.

He'd thought the same thing about all of his nieces and nephews at some time, but today the notion brought no comfort because he knew now that his daughters would not share Claudia's sloping cheekbones and small, proud nose.

Hard on the heels of this depressing acknowledgment, the phone rang. The tension in the room ratcheted as tight as a drum as Stavros calmly reached out a hand and lifted the receiver.

"Mandalor residence," he said.

Leandro only realized he was holding his breath when it hissed out of him as his father's mouth stretched into a big grin.

"Wonderful news! Wonderful!" he said, waving his free hand exuberantly.

Covering the mouthpiece, he spoke to the room.

"Mother and babies are well. The bubs don't even need the special beds, Dom says." Stavros sounded proud, as though the entire Mandalor family could take credit for this achievement.

"And what about Betty? Did she need any stitches?" Alethea asked.

"Stitches? Why would she need stitches?" Stavros frowned.

"Because the— Give the phone to me!" Leandro's mother said, flushing red and snatching the receiver from her husband's hand.

Alethea interrogated her middle son for a few minutes before reluctantly ending the call. In the meantime, Stavros had been busy pulling out the shot glasses. Splashing the ouzo bottle from glass to glass, he finished pouring with a flourish.

Leandro accepted his glass, wondering vaguely what his stomach was going to make of hard liquor at nine o'clock on a Saturday morning.

"Here's to our new family members—Christopher and Jason Mandalor," Stavros said, raising his glass high, sticky ouzo dripping from his over-full glass.

Leandro raised his own glass and tossed back the liquorice-flavored mouthful in one shot. Isabella gave a small cheer of relief and hugged her husband, and his parents gave each other fond hugs. His sisters clinked glasses, and under the table, the children sent up a cheer of their own.

His throat burning, Leandro was suddenly acutely aware of the empty space at his side.

It had taken him nearly a year to get over the failure of his six-month marriage to Peta. His time with Claudia was ridiculously short by comparison, but he knew he would be stinging from her loss for far longer.

I thought she was the one.

Standing amongst his family, marveling at the birth of two new tiny beings into the world, he understood absolutely that she'd been right to end things. This was his world, and she didn't want any part of it.

Forcing a smile, he reached for the ouzo bottle and topped up everyone's glass.

"To new life," he said, raising his glass.

A MONTH LATER, Claudia rubbed her eyes as she, at last, ended a phone call with one of the show's most experienced directors. It was Monday night, and she'd spent the past two hours talking the woman out of resigning over a disagreement she'd had with their production manager. Now she had to call the other woman and convince her not to resign, also. The joy of working with volatile creatives.

She was reaching for the phone again when someone whisked it out of her reach. She glanced up to find Sadie hovering over her desk, the receiver clutched to her chest. Rather incongruously, she also held a stack of plates and a fistful of cutlery. Grace stood in the doorway behind her holding two carrier bags that gave off the distinct aroma of takeaway Chinese food, and Claudia realized she was about to be on the receiving end of an intervention.

"No more work," Sadie said bossily, proving Claudia's theory. "It's seven, and it's time to stop."

"Guys, I need to call Sally-Anne before she takes a job with someone else," Claudia said wearily.

She'd been feeling so tired lately. Partly because she was having trouble sleeping, but also because she just wasn't getting the same kick out of work that she used to.

"Sally-Anne is not leaving this show, she loves it more than her own children and she would go insane if she didn't have us all to boss around. Let her wait until tomorrow and then she'll feel a bit stupid about what happened and all will be well," Grace said, unpacking the bags and laying out a daunting array of boxes.

"Good Lord, did you buy the whole restaurant?" Claudia asked.

"Some of us are eating for two," Sadie said, patting the cutest baby bump the world had ever seen. From behind, she didn't look as though she were pregnant at all, but her belly had popped out in a gentle bump in the last two weeks.

"And some of us aren't eating at all," Grace said meaningfully.

Claudia frowned and shifted some paperwork around on her desk.

"I'm eating," she said defensively.

"Not enough. So here's the deal—either you eat, or you talk to us. One or the other, although to be honest we'd love you to do both," Grace said. "We're worried about you."

"There's no need to worry about me. I'm fine, more than fine," Claudia said.

"Bullshit," Grace said, pulling up a chair.

"You're a bag of bones, Claud," Sadie said, prying the lid off a container of steamed rice. "How much weight have you lost?"

"I don't know. I haven't weighed myself in months. I've just been busy, that's all."

"You've been throwing yourself into work like a

complete obsessive, running yourself into the ground. We all know this is about Leandro, and if you still don't want to talk about it, that's fine—but you have to eat," Grace said.

Sadie shoveled rice, kung pao chicken and beef in black bean sauce onto a plate and pushed it toward Claudia. Claudia's stomach rumbled and she picked up a fork. It wasn't that she had no appetite, or that she hadn't been eating. It was more that she could only eat so much. A few mouthfuls, and she'd had enough. But she knew that was not going to satisfy her friends tonight.

"Have you heard from him at all?" Sadie asked.

Claudia stiffened. "Look, this is all very sweet, guys, but I'm not hung up on Leandro, okay?"

Even as she said it she could feel a blush rising into her cheeks. She'd never been good at lying to her two best friends. Ever since she'd met Grace and Sadie at the University of California Los Angeles all those years ago, they'd been the ones she turned to in good times and bad. No one knew her like these two women.

Neither Sadie or Grace called her on her lie, however. For a moment there was just the clink of cutlery on plates as they ate in silence, then Claudia put her fork down and sighed heavily. A part of her wanted to talk, even though she was afraid of how much pain she'd been holding inside her. She'd expected to walk away from her fling to Leandro and get on with her life. That's what she'd always done in the past. But he had touched something inside her, made her dream dreams she hadn't even known she'd wanted.

"I haven't spoken to him. Haven't seen him, nothing. Which is what I wanted. And, anyway, it didn't end too well. He was angry with me, and I got angry back."

Picking up her fork again, she pushed her food around

on her plate, getting mad all over again as she recalled his parting words to her.

"He said I was a coward because I didn't want to have a relationship that I already knew was doomed to failure. I was doing the smart thing for both of us, and he just couldn't see it," she said hotly.

"Why was it the right thing, Claud?" Grace asked quietly.

Claudia stared into Grace's clear green eyes.

"Because it had no future. You guys know me. I don't want marriage and kids and a house in the suburbs."

Sadie made an unconvinced noise.

"What's that supposed to mean?" Claudia asked.

"It means I think you want to love and be loved just as much as everyone else in the world. But you think your childhood makes you a bad risk," Sadie said.

"I *know* it does. You guys have met my mother," Claudia said, feeling distinctly under attack. Sadie and Grace knew all the things she'd been through—hell, hadn't they walked the streets with her just weeks ago, looking for her mother?

"You're not your mother, Claudia," Grace said.

"But I could be. She had a career before she met my father. Then they got married, and the babies came, and she fell apart. She hated being at home. She couldn't handle us kids. And she felt she'd given up too much to be a wife and mother. So she drank. And she never stopped."

"Who's to say the same thing will happen to you? You've had a completely different life from your mother's. You're more educated, more affluent, you don't drink *at all*, Claudia. And you're self-aware, you know what the issues are. Don't all those things mean you have the best chance in the world of not being like your mother?" Grace said.

"And what if they're not enough? What if there's some gene that's just waiting to switch on inside me, or some innate, subconscious learning I took in with my mother's breast milk? What if it's just *in* me, like it was in her?"

A hundred ugly memories rushed up to haunt her—the time Talia had flown into an alcohol-induced rage and screamed at her and her brothers until they all cowered in the corner, scared of the banshee who had once been their mother. The time her mother had insulted her and told her off in public because Claudia had dared to move the wine bottle out of her mother's reach. She'd been just thirteen, and the memory burned still. Then there were the many, many times her mother had lain on her bed sobbing uncontrollably for hours, lost in private misery.

Quivering with emotion, Claudia leaned across the desk, her finger stabbing the air to emphasize her point. "I will *never, ever* put children in that situation, do you hear me? I never want another kid to go through what George and Cosmo and I had to go through," Claudia said, her voice breaking. "Never."

Tears threatened, but she choked them back. It would be so much easier if she hated her mother. But she didn't. She loved her with all her heart for the gentle times between her despair and her rages. The elaborate cakes she'd baked for birthdays, the games she used to play with them, her insistence in believing that if Claudia wanted to be a producer, she could make it, despite the odds. She loved her mother desperately—which was why it hurt so much every time Talia let them all down.

Springing up from her chair, Sadie rounded the desk to rub Claudia's back.

"We didn't mean to upset you, Claud," she said softly.

"We love you more than anything, you know that. We just want you to be happy," Grace said.

"I am happy," Claudia said.

There was a speaking silence for a beat.

"Okay, I'm miserable at the moment, but I'll get over it," Claudia conceded. " I fell in love with the wrong man. I knew I was doing it, but I still let it happen. And I miss him. I miss him so much my skin aches with it."

She closed her eyes as she thought of the dreams she'd had where she was with Leandro again, lying in his big arms. She'd forced herself out of each and every one of them—the reason her sleep pattern had gone to the dogs— but it didn't stop them from coming.

"Claud, I know you think breaking the cycle is about not having kids, not having a family, but maybe that's the wrong way to look at it. Maybe breaking the cycle is about doing all those things, but making sure that your kids never know what it's like to live like that," Grace said.

Claudia felt a thrill of fear, followed by a surge of anger.

"And whose lives am I gambling with? Children can't choose their parents. They're utterly defenseless. What if I'm not strong enough, like my mother? Who pays the price then?" she asked.

Grace and Sadie both looked a little pale, and Claudia realized she'd been yelling.

"Sorry. I'm tired, and you're right, I haven't been looking after myself. I'm just going to go home and get a good night's sleep," Claudia said, running a hand through her hair.

Without saying a word, Grace started to scrape Claudia's virtually untouched meal into one of the take-away containers.

"It's not pretty, but it will taste just the same," she said as she handed the box over to Claudia. "We had a deal remember—talk or eat."

Claudia dredged up a smile. Even when she was being stubborn and horrible and incommunicative, these women still loved her.

"I'll eat it, I promise."

They all stood, and Claudia gave them each a fierce hug.

"You're the best, and I'm sorry for being such a psycho at the moment. I'll be fine."

Sadie and Grace both nodded, and Claudia grabbed her handbag, briefcase and the Chinese food then escaped to her car.

Only when she was alone did she let her shoulders sag. She felt so...*alone* at the moment. Despite her friends. Despite filling every waking moment with work. Leandro had shown her how it could be—how it felt to never be alone, even when that other person wasn't physically with her. He'd filled all the empty places in her heart and her life and now that he was gone, she was painfully aware of all that was missing.

Knowing that Sadie and Grace would be walking out to their cars any minute, also, Claudia forced herself to pull it together. She'd been strong all her life. She wasn't going to fall in a heap now.

Her thoughts shifted to her mother as she pulled out into the traffic. Talia had surprised the world and listened to her doctors when she recovered from her alcoholic binge. She'd been receiving treatment at a residential rehabilitation center for three weeks now. Part of the process required that she have no visitors for the first two weeks, and last week her father had gone to see her for the first time. Her brother George reported that her father had been shaken by the experience—apparently Talia had been edgy and easily agitated, nothing like her usual self. The fact that her usual self was usually well-sedated thanks to several glasses of strong drink was something that they'd both left unsaid. As usual.

But her mother was in treatment. Even though Claudia had taught herself not to care, not to believe in second chances where her mother was concerned, there was a tiny part of her soul holding its breath in hope. If only…

She shook her head as she stopped at a traffic light in West Hollywood. She was so stupid, so ready to step on the roller coaster ride of faith and betrayal again. How many times would she have to get slapped in the face by the same reality before she learned to duck?

The sound of laughter drew her attention to the sidewalk seating of a popular eatery to her right. It was a warm night, and the tables were overflowing with Los Angelenos filling up on cool drinks and fancy food. Claudia thought of her Chinese takeaway and the empty house she was going home to. She really had to make an effort to pull herself out of the doldrums. She wasn't a wallower, and it was time to stop acting like one.

Her eye was caught by the colorful shimmer of a bright pink and turquoise summer dress on a dark-haired woman weaving her way through the outdoor tables. Claudia looked down ruefully at her own black-on-black ensemble. Maybe she should think about breaking out of her little black box, also.

Still waiting for the light to change, she idly followed the sway of the other woman's hips as she walked. The man waiting for her stood politely as she approached, and a lurch of adrenaline kicked into Claudia's belly as she recognized him.

It was Leandro. Leandro, out with another woman. Claudia's gaze darted to the woman again, taking in the olive skin, the long curly dark hair, the sexy figure. Jealousy ripped through her like a knife. She wanted to get out of the car, stride across the sidewalk and forcibly drag the woman away.

Claudia shot her gaze back to him, greedily taking in his easy smile, the charming tilt of his head as he asked his dinner companion something, how broad his shoulders looked in a crisp white shirt.

The angry honk of a car horn rocketed her from her trance. The light had changed. Some time ago, she guessed, since the guy behind her was swearing and giving her the finger. She pressed her foot down on the accelerator reflexively, sending the Cayenne racing out into the intersection with a burst of noisy speed.

Leandro had moved on. It was time for her to do the same.

10

LEANDRO GLANCED away from the woman sitting opposite him and out into the street, his attention drawn first by the belligerent honk of a horn, then the overzealous revving of a car engine. Personally, he hated dining in sidewalk cafes at busy intersections, but his date had chosen the venue and the table so he was playing nice. His whole body went on alert as he caught a glimpse of the tail end of a silver Porsche Cayenne disappearing across the intersection.

He hadn't caught the number plate, but it might have been Claudia. His thigh muscles bunched, ready to propel him to his feet and out into the street so he could get a better look—then he realized what he was doing. Did it matter if it was Claudia? Not at all, was the correct answer. The sensible, sane answer.

He hadn't seen her, heard her voice, spoken her name for more than four weeks. And tonight he was out with another woman—Stella Diodorus, to be exact. Who was very attractive, very warm, very nice. If he played his cards right, he might even stand a chance of getting invited back for coffee after dinner, if he was reading the attraction in her brown eyes correctly.

If only he wanted to play his cards right. The truth was, he wasn't interested in any woman who wasn't Claudia.

And, truly, that was the most unmanning aspect of being a forlorn, love-crossed idiot—he'd gone from having earth-shattering, bone-jarring, back-clawing sex with a women he adored to nothing. Zero. Zilch. And because he couldn't muster so much as half a hard-on for anyone else, he was pretty much stuck in limbo-land, never to be satisfied by the woman he wanted, not able to get off with anyone else because he just wasn't interested. Talk about a vicious circle.

Because he felt like such a grade-A turd to be thinking about Claudia while he was out with Stella, Leandro flashed his dinner companion a big smile and reapplied himself to their conversation with renewed zest.

"So now you're fully qualified, what next?" he asked, picking up on the comment Stella had made before the ghost of Claudia had cast its shadow over their meal. Well, his meal, anyway.

"I have to wait for my results first, but then I'll start looking for a teaching position. The school I did some of my training at said they were keen to have me back, but we'll see if they're prepared to put their money where their mouth is," Stella said, breaking a bread stick in two and nibbling on the end.

He forced himself to concentrate on how attractive she was—the smoothness of her skin, the fullness of her plump mouth, the gentle sparkle in her eyes. She'd turned heads when she returned from the powder room, and he knew there were plenty of guys sitting around him right now who wouldn't mind trading places with him.

"So you like teaching more than being a beautician?" he asked.

She screwed up her nose at him.

"Are you kidding? Why do you think I just slogged

through six years of night school? If I never do another manicure in my life I will die a happy woman," Stella said expressively.

"You know, I've often thought that being a producer is a bit like being a teacher," Leandro said.

"Yeah, how?" Stella asked, her half-smile indicating she was prepared to be entertained.

"Well, basically the show is like a big classroom. You've got the actors—they're the popular kids. Then there's the geeks and jocks, otherwise known as the crew. And finally there's the sensitive outsiders, the writers. Sometimes they all get along really well, and other times it's anarchy and I have to hand out a few detentions," he said.

Stella laughed and ate some more bread stick.

"You know, I have no idea what a producer actually does. I mean, I know I live in L.A. and that's almost sacrilegious, but whenever you see the credits at the end of a show, there are about a million producers. They can't all run the show, right?"

Leandro spent the next ten minutes giving her breakdown on the different kinds of producers that were typically involved in a television production.

"…but, of course, I'm the only one who counts," he said as he finished his one-man tour of the industry.

Stella laughed.

"You've got a good sense of humor, Leandro," she said.

Why did his thoughts instantly divert to Claudia? Why did he suddenly remember how funny *she* was, how sassy and cheeky and daring?

If he thought he could get away with it, he'd give himself a slap on the side of the head. He wanted Claudia out of his mind, his memories, his heart. He wanted his libido back. He wanted to look forward instead of back.

"What did you want to order?" he said. "I was thinking of the lasagna."

"I love lasagna," Stella said. "Will you think I'm a terrible copycat if I have it, too?"

"I will, but I'll try to hide it," he said, tongue-in-cheek.

For a moment she stared at him, then she got it.

"See, you are *so* funny," she said, cracking up again.

She was a nice woman. If tonight went okay, he was going to ask her out again. He made the resolution on the spot. He might not be on fire for her the way he had been with Claudia, but he was still recovering from having his fingers spectacularly burned. Maybe fire wasn't all it was cracked up to be at the end of the day, anyway.

BECAUSE SHE'D promised Sadie and Grace that she would eat, Claudia dutifully nuked the Chinese food in her microwave when she got home and sat in front of the TV chewing mechanically on whatever happened to wind up on the fork whenever she stuck it in the box. By the time she'd hit her limit, she'd put a sizeable dint in the huge portion Grace had packed her. She figured that covered her obligation to her friends, and dumped the rest in the trash.

She couldn't stop thinking about Leandro and the Other Woman. About what would happen when they left the restaurant. Would he drive back to her place and make love to her? Or would he be so worked up, so hot for it that they'd do it in the car, the way she and Leandro had on more than one occasion? Maybe he'd take her back to his place and wash her slowly in his big, deep tub. And maybe then he'd lay her out on his bed and use his tongue and hands to send her thundering toward climax again and again and again.

Claudia was caught between being aroused at the sensual memories she was reliving and nauseated by the thought of him touching another woman. God, she hadn't even looked at another man in the past month, let alone gone on a date. So much for him loving her, wanting to have a future with her.

Realizing how screwed up her logic was, she groaned out loud and switched the television off. No man had ever turned her life upside down the way Leandro Mandalor had. He'd rampaged in, shaken her up, and then left her reeling. And here she was, four weeks later, still staggering around trying to work out which way was up.

A feeling that only intensified when she began preparations for bed. Brushing her teeth at the vanity, she opened a drawer to search for floss and caught sight of the full pack of tampons she'd bought last week in preparation for her period.

And never used.

Because her period had never come.

Her hand froze mid-brush, toothpaste dripping down her front as she did a mental check. She'd been due last week, and it was now Thursday of the following week.

She was late. A week late. She was *never* late. Ever.

Spitting the toothpaste out in a flurry of panic, Claudia gave her mouth a half-assed rinse and strode out into the living room to grab her briefcase. Leafing frantically back through her diary, she stared at the small red cross she'd placed in her diary six weeks previously.

She was definitely late.

She closed her eyes as a wave of nausea swept over her. A memory flashed across her closed eyelids—Leandro coming home from his three days in New York, the two of them not even making it past the foyer before they dropped to the floor to make love. Without a condom. Her own words sounded in her head: *I'm safe.*

Apparently not.

On top of discovering that Leandro was seeing someone else, the realization that she could, in fact, be pregnant was the final encouragement her stomach needed. Hand pressed to her mouth, she barely made it to the kitchen sink before she threw up.

Rinsing her mouth out afterwards, she tried to calm her crazily circling thoughts.

The first thing to do was to confirm that she actually had something to throw up about. Snatching up her car keys and purse, she shot out the door. She was so harried she couldn't remember the location of the nearest late-night drugstore, and she drove twenty minutes in the wrong direction before she remembered there was one near her house. Inside, the fluorescent lighting was too bright, the aisles too long, the signage incomprehensible. The last thing she wanted to do was ask for help, however, and she finally tracked down the right aisle through a process of elimination.

Another daunting task awaited her—choosing a pregnancy test. There were no less than six brands on offer, and she glared at them, resenting the world for making this situation even more stressful than it needed to be. Swearing under her breath, she snatched the nearest one and took it to the register. It wasn't until she was back home, her heart beating a rapid, panicky tattoo against her breastbone, that she read the back of the pack and realized she would have to wait until morning to do the test.

"Shit," she said, throwing the box across the room in frustration.

Immediately she dashed across to inspect the contents of the box for damage. All she needed was to wait all night and then find out that her temper tantrum had rendered the stupid test unusable.

As far as she could tell she hadn't broken anything, and she placed the box carefully on her kitchen counter and spent the next fifteen minutes reading the simple instructions over and over. In a nutshell, all she had to do was wake up in the morning and pee on a stick. Not rocket science.

It was the results that were going to be hard to take. If she was pregnant.

If she was pregnant, she would have a termination, she told herself briskly. There was no question about it. Hell, it wasn't even an issue. Right? Just so she'd have all the information at her fingertips tomorrow morning, she grabbed the phone book and looked up the location and number of the nearest family planning clinic.

Then she booted up her home computer and spent an hour surfing the net, checking up on any health issues she should know about. But it all seemed pretty straightforward. Day surgery, in and out. She'd need a single day off work. No one would need to know. No one like Leandro, for example.

This last thought resounded in her mind as she stripped down to her panties and pulled on an oversize T-shirt for bed.

As soon as she settled beneath the quilt and closed her eyes, her thoughts went to the one place she'd resolutely refused to let them go.

She might be pregnant with Leandro's baby. Unbidden,

an image popped into her mind's eye—a little boy with big dark brown eyes, curly black hair and a mischievous smile.

She erased the image through an act of will and rolled onto her side, punching her pillow into shape. If only it were as easy to pummel her thoughts into submission.

She didn't want children. They'd never been a part of her plans. She'd spent half an hour tonight explaining exactly why she couldn't—wouldn't—have children to Sadie and Grace. End of debate, discussion over.

All she wanted was to go to sleep and wake up and be able to know for sure one way or the other. Instead, for the next few hours she lay staring at the ceiling, her thoughts and stomach churning. She thought about Leandro and the beautiful woman. She thought about her mother. She pressed her hands to her breasts and tried to decide if they were tender or if she was just imagining it.

For a while, she seriously considered going back to the drugstore to buy a test she could use immediately, but by then it was so late she figured she only had a few more hours to wait until she could legitimately call it morning.

She must have eventually drifted off to sleep, because she woke with a jerk when she heard a car door slam out in the street and saw that it was nearly seven in the morning. Her dreams had been a disturbing muddle that she didn't want to examine too closely. She didn't want to examine anything too closely. She just wanted to find out the truth, and get on with doing what had to be done.

Adrenaline racing through her body, she reread the instructions just to make sure that she hadn't forgotten anything. She hadn't—peeing on a stick was still the order of the day.

Hands shaking, she padded back into the bathroom,

removed the test stick from its wrapper, pulled down her underwear and sat on the toilet. She was about to get down to business when she registered the blood on her underwear.

She had her period.

She'd just been late.

She wasn't pregnant with Leandro's baby.

Out of nowhere, a flood of tears washed up and over her, taking her utterly by surprise. Sitting on the toilet, pants around her ankles, she tasted the bitter irony of the moment.

Because she wasn't crying with relief—she was crying with *disappointment*.

"God, you're such an idiot!" she sobbed into her hands.

She'd had her bluff called in the most spectacular of ways—and been busted for the fraud she was.

Deep down inside, she wanted children. She craved a family. She wanted all the warmth of hearth and home that her brothers enjoyed.

Beneath the bravado, beneath the fear, she wanted it all. Worse, she wanted it with Leandro, the man she'd rejected, the man who was now dating another woman because Claudia had sent him packing.

He'd been right about her from day one—she was a coward. She'd been so scared of having the same weaknesses as her mother that she hadn't been prepared to take the leap of faith. All her posturing about how different she was from her mother, how independent she was, all her bravado and tough talk—all just part and parcel of her running scared from the real challenges of life.

Grace had said it last night. Breaking the cycle wasn't about not having children—it was about having them and ensuring they never knew what it was like to have an alcoholic for a mother. Because wasn't Claudia paying the ultimate price for her mother's illness if she curtailed her life's experiences out of fear?

"Talk about a screwup," she said to her bare knees. "Way to go, Einstein."

Dragging a loop of toilet paper off the roll, she blew her nose noisily and mopped at her eyes. Pulling off her T-shirt, she stepped into the shower and scrubbed away the last remnants of years of self-delusion.

The woman she saw in the mirror afterward looked chastened and scared and angry at herself. And she was—because she'd blown it big-time. She'd had the love of an amazing man and all the ingredients for a lifetime of happiness and contentment. And she'd stuffed it up. She'd cut Leandro loose, and pushed him into the hands of a voluptuous siren.

Hands down, it was the dumbest thing she'd ever done. And the truly terrible thing was, she'd have a lifetime to regret it.

LEANDRO WAS TAKING his first mouthful of coffee for the day when his publicity head rapped on his open office door.

"We've got a problem," Michael said, looking grim. He held out an unlabelled CD-ROM. "I've just burned this off the Net, you need to see it."

A tickle of prescience raised the hairs on the back of Leandro's neck. He had a feeling that he already knew what was on the disk. The wonder was that it had taken this long to gain notoriety.

Keeping his face carefully blank, Leandro inserted the disk into his computer and waited for the media player to pop up. The sounds of a man and a woman having sex filled his ears before the image came on screen, and he knew his fears had been justified.

Wes and Alicia's bedroom antics had gone public. A veritable shit storm was about to rain down on *Heartlands* and *Ocean Boulevard*. And, insanely, his first thought was for how he could protect Claudia from the worst of it. He shook off the impulse impatiently, angry with himself. Claudia was tough. She'd just shown him exactly how tough and cool she could be. She didn't need him to protect her.

"She's eighteen, right?" Michael asked worriedly. "Please tell me she looks eighteen."

"She's seventeen, I'm pretty sure," Leandro said.

Michael peered more closely at the screen.

"Are you sure? I think we can sell her as eighteen," he said.

Leandro opened his mouth to tell Michael that it would be hard to dispute the actress's well-known birth date but stopped as a thought suddenly occurred to him.

"Do we know who she is?" he asked carefully.

"Some bimbo with great tits, same old, same old." Michael shrugged. "The important thing is how we spin this. We need to get Wes in, get our stories straight, and handle this right."

Leandro stared at his PR guru for a second, then turned back to the video footage and tried to look at it through new eyes. He couldn't quite believe that Michael hadn't recognized Alicia. It was true that what she was doing on camera was almost in direct opposition to the way she normally appeared to the world. But was it really enough to ensure that no one else would recognize her either?

He decided to test his theory a little.

"I don't know, I think she looks a little familiar," he said slowly.

Michael stared at the screen again. "Blond, big boobs, nice ass—she looks like every other wannabe in town," he said dismissively.

For a moment Leandro was gripped with an utterly in-appropriate urge to laugh. All the trouble he and Claudia had gone to, to ensure this footage never saw the light of day, and Alicia Morrison was apparently unrecognizable. With only one star in the offing, the footage became a hell of a lot less titillating. In fact, he was willing to bet that Wes's reputation would only receive a boost from distribution of the scenes. After all, he was only doing what most guys dreamed of doing—making it with a gorgeous girl. A gorgeous, anonymous girl. If they played this right, there'd be no trading off the fact that *Ocean Boulevard* and *Heartlands* were in opposition, no fuss made about the known disparity in Wes and Alicia's ages. The story would still be tabloid-worthy, of course, but it would be a flash in the pan, over in a day or two. In a few months' time, Wes would join the ranks of Tommy Lee, Rob Lowe and Charlie Sheen as a bona fide pants man.

Getting a grip on his wayward sense of humor, Leandro reached for the phone. Wes was scheduled to be on set this afternoon, so he was probably already in makeup or lounging in his dressing room. His finger poised to dial, Leandro looked up at Michael. The less anyone knew of the truth, the better.

"You should go start on a statement. I'll break the news to Wes," he said.

Michael nodded his understanding and strode out the door, a man on a mission. Rising to shut the door for privacy, Leandro dialed Wes's extension.

To his credit, Wes sounded disturbed by the idea that Alicia was about to become tabloid fodder.

"She's a nice lady," Wes said in his soft Texas drawl once Leandro had filled him in on the situation.

Leandro averted his eyes from the not-very-ladylike pose Alicia had assumed on-screen.

"I think we can weather this if we just play it cool," Leandro said. "Most people are going to find it hard to re- concile who they think Alicia is with what's on that tape. If anyone makes the leap, we'll just deny it. When it's just about you, this will be a two-day story and die a natural death. Think you can do that?"

"Are you kidding? I'm an actor, man," Wes said confi- dently. "I lie for a living."

Satisfied that Wes's end of things was covered, Leandro ended the call and picked up his cell phone. He'd never actually got around to deleting Claudia's numbers from his phone memory, and he had her number on screen in a blink.

He was about to press speed dial when he realized what he was doing—protecting her. Going out of his way to shield her despite the fact that five minutes ago he'd just decided she could fend for herself.

There was only one word for it: *pathetic.*

Despite his misgivings, his finger descended on the button. He couldn't help himself. For good or for ill, he wanted to help her. Probably that made him a sap, and hearing her voice would probably set him back four weeks in recovery time, but he was powerless to resist the urge.

Sir-bloody-Galahad, he thought sourly. *Gallant to the death.*

"CLAUDIA."

Her hand convulsed around the phone receiver as she recognized the low bass of Leandro's voice.

"Leandro," she said, her voice shaky. She almost dropped the phone as she tried to loosen her death grip.

After the epiphany she'd had this morning, hearing his voice was almost too much.

"We have a problem, but I'm calling to let you know I think we've got it covered," he said. "Wes and Alicia are on the Internet."

"No," Claudia breathed. This was the last thing she needed right now. Hadn't life thrown enough crap at her lately?

"Relax. Like I said, I think we've got it covered. My PR guru Michael is the one who brought it in. He has no idea it's Alicia," Leandro said.

Claudia was so busy savoring every low syllable that came from his mouth that she almost missed the meaning of his words.

"What, you mean…you mean he didn't recognize her?" she asked.

"That's right. I hinted around a bit to see if he would twig, and he didn't. And this guy is a PR mastermind. He knows everyone, keeps on top of all the gossip. If he doesn't recognize Alicia, I think we've got a solid case for denying her involvement, should her name ever come up. If we stick to the line, no one will ever know for sure if it's her or not."

Claudia frowned. "That's very generous of you," she said.

He was doing her a favor. A big one. It was the last thing she'd expected of him given the way they'd broken up.

"Alicia's just a babe in the woods. And Wes is keen to protect her," he said offhandedly.

The small flare of hope in Claudia's heart wavered at his cool tone. She reminded herself that she'd seen him out with a beautiful woman last night. She'd had her chance and blown it.

"I take it you'll be working with Wes to release a statement?" Claudia said.

"We'll wait till it makes the tabloids first. There's no point handing the story over on a silver platter. We might get lucky still and the tabloids miss it altogether."

They both knew that was highly unlikely, however. The tabloids fed off scandal; it was their bread and butter. They had people trawling the Web constantly, looking for gossip, innuendo, images.

"I really appreciate this, Leandro. And I know Alicia will thank you on bended knee," she said.

"It's best for all of us this way."

There was an awkward silence. Because she wanted to stretch the moment, she stumbled into speech.

"How, um, are your parents? Is your mom still happy with her new haircut?" she asked, wincing as she heard how awkward she sounded.

"They're well, and she loves it."

"And Dom and Betty?" she asked, closing her eyes so she could concentrate on his voice and allow the memories to wash over her.

His deep, rolling laugh. The wicked glint in his eye. The gentleness and compassion in his touch. The hungry need of his body.

"Betty's good and the babies are doing fine," he said.

She frowned.

"I thought they weren't due for another month or so?" she asked.

"They came early. Seven weeks early, in fact. It was a bit scary there for a while, but they're thriving now."

"Well, that's good," she said lamely. Dom must have been beside himself. All of them must have been—they were a close-knit family, and she knew without actually being there that they would have pulled together.

She'd run out of questions, bar the most important one.

"And how are you?" she asked, her voice almost breaking on the last word.

There was a profound silence on the other end of the line, then she heard a deep sigh.

"I'd better go deal with this situation," he said.

"Sure. Okay. Thanks again for what you're doing. I owe you one," she said.

"Goodbye, Claudia."

She sat holding the phone for a long time after the call ended. She needed to call Alicia and alert her to the state of play. No doubt the young girl would be hysterical at the news that she was about to become an Internet porn star, incognito or not.

But all Claudia could think about was Leandro, and that silence when she'd asked him how he was.

Last night and this morning, she'd been so sure that she'd burned her bridges with him beyond all repair. Who would want to take on someone so messed up, after all, great sex or no great sex, love or no love?

But he hadn't answered her question. Which meant…what, exactly? The rational, cynical part of her brain told her it meant nothing. He might be distracted at work—she *knew* he was distracted, he had a looming crisis on his hands. And there was always the chance that he felt awkward about mentioning he was seeing someone else.

Or he might not be over her.

Which meant that maybe she hadn't ruined her life, after all.

Grabbing the phone, she buzzed Grace's office.

"Grab Sadie and get in here. I need help," she said briefly before slamming the phone down.

All of a sudden, the dull, heavy feeling that had been dogging her for the past four weeks was gone. She felt energized, invigorated. She'd stuffed things up royally with Leandro. She'd been dishonest with herself and him, and she'd been so crippled by the hurts from her past that she'd been too scared to have a full life of her own.

But she'd always risen to the challenges in her life. She'd insisted on joining the girls' basketball team in junior high, even though she was so short the coach had laughed in her face. She'd practiced her jump shot for hours until she became the highest scorer on the team. When the production company she'd been working for straight out of high school had folded, she'd reimagined her career trajectory and applied for a placement at UCLA, lobbying the dean of students until he gave her what she wanted.

She had always been a fighter. But lately, it felt like she'd forgotten how.

That was about to change, because she'd never wanted something this much in all her life.

THE FOLLOWING SATURDAY, Leandro stretched out his calves and hamstrings, the sun beating down fiercely on his back.

Beside him, Dom was doing jumping jacks—his version of a warm-up prior to them tackling the fire trails of Griffith Park.

"It's going to get pretty hot," Leandro said. "Maybe we should take one of the lower trails, take it easy?"

Dom gave a meow and pretended to claw at the air.

"What's that supposed to mean?" Leandro asked, although he had a fair idea what his brother was inferring.

"It means you're a pussy. You're afraid that I'm going to beat you again now that I'm getting some form," Dom said.

Leandro smirked. He ran four days a week. To his knowledge, the only time Dom got his heart rate above ninety was when he raced into the kitchen to grab the cookie jar.

"You been training in private?" Leandro asked.

"No."

"So coming here with me is the only exercise you get?"

"That's right."

Leandro grinned. "Let's see what you've got, Junior."

"Don't call me that. You know I hate it," Dom said as they broke into a jog.

"Exactly," Leandro said.

Dom shot him an annoyed look and Leandro laughed. It felt like the first genuine laugh he'd had in weeks. Ever since Claudia, there hadn't been many reasons to feel that good.

"How'd your date go with Stella?" Dom asked, his face already red from exertion.

"She's nice."

"Gonna ask her out again?"

"Maybe. Probably."

"She's wrong for you, you know," Dom puffed.

Leandro did a double take. "Excuse me? Are you not the guy who was practically pimping this woman to me? *Handpicked by people who love you.* I believe those were your words."

"Yeah, but we decided that you did a much better job handpicking your own woman," Dom said.

Leandro remained silent, knowing Dom was talking about Claudia. Dom had been probing for weeks to find out what had caused the breakup.

"If you could get her back, would you?" Dom asked.

"It's not a matter of anyone getting anyone. We want

completely different things. Sometimes loving someone isn't enough."

"So you do still love her?" Dom gasped, really struggling now as they neared the highest peak in the fire trail.

"I swear, you're breast-feeding those kids alongside Betty, aren't you?" Leandro said. "Since when did you turn into such a gossip?"

"Answer…the…question," Dom wheezed.

"Yes. I still love her. Happy? Now you know what a miserable sap I am," Leandro said as they arrived at the crest.

He stopped in his tracks when he saw who was standing there. Wordless, he turned to Dom.

"Did you…?" he asked, but Dom just grinned and waved.

"See you later, Senior," he said, taking off down the fire trail.

Leandro turned to face Claudia.

"Hi," she said. She gave him a tight little smile.

"What are you doing here?" he asked.

God, she looked good, like all his fantasies rolled into one delicious body. Black leggings covered her small, slim legs, and she wore a bright red tank top with some sort of high-tech sports bra peeking out beneath it. She didn't look as though she'd been running, however. She looked cool as a cucumber. And sexy. Very, very sexy.

"Dom told me you'd be here today," she said.

He'd already guessed that part. The question was, why was she here?

Wiping sweat from his eyes, he tried to stop himself from visually feasting on her. It had been so long, too long. She'd lost weight, he registered as he scanned her again. She looked smaller, more delicate. But her eyes were blazing with the same energy that had always captivated him, and her mouth was as full and sensuous as always and her breasts looked as touchable and desirable as they'd ever been.

"I wanted to talk to you. This seemed like a good place to get a few things out in the open. Do you want some water?" she asked.

She was nervous. He'd never seen her nervous before. He found it…very endearing.

Quickly he reminded himself of the facts of their situation. As much as it had burned him up that she'd drawn a line under their relationship, in his gut he knew she'd done the right thing. There could be no lasting future between two people with such disparate dreams in life.

Still, he took the cold bottle she passed him and swallowed half of it in one long glug. Then he dropped the bottle to his side and eyed her neutrally.

"What did you want to get out in the open?" he asked.

She took a deep breath, glanced over his shoulder at the sprawl of Hollywood below, then met his eye dead-on.

"My mother is an alcoholic, has been ever since I was a child," she said boldly. "She was a bazouki player back in Greece, one of the few successful women players. Then she met my father, and they married and came to America. I don't know if she hated it here, if she felt isolated or if she simply hated being at home all the time with us kids. But she started to drink. And, I guess, she couldn't stop."

She was wringing her hands together, even though she still held his eye. He could see the tension in her small frame, knew how hard this was for her.

"She doesn't talk about it, but her mother used to drink, too, I know. Maybe she didn't know any better. Or maybe she had no control over it. Either way, it was a bad way to grow up. Either she was crying and threatening suicide, or she was raging and throwing things and yelling at us. Then there would be times when she didn't drink, and we all would think that it was over. But she had no control over it, and she always started again. Always.

"I spent my childhood cleaning up after her, covering for her from my dad until I realized that he knew, and he loved her anyway. He did his best to shield us, but he was too proud to ever ask anyone else for help."

She took another deep breath, smoothing her hands down the front of her thighs.

"I'm not telling you this because I want you to feel sorry for me, but because I don't want there to be any more secrets between us. My mother is an alcoholic, and all my life I have been terrified that I would end up just like her, the way she has ended up like her mother. Everything I do has been predicated on me walking outside of her footsteps. But only the other day did I realize that I was denying myself one of the most fulfilling, amazing experiences a person can have because of my fear of what I might become."

He took a step toward her as he saw that she was crying. Big, fat tears that rolled down her cheeks unheeded.

"Leandro, I thought I was pregnant. I thought I was going to have your baby. And it was only then that I realized I wanted it more than anything in the world. That I wanted you and everything you had offered me. I thought I'd blown it, but then the thing with the tape came back to bite us on the ass and I wondered…"

She trailed to a halt then, wiping the tears away with her hands.

"I wondered if you still loved me enough to give me a second chance," she asked in a small, uncertain voice.

He felt as though he'd been punched in the gut. All of

it—her story, her pain, her revelation about the baby that might have been, her tremulous question. He couldn't believe it. He couldn't believe that the one thing he wanted more than anything in all the world was actually within his reach.

"Are you freakin' kidding?" he asked incredulously, then he lunged forward and scooped her into his arms.

She felt so good pressed against him, so precious, that he just lay his cheek against the crown of her head and hung on for dear life.

"Are you freakin' kidding?" he repeated in a whisper. "Do you have any idea how much I've thought about you? How hard it's been, knowing you were it, that I was never going to meet someone else like you, but I couldn't have you?"

"I'm so sorry. I'm so dumb. I just didn't get it," she said, her hands clutching at his shoulders. "Leandro, I love you. I love you, and I will never stop loving you. I want to have a family with you. I want to be part of your family. I want everything we can have together, everything."

"Yes," he said simply, and then he kissed her.

Between them they tasted of salty sweat and tears, and he'd never tasted anything better in his life. Angling her head backward, he slid his tongue into her mouth and reminded himself of the heaven that lay within. Her tongue danced with his, mated, teased, challenged. Her hands slid up and down his back, then down onto his butt as she strained toward him.

Groaning low in his throat, hard as a rock after a month of being a dead man below the waist, he cupped her butt with his hands and lifted her against his erection.

"Sweetheart, it is so great to see you, but you chose one helluva spot for a reunion," he said against her ear.

She laughed, her body vibrating with the sound. Then she slid away from him and pointed to a backpack and blanket lying near the edge of the trail.

"A little presumptuous, I know. But a girl has to hope…" she said.

"She certainly does," he said, moving toward her with intent. "Let's go find somewhere off the beaten track."

They were too impatient to walk far. As soon as they found a halfway clear patch between a circle of dense trees and scrub, Claudia spread the blanket out and tossed her backpack to one side.

He had her in his arms again in a second flat. Sliding his hands into her hair, he kissed her and kissed her, needing the reassurance of knowing that this was happening, that he really was this lucky. Soon kissing was not enough, however, and his hands began to roam, smoothing up her rib cage and onto her breasts, sliding over her butt and between her legs. She murmured and moaned and he felt the damp heat growing between her thighs, even through the fabric of her leggings.

Gaining access to all the areas he needed to touch and taste proved to be a time-consuming task. Her sports bra had about a million clasps and catches, and he had to slide it over her head before he could get his hands and mouth on her breasts. Then she had to toe off her shoes and roll down her leggings before they could get any more intimate.

"Ten points on the blanket, negative five for the sports gear," he growled against her stomach as he nibbled his way down her body.

She just gasped and threaded her fingers through his hair and wrapped her legs around his back.

He wanted to go slow, to make this moment last forever, to ride the realization that he was going to wake up with this woman, hold this woman in his arms, love this woman for the rest of his life. But primitive instinct demanded more. He wanted to take her, claim her, bury himself inside her.

Shucking his running shorts with efficient haste, he centered himself in the cradle of her thighs, the head of his erection probing the moist plumpness of her inner lips.

"Condom," he said instinctively.

She just smiled up at him and lifted her hips. He grinned back at her, then closed his eyes as he slid into the exquisite, wet, tight heat of her.

"I love you," he said as he began to move. "I love you."

"Yes," she breathed.

He figured he had about sixty seconds left in him, between her writhing body, the slick pressure between her thighs, and the four weeks of pent-up need rising inside him. Pumping into her furiously, he sucked a nipple into his mouth and tongued it firmly, savoring her taste and the animal cry she made. He felt her body flex like a bow, and then she threw her head back and he felt her body tighten and release around his.

"I love you," he said between clenched teeth as his own passion rose up to take him. She stared into his eyes, and she pressed her palm against his cheek as he spun off into pleasure, his body shuddering into hers powerfully.

They lay in the dappled sunlight not speaking for a long time afterward, hands soothing each other's bodies, lips meeting for frequent, lingering kisses full of unspoken tenderness and promises.

"I knew the moment I met you that you were trouble," he finally said, pressing a kiss into the nape of her neck.

"Oh yeah? I thought you were trouble, too—my kind of trouble," she said.

When he looked into her eyes, he saw so much love and vulnerability and hope there that it nearly slew him.

"Definitely. The kind of trouble I could handle a lifetime of," he said.

"Deal," she said. She offered him her hand, her mouth quirked into a lopsided smile.

"I think we can do better than that," he said.

And he proceeded to show her how much better.

Epilogue

TAKING a deep breath, Claudia stared at the rustic door in front of her. She felt rather than saw Sadie and Grace join her on the stoop, and knowing they were there for her gave her the courage to knock.

The Safe Ground Residential Treatment Center was situated in Monte Nido in the Hidden Hills area of Calabasas, and the house before them was a rambling mountain home, the sort of house that had been added on to a dozen times over the years. Claudia knew that it accommodated forty patients, all of them alcohol or drug addicts. Her brothers had described the rooms inside to her—the big hall with a Ping-Pong table, old couches and shelves of books, the industrial-sized kitchen staffed by the residents, the rambling backyard full of outdoor seating for visitation day. They hadn't seen the dorms where their mother was sleeping, since those areas of the house were for residents only, but Claudia felt she had a good idea of what to expect from the center itself.

It was her mother she was unsure about.

The door opened, and a slight middle-aged woman gave them an inquisitive smile.

"I'm Claudia Dostis. I'm here to see Talia Dostis," Claudia said.

"You're on our list. Please come in," she said.

It took a few moments for them all to sign in and be taken through the rules. Finally, the woman led them through a series of cool, dim rooms until they reached a door to an outside porch. Stretching out behind the house was a broad expanse of lawn, already littered with other family groupings on visitation.

"Talia, someone to see you," the woman called.

Behind her, Sadie and Grace placed a hand each on her shoulders, silently reassuring her that they were there for her. Leandro had wanted to come, but Claudia didn't want him to meet her mother like this. For the first time in years, she'd allowed herself to believe that her mother might stand a chance at beating her demons, and she wanted Leandro to meet the woman Talia Dostis could have been, should have been.

And, somehow, it felt fitting that Sadie and Grace should be here with her. They'd been through so much together over the years. They were her conscience, her courage, her compassion.

A woman was walking toward them, her steps slow but determined. Claudia stared at the healthy glow of Talia's makeupless skin, noted the clarity of her dark brown eyes, and the fact that her mother no longer had bones poking angles in her skin.

"Claudia," she said.

It had been so long, Claudia didn't know whether to embrace her or not. Her mother seemed equally uncertain. They settled for touching each other's arms, the contact fleeting but genuine.

"I've saved us a table," Talia said.

"We'll wait here," Sadie said quietly as Claudia began to follow her mother.

"You're very welcome to join us," Talia said warmly.

Sadie and Grace just smiled and shook their heads, waving them off. Claudia followed her mother to a rustic picnic bench and chairs in the shade of an old oak tree.

They sat opposite each other and simply stared at each other in silence for a long time, each cataloguing the other's precious features.

"You look well, Mama," Claudia said.

"I feel well, but there's a long way to go," Talia said. "Thank you so much for coming, Claudia. I know how hard I've made it for you to believe in me."

Claudia shrugged uncomfortably. Her mother had been in treatment for nearly eight weeks now. She'd told herself she wasn't going to buy into the fantasy of her mother's recovery, but having Leandro in her life had made her brave. If her mother slipped again…Claudia would deal with it.

"I want to believe," she said now.

Talia nodded, blinking away sudden tears.

"I wanted you to come because I wanted to tell you something. You were right to do what you did, to pull away from me. I know I didn't respond at the time, but I thought about what you'd said, about what you'd done every single day. I wondered how you were, I asked your brothers all the time, I watched your show. When I saw you accepting that award on television, I was so proud of you. But I knew I had no right to be. What have I ever contributed to your success, after all? You have thrived despite me."

"That's not true. There were many, many good times," Claudia said.

Talia reached across the table, and Claudia met her halfway. Their hands met, their fingers meshing tightly.

"My children are my greatest achievement, and I failed you terribly. But I'm not going to let the past defeat me anymore. I want you to know that. And I want to thank you for having the courage to do what you did. Without you, my brave girl, I wouldn't be here today."

Afterward, she wasn't sure who stood first, her or her mother. It didn't matter; within seconds they were in each other's arms.

They talked some more, Talia explaining the ins-and-outs of rehab life, the rules, the problems, the triumphs. Sadie and Grace came to join them, and all too soon their two hours were up.

Claudia was silent on the drive home, simply listening to Sadie and Grace talking softly about work, Sadie's baby, the renovation plans Mac and Grace had in mind.

Leandro exited the house as they pulled up, and she stepped into his arms and pressed her head against his big, broad chest.

She was home. And she had a family of her own at last—a fresh start, a chance to do things right.

Leandro tilted her chin up and kissed her, and she felt the old passion roar to life. This man…this man had saved her from herself.

"Thank you," she whispered to him.

Then she followed him inside to begin the rest of their lives.

* * * * *

Mediterranean Nights

Join the guests and crew of Alexandra's Dream, *the newest luxury ship to set sail on the romantic Mediterranean, as they experience the glamorous world of cruising.*

A new Harlequin continuity series begins in June 2007 with
FROM RUSSIA, WITH LOVE
by Ingrid Weaver

Marina Artamova books a cabin on the luxurious cruise ship Alexandra's Dream, *when she finds out that her orphaned nephew and his adoptive father are aboard. She's determined to be reunited with the boy...but the romantic ambience of the ship and her undeniable attraction to a man she considers her enemy are about to interfere with her quest!*

Turn the page for a sneak preview!

Piraeus, Greece

"THERE SHE IS, Stefan. *Alexandra's Dream.*" David Anderson squatted beside his new son and pointed at the dark blue hull that towered above the pier. The cruise ship was a majestic sight, twelve decks high and as long as a city block. A circle of silver and gold stars, the logo of the Liberty Cruise Line, gleamed from the swept-back smoke-stack. Like some legendary sea creature born for the water, the ship emanated power from every sleek curve—even at rest it held the promise of motion. "That's going to be our home for the next ten days."

The child beside him remained silent, his cheeks working in and out as he sucked furiously on his thumb. Hair so blond it appeared white ruffled against his forehead in the harbor breeze. The baby-sweet scent unique to the very young mingled with the tang of the sea.

"Ship," David said. "Uh, *parakhod.*"

From beneath his bangs, Stefan looked at the *Alexandra's Dream.* Although he didn't release his thumb, the corners of his mouth tightened with the beginning of a smile.

David grinned. That was Stefan's first smile this after-noon, one of only two since they had left the orphanage yesterday. It was probably because of the boat—according to the orphanage staff, the boy loved boats, which was the main reason David had decided to book this cruise. Then again, there was a strong possibility the smile could have been a reaction to David's attempt at pocket-dictionary Russian. Whatever the cause, it was a good start.

The liaison from the adoption agency had claimed that Stefan had been taught some English, but David had yet to see evidence of it. David continued to speak, positive his son would understand his tone even if he couldn't grasp the words. "This is her maiden voyage. Her first trip, just like this is our first trip, and that makes it special." He motioned toward the stage that had been set up on the pier beneath the ship's bow. "That's why everyone's celebrating."

The ship's official christening ceremony had been held the day before and had been a closed affair, with only the cruise-line executives and VIP guests invited, but the stage hadn't yet been disassembled. Banners bearing the blue and white of the Greek flag of the ship's owner, as well as the Liberty circle of stars logo, draped the edges of the platform. In the center, a group of musicians and a dance troupe dressed in traditional white folk costumes performed for the benefit of the *Alexandra's Dream*'s first passengers. Their audience was in a festive mood, snapping their fingers in time to the music while the dancers twirled and wove through their steps.

David bobbed his head to the rhythm of the mandolins. They were playing a folk tune that seemed vaguely familiar, possibly from a movie he'd seen. He hummed a few notes. "Catchy melody, isn't it?"

Stefan turned his gaze on David. His eyes were a striking shade of blue, as cool and pale as a winter horizon and far too solemn for a child not yet five. Still, the smile that hovered at the corners of his mouth persisted. He moved his head with the music, mirroring David's motion.

David gave a silent cheer at the interaction. Hopefully, this cruise would provide countless opportunities for more. "Hey, good for you," he said. "Do you like the music?"

The child's eyes sparked. He withdrew his thumb with a pop. *"Moozika!"*

"Music. Right!" David held out his hand. "Come on, let's go closer so we can watch the dancers."

Stefan grasped David's hand quickly, as if he feared it would be withdrawn. In an instant his budding smile was replaced by a look close to panic.

Did he remember the car accident that had killed his parents? It would be a mercy if he didn't. As far as David knew, Stefan had never spoken of it to anyone. Whatever he had seen had made him run so far from the crash that the police hadn't found him until the next day. The event had traumatized him to the extent that he hadn't uttered a word until his fifth week at the orphanage. Even now he seldom talked.

David sat back on his heels and brushed the hair from Stefan's forehead. That solemn, too-old gaze locked with his, and for an instant, David felt as if he looked back in time at an image of himself thirty years ago.

He didn't need to speak the same language to understand exactly how this boy felt. He knew what it meant to be alone and powerless among strangers, trying to be brave and tough but wishing with every fiber of his being for a place to belong, to be safe, and most of all for someone to love him....

He knew in his heart he would be a good parent to Stefan. It was why he had never considered halting the adoption process after Ellie had left him. He hadn't balked when he'd learned of the recent claim by Stefan's spinster aunt, either; the absentee relative had shown up too late for her case to be considered. The adoption was meant to be. He and this child already shared a bond that went deeper than paperwork or legalities.

A seagull screeched overhead, making Stefan start and press closer to David.

"That's my boy," David murmured. He swallowed hard, struck by the simple truth of what he had just said.

That's my *boy*.

"I CAN'T BE PATIENT, RUDOLPH. I'm not going to stand by and watch my nephew get ripped from his country and his roots to live on the other side of the world."

Rudolph hissed out a slow breath. "Marina, I don't like the sound of that. What are you planning?"

"I'm going to talk some sense into this American kidnapper."

"No. Absolutely not. No offense, but diplomacy is not your strong suit."

"Diplomacy be damned. Their ship's due to sail at five o'clock."

"Then you wouldn't have an opportunity to speak with him even if his lawyer agreed to a meeting."

"I'll have ten days of opportunities, Rudolph, since I plan to be on board that ship."

* * * * *

*Follow Marina and David as they join forces
to uncover the reason behind little Stefan's unusual
silence, and the secret behind the death of his parents....*

*Look for
FROM RUSSIA, WITH LOVE
by Ingrid Weaver,
in stores June 2007.*

Mediterranean
NIGHTS™

Tycoon Elias Stamos is launching his newest luxury cruise ship from his home port in Greece. But someone from his past is eager to expose old secrets and to see the Stamos empire crumble.

Mediterranean Nights
launches in June 2007 with...

FROM RUSSIA, WITH LOVE
by *Ingrid Weaver*

Join the guests and crew of *Alexandra's Dream* as they are drawn into a world of glamour, romance and intrigue in this new 12-book series.

MN1

REQUEST YOUR FREE BOOKS!

2 FREE NOVELS PLUS 2 FREE GIFTS!

HARLEQUIN®

Blaze®

Red-hot reads!

HARLEQUIN®

Blaze™

COMING NEXT MONTH

#327 RISKING IT ALL Stephanie Tyler
Going to the Xtreme: Bigger, Faster, Better is not only the title of Rita Calhoun's hot new documentary, but it's what happens when she falls for one of the film's subjects, undercover navy SEAL John Cashman—the bad boy who's very, very good....

#328 CALL ME WICKED Jamie Sobrato
Extreme
Being a witch isn't easy. Just ask Lauren Parish. She's on the run from witch-hunters with a hot guy she's forbidden to touch. Worse, she's had Carson McCullen and knows *exactly* how good he is. Maybe it's time to be completely wicked and forget all the rules.

#329 SHADOW HAWK Jill Shalvis
ATF agent Abby Wells might be madly in lust with gorgeous fellow agent JT Hawk, but she's not about to do something stupid. Then again, walking into the middle of a job gone wrong—*and* getting herself kidnapped by Hawk—isn't the smartest thing she's ever done. Still, she's not about to make matters worse by sleeping with him. *Is she?*

#330 THE P.I. Cara Summers
Tall, Dark...and Dangerously Hot! Bk. 1
Writer-slash-sleuth Kit Angelis is living a *noir* novel: a gorgeous blonde walks into his office, covered in blood, carrying a wad of cash and a gun and has no idea who she is. She's also sexy as hell, which is making it hard for Kit to keep his mind on the mystery....

#331 NO RULES Shannon Hollis
Are the Laws of Seduction the latest fad for a guy to snag a sexy date, or a blueprint for murder? Policewoman Joanna MacPherson needs to find out. Posing as a lonely single, she and her partner, sexy Cooper Maxwell, play a dangerous game of cat and mouse that might uncover a lot more than they bargained for....

#332 ONE NIGHT STANDARDS Cathy Yardley
A flight gone awry and a road trip from hell turn into the night that never seems to end for Sophie Jones and Mark McMann. But the starry sky and combustible sexual heat between the two of them say they won't be complaining.... In fact, it may just be the trip of a lifetime!

www.eHarlequin.com

HBCNM0507